"I'm relying on you, Jane."

Stuart's request that she accompany Della to Switzerland was almost a command. "With proper nursing care, Della could recover completely."

Jane remembered that once, long ago, when he had loved her, Stuart had relied on her in vain. But now, she *had* to refuse this job, she thought wildly. Being with the woman he had come to love in her place would be unending torture. "I feel it might be better if you employed someone else," she said.

"That's out of the question. Della has specifically asked for you." His expression made it clear that he was totally indifferent toward Jane, but would do anything for Della.

Suddenly angry, Jane threw caution to the winds. "Very well," she said simply. "I'll go."

OTHER
Harlequin Romances
by JEAN S. MacLEOD

The Silent Valley

by

JEAN S. MacLEOD

Harlequin Books

TORONTO•LONDON•NEW YORK•AMSTERDAM
SYDNEY•HAMBURG•PARIS•STOCKHOLM

Original hardcover edition published in 1953
by Mills & Boon Limited

ISBN 0-373-00431-1

Harlequin edition published July 1958
Second printing September 1958
Third printing February 1971
Fourth printing March 1972
Fifth printing February 1974
Sixth printing May 1977
Seventh printing September 1979

To
Topsy

Printed in Canada

CHAPTER ONE

WHEN STUART HEMMINGWAY had been turned down by the girl he loved four years ago, he had taken it bitterly. He had told himself, on that dark January night, standing on the high ridge above Norchester with the bleak wind in his face, that there was nothing of faithfulness in life, no trust, only selfishness and disillusionment, and when the mood of passionate self-pity had passed he told himself that nothing mattered now but success. That he must have, to bolster up his shattered self-esteem.

An hour before he had been standing at a cross-roads in life. Along one way lay the comparative security of routine hospital work; upon the other lay the chance to specialize. He had been offered the job at the Zurich clinic several weeks before and he had known that was the way for him to go, but Jane had not seen eye to eye with him. He had sought her out full of a boy's enthusiasm, confident in the future, confident in his own ability and the sheer animal strength which would carry him through, as it had carried him through his student days. Jane had advised him to accept the Zurich job because his heart was in it, but she had refused to go with him.

Chagrined and bitterly disappointed, he had stormed and accused her. Her puny love, he had called it, unable to face the uncertainty, the near-poverty of beginnings, and she had stood, white-faced, and let him have his say. When he had finished she had told him that she would wait for him, but he had flung away from her in angry denunciation, telling her that it was then he needed her, not in some secure tomorrow. He had said that he understood, that he saw that the sacrifice was too great for her to make.

"There are people who give and others who take, all through life!" he had flung at her in his wild frenzy of disappointment. "It's easier to be one of the taking kind, apparently!"

Jane had not answered that, and he had wondered bitterly, then, how much he really knew about her.

A nurse at the City General, where he had just completed his training, she had lived outside the town and he had never thought very much about her background. He knew that her father was dead and that her mother divided her time between her own home and that of a married daughter somewhere in Devon. He had intended to meet her family one day, but it had never quite come about.

5

All that was behind him now, four years away, yet the bitterness still remained, crystallized rather than softened by the success he had made of his career—success beyond his wildest dreams. He told himself that he looked at life more sanely these days, that passion had become mellowed by experience and that ideals, for him, were things of the past, yet he had come back to Norchester because of an ideal.

Standing before the fireplace in Sir Gervaise Cortonwell's library, he recalled how much he owed to the man whose portrait in oils adorned the alcove above the wide marble mantelpiece, and some of the coldness of reserve passed from his face as he looked into the painted eyes.

He was still studying the portrait when its owner came into the room.

"Stuart, my boy! It is good to see you again." Sir Gervaise held out a hand which the younger man clasped eagerly. "I'm sorry to have kept you waiting these few minutes, but I had a consultation. I'm still old-fashioned enough to do all my private work from the house." He crossed to the cocktail cabinet against one of the walls. "What will you have? You're not starting in at Conyers till tomorrow, I hear, so there's no need to worry about a steady hand!"

Stuart made his request for a dry martini, and when Sir Gervaise handed him his glass he raised it to the light.

"To you, sir," he said.

The older man's eyes gleamed and he lifted his own glass high.

"To your continuing success, my boy!" he answered. "There's no limit to the road you can travel now."

"Thanks to you!" Stuart put his glass down on the small Sheraton table between the two windows. "I'm not very good at saying this sort of thing," he added almost apologetically, "but I am most definitely grateful for all you've done for me."

"I owed it to your father, my boy," Sir Gervaise said in a voice that was just a little pompous. "But that's an old story." His eyes went to the window, ranging across the neat flower beds in the garden beyond. "We were together during the war and his gallantry was the means of sparing my life, so it was as little as I could do to see that your training was completed afterwards. Your mother didn't live very long after he was killed. She was never an ambitious woman, but your father would have been proud of you today."

6

The slight, underlying note of contempt with which he invariably referred to women angered Stuart for a moment, but when he remembered the vain, self-seeking creature who had been Sir Gervaise's wife he fancied that he understood. His own mother had been generous in her loving, generous to a fault, perhaps, and her death had been a great blow to him, but it seemed that she had not cared over much about living once the light of her life had gone.

In some ways he had imagined Jane Calvert to be like his mother, but he had come to know better. There had been a hardness about Jane which had shut out generosity. Otherwise, how could she have failed him?

He pulled his thoughts together. He was thinking far too much about the past today, although perhaps that was only natural when he had just returned to Norchester after four years.

"I wanted to talk to you about Della," Sir Gervaise said when they had moved across the richly-carpeted hall to the dining room where their lunch was set. "We won't be interrupted. She's gone to Malvern for the day, to buy clothes or some other woman's diversion."

He unfolded the napkin lying on his plate and rose to attend to the madeira on the sideboard, the perfect host, tall, stooping a little, a slight air of preoccupation about him which Stuart put down to anxiety about his exuberant offspring.

"Frankly," he went on when the first course had been put before them, "I'm worried about that girl of mine. She ought to have been a boy." There was irritation as well as affection in his voice. "Last year she was off again on one of her mad skiing holidays, this time to Iceland, and she made the return trip on a trawler. They met foul weather in the Minch and she was ill for days. There was no adequate accommodation, of course, and she came back with a cough which she has never quite cleared up. I've had her to Sir Aukland Trevor," he ended somewhat despondently.

Stuart's expression sharpened at the mention of the famous lung specialist's name, but before he could say anything his host added:

"It's your line, too. I want you to take her in hand. She'll listen to you, I think. There's nothing very serious, you understand, but they have found a patch on the right lung."

Stuart nodded.

"I'll have a look at the plates," he said. His face had gone slightly pale under its fine coating of tan and his lips had firmed. This, at least, was something he could do for the Cortonwells, but it was difficult to imagine anyone like Della in such a plight. He concluded that her father's anxiety was naturally a little exaggerated. "Do you wish me to see her at Conyers—professionally, I mean?"

"I don't quite know." Sir Gervaise hesitated. "Perhaps it would be best. You know how difficult Della can be."

Stuart smiled. When his mouth was relaxed he looked years younger and a certain tension went out of his expression as the habitual aloofness faded in his grey eyes.

"I know how intelligent she is," he answered. "We've met frequently in Switzerland these past few years, you know."

"Yes, she told me." Sir Gervaise regarded him keenly, almost speculatively. "It was Della who supplied us with all the important news about your career," he added. "But for that daughter of mine, we would never have heard of your amazing progress until your appointment struck the local Press!"

Stuart smiled whimsically.

"And I thought I had kept in touch!"

"Oh, yes! The usual enigmatical notes that told us nothing we wanted to know!" Sir Gervaise smiled at him indulgently. "Anyway, I'm glad you and Della were good friends," he said.

The hint of anticipation was there again, the note of eagerness in the well-bred voice, as if Sir Gervaise hoped the friendship had already developed into something deeper, but if his guest was aware of the expectant undercurrent, he made no sign. Long ago he had schooled himself to keep his emotions in check—as long ago as the day on the ridge out there above the old town when he had faced disillusionment and despair and thrust them both determinedly behind him—or so he thought.

They spoke of his temporary appointment at Conyers. The Board of Management had invited him to work there while he remained in Norchester, putting a comfortable consulting room at his disposal in the hope that he would eventually settle in the town and add his personal brilliance to their name. For some time the Board had been painfully aware of their dwindling finances, and it was necessary to maintain a steady flow of private patients. A name like Hemmingway's would greatly enhance their reputation and a brilliant operation or two would soon restore their

8

fading prestige. People were still snobbish enough, or fearful enough, to pay for individual attention when they were ill, and a certain type of young mother liked to have babies in luxurious surroundings. The maternity wing still continued to pay its way, and moneyed old ladies died without being too great a burden on their relatives.

"How long can we hope to keep you?" Sir Gervaise asked. "Until the call of the Swiss clinics becomes too great again, I suppose?"

"At least until Doktor Frey expounds a new theory and is ready to put it into practice!" Stuart smiled as he rose from his chair. "And now, if you'll excuse me, I must go. I haven't really settled in at my hotel yet, and my books are still to unpack."

Sir Gervaise moved with him to the door.

"Why not come over here?" he asked. "I know we're a semi-bachelor establishment, but that ought to suit you."

Stuart had half expected the invitation, but for some peculiar reason he shook his head.

"I won't inflict myself on Della," he said. "She may feel that she is being hedged round by the medical profession at present."

Going out to the main door, Sir Gervaise put a hand on his arm.

"She'll count on you in this, my boy," he said rather unevenly. "Della's not so hard-boiled as she may seem."

Which, agreed Stuart, was possibly quite true. The strange part was that he hadn't expected Della's father to realize it.

During the past hour he had been unsure of himself with Sir Gervaise for the first time, recognizing some hidden quality in his benefactor to which he could not put a name and which a youth's gratitude and adoration might conceivably have overlooked. Suave, charming and talented, Sir Gervaise got his way in most things without being considered ruthless, but "ruthless" was the word which had just sprung unbidden to Stuart's mind. His own incisive brain had cut straight to the root of a problem which he might have to consider more fully in future, although at present it was easy enough to give the older man his promise.

"I'll do all I can for her," he said.

He felt that he owed that much at least, to the man who had treated him as a son for the greatest part of his student days, and he went away remembering Sir Gervaise's obvious pride in him when he had graduated with honors, and, later, when he had taken his surgeon's degree. Yes, it was the least he could do to look after Della Cortonwell and see her safely through the next few exacting months, although he was quite sure that she would be a most difficult patient.

CHAPTER TWO

To JANE CALVERT, treading the long corridors of the Conyers Park Nursing Home, the past was like an unpleasant dream which she had done her best to thrust behind her, but incidents from it came up to haunt her at the most unexpected times. A trick of nostalgic memory was to invade the mind on the wings of a half-forgotten melody, or in a word, or at the fleeting glimpse of a half-turned head, but quite often she let her defences down and confessed that the memory itself was ever-present in her heart.

She had lived with it, day by day, had known regret, and loneliness and tears, but she still believed that she had done the right thing, the only possible thing, when she had refused to marry Stuart.

There was no reason why her mind should have plunged deep into the past because she had been summoned to Matron's room, she tried to assure herself as she ran down the stone staircase connecting the first and second floors. Rather, it should have been wrestling with the future, wondering what had gone wrong and how she had become involved. There could, of course, be the possibility that she was about to be promoted.

She smiled to herself at the idea. Promotion meant much these days. It would mean greater security for Hazel and small, golden-haired Linda Jane, and it might lead to new conquests in her own career. She felt that her career mattered to her more now than it had ever done. She had been three years at Conyers and a year ago she had been made Sister in charge of the West wing.

Chronics! she thought with a wry smile, but she had gained a fund of useful information in dealing with them and a vast insight into the complexities of human relationships.

She tapped on Matron's door, and without hesitation a voice said:

"Come in!"

A woman in her early fifties, in a well-cut sage-green frock, sat behind the mahogany desk set at an angle across the window, and her eyes regarded Jane critically as she crossed the carpeted floor.

"Sit down, Sister." She glanced at her watch. "I know that you have just come off duty, but I won't keep you many minutes." The dark eyes under their heavy brows did not leave Jane's face. "I suppose you will have heard that Sister Harrison has handed in her resignation? She is going to be married."

Jane wondered if there had been the faintest suggestion of dryness in Matron's tone when she offered that piece of information, the barest hint of disapproval, and she found herself pondering over the problem of women like Agnes Lawdon who did not marry, who were content to give all of themselves to their chosen careers. Matron must have done that. Had she dried up inside and lost some of the milk of húman kindness in the process? She looked across the desk into Agnes Lawdon's steady eyes, thinking that, if she stayed at Conyers, she might even come to look like Matron in time.

The dark eyes were still regarding her critically.

"I've decided to give you a trial in the theatre," Matron said. "I think that you have the necessary stamina for the work and the necessary intelligence. I've been quite pleased with your progress this past year and I know that you are anxious to succeed. You have the makings of a fine nurse, and I understand that there is nothing to stand in your way. You have no—ties, I gather. You're not—attached in any way?"

Jane's heart twisted with an old, familiar pain, but her grey-green eyes were steady on the brown ones opposite as she said:

"No, I have no ties, Matron. Not in the way you mean."

Agnes Lawdon looked down at the chart lying on the desk before her. It was the first time since Jane had entered the room that she had been free from that penetrating scrutiny, and while she waited she took in the older woman's trim, upright figure, the good carriage of the shoulders, and the consciously-proud lift of the head. Beneath the heavy, greying eyebrows high cheek bones flanked a well-shaped nose and the slight weakness of the mouth was overcome by Matron's habitually compressed lips.

Jane had an instant impression of a woman on guard, which was as swiftly dismissed as Agnes Lawdon said:

"You will start your duties in the theatre on Monday." She rose to her feet, holding out her hand across the desk. "I have the greatest confidence in you, Sister."

Jane felt that her own elation was excusable. There was a feeling of treading on air as she walked towards the door and she could still feel the firm clasp of Matron's fingers on her own. It was like an accolade.

This would make everything so much easier at home! Pride in her work surged up, too, and she knew the gratification of acknowledgement.

"Don't tell me you've been on the carpet and can come out from the Presence looking like that!"

She turned swiftly, waylaid by a tall, fair-haired young man in a white coat with a stethoscope dangling from one pocket and a most unprofessional gleam in his eyes.

"We're not always called to Matron's room to be reprimanded, you know, Tom!" she smiled. "There might possibly be another reason, although I didn't know I was looking particularly pleased with myself."

"Pleased wasn't the word for it, my dear Jane!" he told her. "You looked positively elated! So much so, that I strongly suspect there may even be room for a celebration!"

Jane, already well acquainted with the recurring nature of Doctor Sark's celebrations, endeavored to curb her natural excitement. Tom was apt to forget that they were still within the confines of Conyers and that he was, ostensibly, still on duty.

"I'm going into the theatre," she told him with the necessary dignity. "Naturally, I'm pleased about it, though I should hate to tell you how nervous I feel!"

"You needn't be," he told her. "You can get away with anything, Jane."

For a moment she wished that he would be more serious, and then she reflected on the impossibility of trapping sunlight. He was like quicksilver—gay, irresponsible, light-hearted Tom! He would never make a good doctor, although for some reason Matron imagined that he could do no wrong.

"Well! Well! Well!" Tom regarded her with a quizzical half-smile and his head slightly on one side. "Our little Jane wallowing among the blood and gore and liking it! May I suggest that it takes all sorts to make a world?"

"And may I remind you that you are still on duty and I am not? I want to carry the good news back to my family."

He glanced down at his watch.

"Let me help you carry it," he suggested. "Give me five minutes and I'll drive you out to Heppleton much more quickly than you could possibly go by bus."

Jane hesitated.

"Why should you?" she asked.

"Because I want to. I thought I might be in on this celebration."

"There isn't going to be a celebration."

"Oh, isn't there? You've no idea what can happen when Doctor Sark is in charge!"

"Unfortunately, I have," Jane remarked dryly, but she smiled and waited for him to find his coat.

Going out into the sunshine of the late October day she still felt that strangely elated sensation, yet deep down beneath it was the realization of all her new position would mean. Harder work, certainly, but more rewarding work. Her mind fastened on after-care, but she knew that she had always wanted to be in the theatre, to be there at the actual working of the miracle. Surgery was her real bent.

Then, suddenly, devastatingly, she was conscious of fear, the fear of inadequacy, the dread that she might not have so much to give as Matron believed. I know nothing, she thought. I'm a babe where operating is concerned, and have I really the stamina to see it through?

Shaken, she walked beside her gay companion in silence, but silence was rarely allowed to deepen when Doctor Sark was around.

"Let's make it something worth while," he suggested. "A weekend jaunt. We could have all day on Sunday." He had not stopped to consider that she might want to spend her one full day off duty with her family, although his voice sobered a little as he suggested: "I'd like to take you down to the sea."

She knew that he spent most of his free time down on the Channel, somewhere round about Avonmouth, but apart from that her knowledge of young Doctor Sark was limited. Nobody, Jane realized, knew very much about him really. His background remained a mystery, and he had never taken anyone into his confidence, although he was free enough in other respects.

"Isn't it rather late in the year for walking along the promenade?" she suggested. "I know about the winds that can beat up out of the Bristol Channel, even in summer!"

"Since we're having an Indian summer at present, that wouldn't apply," he assured her as they reached the battered old car standing in the shade of the cloister wall. Conyers had once been a priory, its many rooms and walled garden closed in from the frustrations of the outside world. "Say you'll come, Jane," he pleaded. "I've meant to ask you—quite apart from the celebration."

The suggestion of seriousness in his voice and the fact that the mocking light had disappeared from his eyes made it difficult for Jane to refuse him, but there was Hazel to think about. Thinking about Hazel and Linda Jane had

14

become second nature to her these days. Her grey-green eyes, set under their finely arched brows, mirrored genuine regret as she said:

"I'd like to come, Tom, but my sister has so little company that I spend as much time as I possibly can with her these days."

He made an impatient gesture with his shapely hand.

"One day won't hurt her, surely? You can give her what's left of today."

She shook her head.

"I'll come another time."

They got into the car, and automatically Jane glanced back at the long row of windows which dominated the forecourt of the Home. It would be fatal if Matron saw her driving away with one of the medical staff—especially Doctor Sark!

"She's standing behind the office curtain!" Tom grinned. "Pity, even though it can only be one blot on your escutcheon!"

They laughed, and he set the car at a swift pace through the narrow streets of the old town, out through the west gate to the suburbs sprawling on the hills behind. They could see the blue windings of the Severn as they climbed and the sky above them was dappled with milky cloud. Always Jane was to remember that day—the broad, winding river, the greenness of the land about them, the lovely, undulating Cotswold country touched with the first deep coloring of autumn. The air was still warm, and ahead of them sunlight glinted on the brow of the Malvern hills. Away to the west, they could see the blue mountains of Wales, cradled in haze, deeply impenetrable, like a man's innermost thoughts.

"I'm not taking 'no' for an answer this time," Tom declared when they had reached Heppleton and turned at the village green into the leafy byway which led to Jane's destination. "I'll be here in the morning, as near ten o'clock as makes no difference, and if you can't possibly get rid of that sister of yours, bring her along too. I'll try to be equal to it!"

Laughing, they parted. Jane did not think that he would really be there the following day. Tom was given to promises which, somehow, easily became mislaid.

Walking briskly along the familiar lane, she promptly forgot about Doctor Sark. Her cheeks were flushed again and her eyes bright with excitement as she pushed open the garden gate.

The house lay back from the road, half hidden in a bower of roses that still bloomed along the trellises, while tall chrysanthemums and Michaelmas daisies hedged the path on either side. She glanced up at the window directly above the front door and saw that the curtains were drawn. Too late to say goodnight to Linda Jane tonight!

Her sister met her in the doorway. Hazel Grantham, who had once been Hazel Calvert, was smaller than Jane, and much fairer, but she had Jane's small, regular features and the same direct glance, although her eyes were a wide, clear blue. Her coloring gave her a slightly doll-like appearance which belied her nature, for Hazel was the efficient housewife, never happier than when she was pottering about a kitchen or presiding over the gate-legged table which now stood set for Jane's evening meal in the bay of the dining room window.

"I thought you'd like it in here, Jane," she said as they went into the room. "There's still heat in the sun, and we get it in here all afternoon."

Jane noticed with some surprise that she was to dine alone.

"Have you had yours, Hazel?" she asked, changing the shoes she had worn all day for a pair of comfortable slippers.

There was a moment's hesitation before her sister replied.

"Yes. I had it with Lindy."

Hazel went through to the kitchen to bring in the pie she had baked. It smelt savoury and warm, and was brown and crisp and professional looking. Jane sniffed appreciatively.

"I'm glad I don't have to have all my meals at Conyers," she said. "It's much nicer waiting to have it here."

She had been about to add 'with you,' and thought again how strange it was that Hazel should have taken her meal so early. She wanted to tell her about Conyers and her amazing good luck at being chosen for the theatre, but suddenly she thought that it would keep.

"Lindy behaved all right today?" she asked, going through to the kitchen sink to wash her hands. "No more tantrums over the fruit juice?"

"A minor scuffle, but we came to terms in the end. I'm afraid Lindy responds disgracefully to a bribe!"

Hazel's tone was preoccupied, her thoughts not entirely on the golden-haired little girl in the room above.

"Well, what is it? What's the trouble?" Jane asked,

16

coming directly to the point. "Hasn't the housekeeping quite stood the strain this month, or is it only a leaky gas jet?"

Hazel smiled, but the smile was still distant, as if she could not quite bring her mind down to mundane things like the housekeeping money and gas jets. Besides, Jane thought, she was a faultless housekeeper. The allowance they had agreed upon was never overstepped. They pooled their resources and apportioned everything out quite fairly, and it was only Hazel who felt that Jane should not remain the breadwinner always. They had talked about that not so long ago, but as things were, Hazel was best at home.

Jane watched her as she limped through the kitchen doorway with the coffee pot and cups on a tray. The small infirmity was almost unnoticeable except when Hazel had spent most of the day on her feet, the pin in the knee joint working so well that she walked now with ease.

She laid the tray down on the end of the table.

"Jane," she asked, "would you baby-sit for me for a couple of hours tonight?"

Jane nodded, a little perplexed by the unexpected request, but perfectly willing to oblige.

"You know that you needn't have asked," she said. "I've come home with every intention of putting my feet up."

Hazel said: "You're always so tired when you have been on duty for such a long spell," but she was not really thinking about Conyers, or the chronics, or the varying duties which her sister took in her stride. "Are you still so terribly short-staffed?"

"So desperately so that Matron has seen fit to put me into the theatre."

Jane had tried to sound matter-of-fact, but she had not been able to control the edge of excitement in her voice or hide the gentle pride in her eyes.

"Oh! Jane, I knew you'd get it one day!" Hazel's pre-occupation with her own affairs had been dispersed like mist before the sun. "I'm so glad—so proud for you! Really—we ought to celebrate this."

She hesitated, and Jane said quietly:

"I'm doing that tomorrow. I'm too foot-sore to attempt anything in that line tonight, so off you go and leave me to baby-sit in peace. You know I'll enjoy it."

She could not say why she had suddenly thrust Tom Sark's invitation between them. Something like self-defence had motivated her, the faintest suggestion of disloyalty when she considered Hazel's hastily made plans. There had been no mention of the visit to the cinema, or whatever it was, the evening before, and suddenly she knew that Hazel was going out with a man. She had been full of some inner joy of her own for weeks back, some deep, enriching experience which shut Jane out for the moment.

Strange, bitter jealousy stabbed at Jane's heart, but in the next instant she was ashamed. Why shouldn't Hazel be taken out? She was free. Her husband was dead.

Four years ago George Grantham had been killed in a road accident, and it was only now that his young wife seemed to be taking up the threads of life again with anything like her former spirit. Hazel had a right to happiness, Jane thought. She would not stand in her way. It had been foolish—childish on her part to strike back with the announcement of her intention to accept Tom Sark's invitation for tomorrow. She did not particularly want to go with Tom. She would have been content to spend her day in the garden with Linda Jane.

"I won't be late." Hazel appeared in the doorway in her best coat and a bright woollen cap she had knitted with scraps left over from her small daughter's cardigans. "But don't wait up. Go to bed if you feel tired, Jane."

There was a shining quality about Hazel tonight which banished any suggestion of tiredness on her own part, although she had been up since seven and had probably worked about the house all day. Love, Jane thought—love and happiness combined! It made a wonderful difference. Was Hazel in love again?

She cleared the table, trying to thrust the crowding memory of the past behind her, but it persisted. Had she been wrong? Had she made the one inexcusable mistake? To break faith—that is the unforgivable thing!" She could still hear Stuart's voice, harsh with bitterness, as he uttered the words. It came to her across the years as plainly as if it had been uttered there in the room beside her. Why was she thinking about him so repeatedly tonight? Wasn't it that never a day passed without her thinking of him at one moment or another? Be straight with yourself, Jane, she demanded ruthlessly. Look this thing in the face. You never have and never will love anyone as you loved Stuart Hemmingway back in those old, carefree student days before life cropped up to mock your loving and thrust its harsh demands between you. You'll never live down the injury you did, never be able to forget

the look in a pair of grey eyes when anger and disillusionment had taken the place of love.

Stuart! she thought. Stuart! It's so long ago, and only
a step away!

She was not asleep when Hazel parted with her escort
at the front door, but she had gone to bed. She lay tensed
in the room next to Linda Jane's, listening to a man's deep-
toned voice out there among the shadows of the porch,
remembering that last night when she and Stuart had
walked the narrow path beside the river and she had told
him so decisively that she couldn't marry him. They had
come back to the house and he had said goodbye to her in
the porch, stiffly, resentfully, not even holding her to kiss
her in a final outburst of passion. He had shut himself
away behind a cold barrier of bitterness and distrust, and
that had been the last time she had seen him.

Hazel was up early next morning, a light in her eyes
that there was no mistaking. She made no demur when
Jane said that she was going out at ten and might be away
all day.

"I'll have something ready for you when you get back,"
she promised. "And, Jane," she added dreamily, "would
you mind very much if I asked—someone to tea?"

"Why should I?" Jane was stuffing a fine woollen
scarf into her capacious shoulder bag in case it was chilly
by the sea. "Do I know him?"

Hazel did not seem to think it strange that she should
have guessed the sex of their prospective guest. She was
clearing the breakfast table with that same preoccupied
expression in her blue eyes and she had brushed her fair
hair into a new and more becoming style.

"No, I don't think you do," she said. "Will you be
back in time to be introduced?"

"I may be." Jane stooped to drop a kiss on Lindy's fair
curls. "Be good—both of you! I'm going to the coast with
Tom Sark, by the way."

She had passed on the information with a feeling that
Hazel was making rather too much of a mystery of her own
affairs, hanging a strange new cloak of reserve, of a sudden,
over her actions, but Hazel did not offer any further confidences and the sound of a familiar car broke up their
thoughts.

Tom Sark pulled up at the gate and greeted Jane
eagerly. He was wearing flannels and an old college blazer
and looking amazingly debonair as he sat at the wheel with
his fair hair neatly parted and flattened close to his head,

and there was a sparkle in his eyes which sent her spirits up again.

"I so rarely see you out of a cap and apron, that this is something of an event," he told her. "Your eyes are greyer than I thought," he went on mischievously. "Dark grey with green lights in them, like the sea on an unpredictable day!"

"There speaks the professional charmer!" she chided, getting in beside him. "It's much too early in the morning for compliments, Doctor Sark."

"It's no use!" he groaned disconsolately. "You never have taken me seriously, Jane!"

"Did you ever want to be taken seriously?" she asked doubtfully as they sped away, by-passing the town and travelling swiftly southwards towards the widening Channel.

Surprisingly, he said:

"There are disadvantages about both extremes. Today we are going to make a pact, Jane. The usual hearty badinage is out."

She glanced at him, her face sobering. Handsome to a marked degree, there was still something lacking about Tom to which she had yet to put a name. He was the gay companion, the ever-ready comrade of adventure, and she had rarely seen him without a mocking gleam in his blue eyes, but today he appeared different for some reason. It seemed that he wanted to talk, that before the day was over he would have put their easy friendship on an entirely different footing.

"Have you always lived in Norchester, Jane?" he asked. "Always had—roots in the same place?"

If she had not been so accustomed to his casual approach to life she might have imagined some sort of wistfulness behind the query, but Tom and roots did not quite coincide. Foot loose and fancy free had always appeared to be his motto in the past.

"Yes, I've lived all my life here," she answered. "Before we moved out to Heppleton we lived in the old town, but the house was demolished during the war by a stray bomb jettisoned during a raid on Bristol."

Those days seemed very far away, the days before she had made up her mind about her career, before she had met Stuart Hemmingway and fallen in love. They marked a carefree phase in her life where responsibilities were something for someone else to take care of, but she knew quite well what Tom meant by roots. It was the feeling, going deep, which had made her keep the old home going, the sense of security which lay behind the thought of family and old association, and mutual love and trust.

Trust! The word thrust at her as it had done more than once lately. 'To break faith—that is the unforgivable thing. . . .'

She turned from the thought of Stuart, determined to give her undivided attention to her companion. Tom drove silently for several minutes before he said:

"I've never told you very much about myself, Jane. When I first came to Conyers I wasn't quite sure whether I could settle or not. Sometimes I think I'm not the settling kind."

She waited, not quite sure of what was coming, while he stared at the road ahead with an intensity which suggested that he might have forgotten her for the moment. It was so unlike him to confide in anyone that she felt slightly uneasy wondering where the conversation might lead.

"I—can't remember ever having had a family," he said. "I was brought up by an aunt—my father's sister-in-law, I suppose—who later adopted me." His long, supple fingers tightened over the wheel and she saw that his lips were tightly compressed. "Don't think I'm—belittling the effort she made," he went on staunchly. "No one could have been more kind to me, but I learned when I was quite young that I didn't quite belong."

And resented it, Jane thought, pity welling in her as she glanced at the stubborn chin and taut, indrawn mouth. Children at school could be unconsciously cruel, repeating gossip picked up at the family dining-table. He must have considered himself outside a charmed circle in spite of all that was done for him, but why should he be telling her all this now?

"I want to take you to Crale," he said abruptly. "I want you to meet Ada Sark. She's a remarkable woman. I think you'll like her."

Jane felt uncomfortable for no very definite reason.

"She may not be expecting me," she protested.

"You don't need to be 'expected' when you go to see Ada," he assured her. "She welcomes all and sundry at any hour of the day or night! She says it keeps her young and uninhibited. There won't be any suggestion of intrusion, Jane," he added more seriously. "Say you'll come!"

"If you really want to go——"

She had acquiesced uncertainly. The widening mouth of the Severn had brought them near to their destination, with the blue Mendips strung out across the horizon and the steep cliffs of Devon rising sheer out of Bridgwater Bay. It was a day steeped in sunshine and haunted by the cry of gulls, and Jane knew that the sea held the same deep spell for her companion as it had always done for herself.

"I come here whenever I can," he said, parking the car where they had an uninterrupted view of a tiny bay. "It's coming home, I suppose, in a good many ways, though sometimes I'm not grateful enough to admit it."

She put an impulsive hand on his sleeve.

"Don't wait till it's too late," she begged. "There's nothing so soul-destroying as regret."

He sat staring through the windscreen for a full minute, gazing at the sea, and then he snapped open the car door and got out.

"Come on, Jane, before we go completely morbid!" he advised. "I'm going to walk you right along the front!"

Even at that time of the year there were people strolling along the short promenade, but they soon out-paced the other walkers, climbing high on the cliff, where the view was magnificent. Jane looked across the blue water to the hills of Wales, the Brecon Beacons clear in autumn sunlight, and when she turned Tom pointed out the green length of the White Horse Vale to her, lying far behind them. She felt isolated in a new world of wind and sunlight, content to be there, content to let the problems of Conyers and the future fall behind her as she stood on the narrow pathway above the sea.

Tom came close, imprisoning her arms from behind.

"Jane," he said, "you're part of all this! You and I should come here more often."

She could feel his warm breath on the nape of her neck, knowing that he was about to kiss her, and even as she tried to free herself he had tilted back her head and pressed his lips possessively against hers.

Shaken by the unexpected contact, she faced him, her cheeks gone suddenly pale.

"I wish you hadn't done that," she said. "Not here."

He laughed then, dismissing her protest.

"Jane, you're out of another world! But I love your loyalties and your quaint ideals just the same!" He drew her close. "Jane—marry me," he demanded.

She drew back, aware of the underlying sincerity in the precipitate proposal, liking him, yet knowing that there was only one answer to give him.

"It wouldn't be any use," she said dully. "I couldn't

give you the things you want, Tom."

The laughter died in his eyes and the banter went out of his voice as he said:

"Surely I should be the best judge of that? I'd work, Jane, harder than I've ever done before," he promised. "I'd even stay on at Conyers and let Matron continue to keep a sobering eye on me! We could come here and sail in the summer weather. You'd like it, Jane. You've told me you would!"

"Liking—and marrying someone on the strength of it isn't enough," Jane told him in a small, constrained whisper. "Tom—I'm sorry! I had no idea you felt this way or I wouldn't have come."

She saw something die out of his eyes. His mouth went grim, and once again all the bitter accusation in a man's voice rushed in upon her. Was she repeating a mistake, disillusioning someone for the second time in her life? She looked up at her companion and could not find an answer. Gay, inconsequential, light-hearted Tom! She wished he would take his profession more seriously and not have to bargain with her for continuing diligence.

"Forget it," he said, "at least for today. You haven't really given me an answer, of course. At least, not one that I can accept as final!"

Jane wanted to protest, but she knew Tom too well to make the attempt. He was adept at sweeping aside the unpleasant, the situation he did not want to face.

He drew her hand through the crook of his arm, marching her back towards the straggling row of houses along the water-front.

The promenade was almost deserted now, with only a solitary figure standing beside the iron rail, gazing seawards, as they approached along the narrow road. Something about the woman's erect back and stiffly-held head was suddenly arrestingly familiar to Jane, and then Agnes Lawdon turned and walked straight towards them.

Her surprise was as great as theirs, but not nearly so obvious. Jane saw the momentary dilation of her pupils and the swiftly controlled movement of her lips before she acknowledged them stonily.

"Doctor Sark—Sister?" she said. "Crale appears to be a popular place at this time of year."

Before either of them could answer she had moved on, coldly hostile, completely disapproving of their companionship.

"Of all the pieces of sheer bad luck!" Tom grinned.

"Don't worry too much about it, Jane. It can't make any difference to your appointment now, and she really hasn't any right to interfere in off-duty hours."

"Matron's fair enough in that respect," Jane said slowly, "though I still feel that she minds about this sort of thing. Doctors and nurses shouldn't be too friendly—not when they have to work together!"

"And I'd say 'rot'! to that!" He drew her hand firmly through his arm again. "Matron would like one's profession to mean everything, cancelling out love and all the rest of it, if need be!"

"It *can* mean a lot," Jane answered thoughtfully. "Matron knows that I'm keen on my work, and she's always been—indulgent where you are concerned."

"Indulgent! That may be a nice way of putting it, but you'll have to think of another word, Jane. At times I've almost felt her contempt." He glanced back at the receding figure on the cliff path. "She's a strange woman. I don't think anyone will ever really get to know Agnes Lawdon. She's been visiting my aunt for as long as I can remember, but she still remains an enigma to me."

So, that was the reason for Matron's interest in his career! Jane had sensed that Tom Sark meant just a little more to Agnes Lawdon than the ordinary run of young doctors who had followed one another with amazing regularity at Conyers Park, but she could not have guessed that there was any real friendship between them. The very last thing Matron would show would be favoritism.

Tom led her along the row of cottages until they came to one standing a little way apart, with a narrow lane running between it and its neighbor and surrounded by a red-brick wall. A late hollyhock nodded beside the gate and there were roses still blooming in the neat beds and pansies starring the borders. Rose Cottage seemed shut away in a little, flowering world of its own.

She saw Tom's eyes go eagerly to the upturned boat standing on trestles under the variegated holly tree beside the wall and knew that it was the reason why he came, week after week, to his old home. His love of the sea was inbred. When he looked at it his eyes and his whole face came alive.

A small, stout figure hurried to the cottage door. Ada Sark had seem then open the gate from the kitchen window and she came to meet them. Generous in her giving, she could not wait to make her welcome felt.

Fresh-faced, with small, twinkling eyes, there was much

of Tom in her, although her humor was rich and deep-seated, unsullied by Tom's cynicism. Jane felt that life must have been a great adventure to Ada Sark, her struggles only part of it, and she found herself clasping the plump, work-roughened hand warmly, glad now that she had come.

Ada set their lunch in the sitting-room, as befitted the occasion, for Tom had never brought a young lady all the way to Crale before and she felt that this must be important.

She fussed, and Tom chaffed her while they ate a hearty meal. When it was over he went out to inspect the boat which he was laying up for the winter. Jane watched him haul out a big tarpaulin to batten it down over the trestles.

"Sometimes I wonder if we did right, making him a doctor," Ada Sark said, coming to stand beside her at the window. "He would just as soon have gone to sea. When he was a little lad we used to miss him and he'd be away with one of the local fishermen to watch the boats at Avonmouth. The only book that ever got really worn in this house was Treasure Island, and he would haunt the Bristol quays for hours whenever we went there, living the fitting out of the *Hispaniola* over and over again!"

"What made him finally decide on the medical profession?" Jane asked.

Ada hesitated. Her blue eyes scanned the small front garden with a hint of regret in their homely depths.

"He hadn't complete say. A boy of eighteen can be swayed by firm talk." She sighed, turning back into the room. "I suppose they do need guidance, even at that age," she mused, "but I never thought he was one to go cutting up folk or attending to the sick." She smiled at some inner reflection. "Not that he wasn't a kind enough lad," she added. "He could never bear to see an animal hurt, and, fond as he was of the sea, he was never one to go fishing much. Even as a tiny tot he couldn't take a fish off a hook. That's why I've always had my doubts about this doctoring business. I thought him too sensitive for it, and still do."

Jane, who wouldn't have called Tom sensitive, found herself wondering about the other influence in his life that had steered him so determinedly towards a profession, but Mrs. Sark had apparently no more to say on the subject. She switched the conversation to gardens, and it was not until they were well on the homeward road that Jane realized they had never once discussed Conyers or her work there.

The unexpected meeting with Agnes Lawdon dominated her thoughts most of the way back, and she could see in her mind's eye that tall, rather gaunt figure walking away from them, awkward out of uniform and inexpressibly lonely.

Why should she put that construction on Matron's visit to Crale? There would be no doubt about her attitude in the morning. Stiffly accusing, she would confront Jane with the enormity of the situation, reprimanding her, at least.

She was prepared, then, for the summons that took her to the room at the far end of the downstairs corridor as soon as she reported for duty the following morning. She had left home without seeing much of Hazel, who had been dressing her boisterous young daughter when she got down for breakfast, but she had ascertained that Hazel's day had been enjoyable. The friend had come to tea, but had left early, before Jane and Tom Sark had returned. His name, Jane had learned, was Eric Bridgewater, and he had been in the Navy, which was a link with Hazel's dead husband, George.

Jane could not pretend to be thinking of anything but her job as she walked sedately along the corridor, but perhaps that was equivalent to thinking about Hazel, too. Her work at Conyers was the future for them both.

Or was it? For the first time Jane did not feel quite sure. Security had come to mean much to her, not from any selfish motive, but because security was necessary for Hazel and Hazel's child. If she had only herself to think about her heart might not be thumping so hard now nor would her eyes have held that faint suggestion of anxiety which deepened them to a misty grey. They may have been a little stormy, too, with protest, because she did not consider that she had done anything wrong.

She tapped lightly on Matron's door and was told to come in.

Agnes Lawdon raised her head. The stiff white cap on her greying hair seemed to crackle and her eyes under the heavy, dark brows were frosty.

"You will, I suppose, understand why I have sent for you, Sister," she began without preliminary. "I feel that yesterday afternoon must have been a mistake on your part, knowing how strongly I disapprove of any familiarity between my nurses and the medical staff."

She fixed Jane with level eyes, a sharp demand in her

voice which it was impossible to ignore. Jane felt the hot blood rising to her cheeks and receding again, leaving her drained of sudden anger but with a resolute purpose in her heart.

"Neither Doctor Sark nor myself was on duty yesterday, ma'am," she said with quiet emphasis. "I do not see that any rules which have been made for our conduct in the Home can possibly apply."

There was no obvious change in the fixed expression of the woman on the far side of the desk. She moved her hands a fraction of an inch, gripping both ends of a silver propelling pencil, but suddenly the knuckles were white with pressure.

"Am I to take it that this is a serious love affair, Sister?" she asked.

Jane swallowed hard.

"No," she said, "there's nothing like that. Doctor Sark asked me to go for a run to the coast with him." Her lips curved in a smile. "I believe he considered it in the nature of a celebration. He had heard of my appointment."

Matron did not smile: neither did she look particularly relieved by what she had just heard.

"Considering the nature of that appointment, Sister— the fact that it could be a step to much greater authority— doesn't your conduct strike you as rather odd? You were deliberately flouting rules."

Jane flushed.

"Not as I see it," she answered swiftly. "I'm sorry if you feel that I have been indiscreet, but Doctor Sark and I have known one another for over a year, so perhaps that is why I didn't consider it odd to accept his invitation."

Matron's eyes narrowed a fraction of an inch, as if by added concentration she might penetrate the armor of Jane's reserve, probing beneath the exterior calmness.

"No doubt you feel flattered by Doctor Sark's attention," she observed crushingly, "but I think you should be warned that he is not yet in a position to support a wife. If he is wise, he will not consider marriage for some time to come. Young doctors are notorious philanderers," she added, her mouth suddenly grim, her eyes gone curiously blank. "Surely you are too sensible to make a mistake of that sort, Sister? You have always impressed me as someone greatly interested in her career. A nurse's whole life is bound up with her duty. Within the precincts of Conyers and beyond it there is a code which must be rigidly observed. As I have said, Doctor Sark isn't ready for

27

marriage yet. A woman is often asked to make sacrifices for a man's career, and graduation isn't the end where a doctor is concerned. There are further degrees to be had —specialization to consider."

Her gaze had gone beyond Jane for the first time and it did not seem that she was speaking directly to anyone. Rather, she seemed to be voicing some remote ambition in herself, and Jane wondered if Tom Sark was her protégé.

It was possible. She had visited Rose Cottage for years and her opinions could quite easily have shaped his career, even although Tom had said that in all that time he had never really come to know her. Agnes Lawdon was still an enigma to him, and to many more besides.

In spite of her justifiable anger, Jane was conscious of a deeper reason for Matron's interference than just the routine one of maintaining the stern set of rules laid down for the nursing staff. It seemed personal, something touching this woman as deeply as she could be touched, and she found herself wondering if Agnes Lawdon had ever known a moment of real tenderness in all her fifty-odd years of living. It did not seem possible that love could have touched her at all.

"When you have thought it over," she said in that same coldly precise tone, "you will see that I am right. Men can be such fools, and Doctor Sark is apparently no exception, but a doctor, if he is wise as well as ambitious, marries in the right quarter, even in these days!"

That made Jane really angry. Her chin tilted, she observed as coldly as Matron had done:

"There is just the possibility that he may be in love with someone."

"Love can wait!" Agnes Lawdon cut her short. "It isn't so important as you young people seem to think." There was a hardness about her now which could not be denied. "There are still heights to be obtained in spite of the all-levelling Health Service, post-graduate degrees still continue to speak for themselves." Her eyes held Jane's determinedly. "I am sure that you are far too sensible, Sister, to stand in anyone's way."

The words found their mark. They had even more than the desired effect, for Jane had suddenly gone deadly pale and any argument that was left in her crumbled before them. She moistened her lips and rose slowly to her feet.

"I think you had better know, Matron," she said in a dry undertone, "that Tom Sark has already asked me to marry him and I have refused."

If her confession gave satisfaction at last, there was little sign of it. Agnes Lawdon put down her pencil and lifted a sheaf of papers from her desk which she considered for a moment or two before she made answer.

"Thank you, Sister," she said. "That will be all." Her voice was almost pleasant now. "I am quite sure you are far too level-headed to take a wrong view of the situation. Let me see, now. I want you to be in the theatre by eight o'clock. Mr. Hemmingway is operating here for the first time, and he will not have his patients kept waiting."

She looked up at the small sound that came from the girl on the far side of the desk, a sound that was like protest—or pain. Jane's face was completely colorless and every nerve in her body seemed to have been shattered by a commonplace remark. She felt that she could not move her limbs. Hands, feet, will itself refused to obey her.

"Is there anything the matter, Sister? Do you feel ill?"

Coolly incisive, Matron's voice cut in upon her humbed brain and Jane got out of the room somehow. She reached the corridor, forcing her shaking limbs to carry her as far as the refectory door, where she leaned back against the wall and closed her eyes.

Stuart operating on her first day in the theatre! Stuart there at all! Her pulses began to beat with sledge-hammer insistency, her heart thumping out the heavy rhythm of desperation until she could almost hear its beating in the stillness. She wanted to run from the very thought of meeting him, from the bitterness and rejection that would be in his grey eyes when recognition first leapt between them, yet training kept her there, rooted to the spot, forcing herself to consider it all as no more than a job of work, her accepted duty.

'A nurse's whole life is bound up with her duty.'

Matron's words came back to mock her, filling the deserted corridor, and then it was no longer deserted. Two student nurses rounded a far bend, broke loose from each other's encircling arm, and walked sedately towards her.

Jane should have issued some sort of reprimand, but she was unable to trust her voice. She stood to one side while they entered the refectory.

How early was it, or how late? Automatically she took out her watch and looked at it, seeing the large second hand revolving with unerring swiftness, relentlessly, as if time, also, were mocking her.

A buzz of chatter and laughter issued from the half-open door. She would have to go in some time, but her limbs were still reluctant to make the initial effort and she had to be sure about her voice. Snatches of conversation drifted out to her. It was inevitable. They were discussing the amazing news Matron had just delivered to her in the form of a bombshell. The great Stuart Hemmingway, fresh from his London triumphs, was to operate at Conyers!

"Why do you think he's come back to Norchester?" somebody asked. "It's such a hole!"

"The Cortonwells *could* be the answer." The cool, insolent voice was Clarrie Parr's. Jane would have recognized it anywhere. Clarrie's nursing wasn't serious. It was taken as a joke in the family. The Parrs had plenty of money, but Clarrie had wanted something to do, something romantic.

"Do you mean that Della Cortonwell could be the answer?" someone else asked, taking Clarrie up.

"Could be." There was a pause in which Jane could imagine Clarrie lighting a cigarette and flicking the match expertly behind the gas fire, all completely contrary to Conyers' regulations. "Della's different from anyone else I know. She's a strange girl. All these hare-brained adventures! We often wonder what her next exploit will be, but nobody in their sane mind could possibly guess!"

Clarrie's 'we' invariably put her less fortunate colleagues at a distance. Quite clearly they did not belong to Norchester's exclusive set. There was a small pause, broken by the entrance of a nurse at the far door. Jane moved just inside the room. She could pour herself a cup of coffee from the percolator on the service table against the wall without exciting any immediate comment. All eyes were fixed on Clarrie and the newcomer, a spectacular blonde, already engaged to be married.

"Girls!" she exclaimed dramatically, "you'll never guess who's coming into number seven?"

"The Queen of Siam, or Methuselah himself," Paddy Monaghan suggested from her perch on a window sill. "No one, at any rate, under seventy!" she added disconsolately. "I know all about Conyers after three years in the place! When you've finished washing napkins over on Maternity, you're transferred up here to chronics and that's that! If one happens to die, you get another centenarian in his place!"

"You're wrong this time, Paddy!" Her informer looked triumphant, but in no hurry to impart her information.

"Oh, for heaven's sake, Stephens, spare us the dramatic approach!" Madge Wakeham looked up from her book, a dark line of concentration etched between her heavy brows. "It can't be all that important."

"We're not all immersed in textbooks to the exclusion of everything else," Joyce Stephens retorted coldly. "*You* may not be interested, Wakey, but I'll bet the rest are."

Jane filled her cup, carrying it to the end of the long table where the night staff were just finishing their supper. Someone made way for her, but their interest was elsewhere. Their eyes were fixed on Joyce Stephens, tired though they were, and they were all agog for information.

"It's Della Cortonwell! Three suitcases and Sir Gervaise's Rolls have just arrived at the front door!"

There was a rush for the window, but apparently the Rolls Royce contained nothing but the suitcases, and they fell back.

"How do you know she's coming in?" someone demanded. It might be Sir Gervaise himself."

"Not with that sort of luggage! The first one Huggins brought up was a sky-blue dressing-case."

Huggins was the porter, and Joyce was nothing if not observant.

The night staff returned to their neglected suppers. It was time, thought most of them, that they caught up with some sleep. Clarrie Parr got up and yawned.

"Another two days of this and then I'm off for a glorious twenty-four hours!" she observed, stretching luxuriously.

"You're not on call?"

"Not me! I've thought up a wonderful excuse."

"You'd wriggle out of anything!"

"So would you, if you had my incentive."

There was a lazy exodus towards the door, arrested by a sudden alert from the window.

"Oh, boy! Look at this!" Paddy had ceased to swing her legs from the sill and was twisting round to gaze down into the forecourt where a big yellow car, long and low and rakish, had drawn up in the space left by the departed Rolls.

"Oh, boy! Oh, boy! I wish we had surgeons like that instead of fat and balding Rory McNichol and old Horatius with his smoker's cough!"

Clarrie Parr moved swiftly to Paddy's side, drawing back the curtain a fraction to look out.

"Prepare for it, Paddy!" she announced silkily. "We *have* got a surgeon like that. As from this morning, Della Cortonwell's escort consults exclusively at Conyers Park."

31

"Good heavens, Calvert!" Jane's neighbor jumped up to avoid the stream of dark liquid pouring from the edge of the table. "How in the world did you manage to do that?"

"I'm sorry!" Jane made a frantic attempt to stem the flow of spilled coffee before it could reach the bench and the floor. "I—it slipped out of my hand."

Nobody appeared to be troubling about her explanation. They were crowding to the window again, jockeying for position, peering over each other's shoulder to catch a glimpse of the man and the girl arriving below, and Jane stood behind them, the breadth of the room between her and the triumphant Clarrie, feeling as if her heartbeats were tearing her apart.

"Do you think he'll marry her?" Paddy's clear young voice with its lilting Celtic intonation broke into her thoughts like splintering ice.

'A doctor, if he is wise as well as ambitious, marries in the right quarter, even in these days.'

Matron's cynical observation rang in Jane's ears as Clarrie turned from the window, her lazily-amused glance seeking Jane's across the table.

"Wasn't there a time when you knew Doctor Hemmingway rather well, Sister?" she inquired placidly. "It wasn't really so long ago, was it?"

How deliberately cruel one's fellow man could be! Jane's hand was at her throat, as if she might tear away some constricting band, but she managed to answer calmly enough:

"It's four years ago now. Yes, we knew each other rather well." She could marvel at the calmness of her own voice and she was even able to get up and cross the room under Clarrie's derisive stare. "I'm on duty in half an hour," she said. "I must go and change my coat."

A trail of coffee-stains marred the crisp spotlessness of the white wrapper she had put on less than an hour ago and she could not appear in the theatre like that, but the whole thing was really an excuse to get away from Clarrie's insolent, doubtful eyes. They had never been friends. Jane had tried, but she had been too much aware of the older girl's jealousy to persist after the first week or two, and she knew that her promotion to theatre sister would not have improved Clarrie's feeling for her. Yet all that scarcely seemed to matter as she made her escape into the corridor. It went on in a world outside the seething world of her own thoughts, where Stuart Hemmingway's name had penetrated like a burning arrow shot at random from the powerful bow of chance.

That he should ever come back into her life had seemed impossible, that he should return to Norchester had been equally remote, but now he was here, not only in Norchester but at Conyers, waiting to operate on her first day in the theatre!

The sinking feeling at the pit of her stomach which even the most hardened and experienced nurse feels when she hears that she is to go into the theatre was as nothing to the pain in her heart, to the ache of uncertainty and longing which beseiged it as memory turned back the pages of the past. And deep beneath everything lay the hard core of Stuart's bitterness. He had left her under no delusion about that. He would never forgive her 'so long as he lived.'

She went to her room, changing the soiled coat and transferring watch, scissors and pen to the pocket of the new one with automatic precision, feeling for the chain of safety pins at her belt in the way of routine. At Conyers they wore white coat-overalls over their ordinary clothes, with starched white coifs and neat, low-heeled white shoes.

Trim and neat and desperately efficient, she thought as she faced her pale reflection in the long mirror behind the bedroom door. Who would guess that your heart is choking you because you don't know how to face a man after four years of parting, because you feel that you'll never have the courage to bear it if you see forgetfulness in his indifferent glance!

> 'If I should meet thee
> After long years,
> How should I greet thee?
> With silence and tears.'

Words read long ago, garnered in the past to rise out of that past and strike deeply now! How should I greet thee? In silence; and the tears would be silent, too, dropping like gall in the secret places of the heart.

The eyes that looked back at her from the mirror were suddenly large and frightened, the shadows under them clearly marked on the pale, sensitive face.

Jane turned swiftly away, without looking at the small travelling clock on the mantelpiece, she knew that it was time for her to go.

Sister Oakroyd was in the theatre when she reached it.

"I expect you're nervous," she said, "but don't worry too much. All you'll have to do at first is to see to the doctors' gowns and adjust their masks once they've scrubbed up. After that, it will just be a matter of standing by, watching and collecting used swabs. Pick up as much useful information as you can and try not to worry about the less glamorous bits. After the first incision, you should be all right."

She moved across the theatre, checking the instruments for the sterilizer, counting swabs, cool, practical but withal, infinitely human. Stella Oakroyd was over forty, solid and dependable, and married to her profession now that it appeared that love had passed her by. She exuded confidence and drew to herself the respect and affection of her juniors as sunlight draws up dew. If there was anything she wanted to know, Jane was aware that she had only to ask Stella Oakroyd and the matter would be made abundantly clear. Stella would give her confidence to meet the occasion, but where was she to find the confidence to face Stuart Hemmingway for the first time in four long years?

She was wheeling the oxygen cylinders to the head of the table when the anaesthetist put his head round the door.

"Hullo, Jane! So you're in here this morning? We've made a nurse of you at last, eh?"

"Not yet!" She tried to smile naturally. "There's still today!"

"I've just met Hemmingway." He was speaking more to Stella than to Jane now, but her hands clenched tightly by her sides as she listened. "He's a remote sort of chap. Clever as the dickens, I believe, but almost inhuman in his approach. I suppose all this idolization that's been dished out in the local Press about his cures has gone to his head a bit, though you wouldn't guess it to look at him. In fact," he added as he passed through into the ante-room to scrub up, "you wouldn't be able to guess anything about Hemmingway at all. He's about as coldly enigmatical as they come!"

Jane counted a pile of towels twice and again a third time before she could trust herself to put the requisite number on the card. Six. The black numbers danced before her eyes. She had been up since six o'clock— waiting. How much longer could she wait without showing some outward sign of strain? How much longer could she keep her stretched nerves under absolute control, moving freely but carefully about the white-tiled room, waiting— waiting?

The patient was wheeled in, and she heard Stella and the anaesthetist talking to her. She was a thin, pale woman with enormous eyes.

Sudden panic clutched at Jane's heart as she experienced a terrible cowardly desire to run from the scene. I can't bear it, she thought. 'I'm not a good nurse. Something will happen and I'll disgrace myself. People's lives ought not to be trusted to anyone like me who can't even keep a check on their own emotions!

She felt Stella Oakroyd's hand on her arm.

"You'll be all right. Don't get in a panic. Just watch, and remember that the woman out there wouldn't have a chance if it wasn't for the surgeon's healing knife."

Fear abated then, sinking to a dull awareness of her own inefficiency. How little she really knew!

She turned, adjusting her mask, picking up the others from the sterilizer. Behind her the door opened. She felt paralyzed, unable to turn. Stuart was standing there—the surgeon, ready to operate.

She knew then that this was the only important factor. Jane Calvert could, and must, be submerged in Sister Calvert, the nurse.

Willing her heartbeats to cease their wild hammering, she turned to face Stuart. He was standing just inside the double white doors and immediately she recognized the change in him. The boy she had known had gone and in his place stood a mature man, sure of his success in the world and in absolute control of every emotion. The dark hair springing from the wide, high forehead, was still parted in the same way, but now it was sleeked back to control its natural tendency to unruliness, and the brow seemed heavier, somehow, shadowing the deep-set, penetrating eyes.

Jane looked into those eyes and knew that they masked a man's inmost thoughts as completely as if he had lowered a steely barrier between himself and the world at large.

Her heart gave one sickening twist and lay still. Matron came forward and introduced Stella Oakroyd, but she did not think it necessary to present Jane.

"Dear God," Jane prayed voicelessly, "don't let me faint or do anything foolish like that. He mustn't know. He must never know. He must never know!"

Stuart crossed to the basins and she forced herself to the necessary activity, following with his rubber gloves and waiting while he put them on. Her breath came quickly under the folds of her mask, beating hotly back against her face, and when Matron switched on the great shadowless lamp she felt as if the added light must penetrate through any disguise.

Stuart turned expectantly and she held out his gown for him, fastening the tapes securely behind his broad shoulders, marvelling that her hands should remain steady and sure at her task.

She held out the mask, waiting for him to turn round again, waiting for recognition to leap between them. He bent his dark head and she saw the familiar, angular line of his jaw, the long, straight nose with its arrogantly flaring nostrils, and the firm mouth with a new hardness about the fold of the lips. Her fingers were trembling, but she slipped the mask into place, remembering for one blinding moment the feel of his arms about her, the touch of those cynical lips against her own.

He straightened, looking fully at her for the first time, their eyes, the only visible part of their faces, holding for a second before he turned away to the table where his patient was waiting.

Jane stood rooted to the spot in powerless inefficiency while her errant heartbeats seemed to grow loud in the stillness. Had he recognized her in that brief second and passed her by? She felt Stella Oakroyd's hand beneath her elbow, guiding her to the far side of the table, and then, miraculously, her wild heartbeats were stilled. She had forgotten Stuart, forgotten the past. The miracle of life and death was being enacted before her wondering eyes.

"Scalpel, please."

The quiet voice and steady, purposeful hands moved across the table, Stuart's hands with merciful healing behind them. 'A good nurse's whole life is bound up with her duty.' Matron's words echoed in her ears as she watched Stella Oakroyd's instant response to Stuart's every request, and suddenly she knew that she had it in her to grow like that, absorbed in this great work of healing. To the exclusion of all else? The demand came from nowhere and she could not answer it, did not try to answer it as her busy hands separated swabs and handed towels. The moment was enough. She could see the beads of perspiration gather on Stuart's forehead from the heat of the overhead lamp and once or twice he glanced toward the head of the table where the anaesthetist sat beside his apparatus, but for the most part his head was bent; the broad shoulders, confident and powerful, stooped to his task.

When he straightened, at last, she saw the gleam of

admiration in Matron's eyes, the little unconscious smile of approval curving the thin lips. Gently, the patient was wheeled away. Matron went with the trolley to the anteroom, motioning Jane to follow.

Stuart was standing beside the basins, waiting. Once again Jane reached up to the concealing mask, but her mind was still on the miracle she had seen enacted behind the cream folding doors and she knew that the operation itself had been a brilliant success. Sister, Matron, the anaesthetist had all proclaimed it in an awed sort of silence which held wonder and admiration and envy respectively, and Rory McNichol, who had assisted, would accentuate it for weeks to come as he peered shortsightedly at his octogenarian patients. "A brilliant man! A coming man! Pity he wasn't a little more approachable!"

Jane watched Stuart Hemmingway too, drained, suddenly of all emotion. He did not speak, nor did he look her way again, although she had taken off her own mask as he reached the door. Before her long day was finished, she was physically and mentally exhausted, yet beneath the aching fatigue lay a curious elation. To work like this— to work with him—that might prove fulfilment of a kind!

She saw the years stretching ahead—the Home, Matron, Tom Sark with his laughing eyes and ready quips, and Stuart there and the work they would do together. It was work they both loved, but always there would be the barrier of Stuart's disillusionment standing between them.

It was late when she left the Home. Stuart had not operated again that day, but Rory McNichol had rushed in with an acute at ten minutes to five. Although it took less than half an hour to rid his patient of an appendix which had troubled her for years, it was well after six before Jane switched off the final light and closed the theatre door.

The corridors were deserted. It was that comparatively quiet hour between tea and visitors when patients read or dozed comfortably and even the most provocative bell remained silent. The supper trolleys were set, waiting beside the lift doors, and an air of peace and contentment prevailed.

Going downstairs Jane thought about Della Cortonwell for the first time. The more luxurious, and therefore more expensive rooms, were on the ground floor and the heavy oak door of number seven was ajar. A radio played softly and the fragrance of exotic flowers drifted out to Jane as she passed. She knew an instant's blind jealousy as she thought of the other girl, pampered, beautiful perhaps, surrounded by everything that money could buy and ready to take Stuart's affection as a matter of course. He had probably been to see Della, bringing the flowers and standing in the room beside the high hospital bed looking down at his patient with the cynical twist gone from his lips, erased by a tolerant half smile. Or had the suave, attentive consultant gone down before the man and Della's color been heightened by a lover's kiss?

She tore her thoughts away from such a scene, changing her soiled wrapper for her tweed coat and running a comb through the thick dark waves of her auburn hair.

How pale she looked! Theatre work had its own peculiar reactions and her first day had been a heavy one, although she would not have missed it for worlds.

The nurses used a back entrance which joined the drive near the main gates and as she reached them a car came swiftly up behind her, a long, rakish, yellow car with a single occupant. It drew up before the archway leading to the busy thoroughfare beyond, but Jane had reached the gates before it pulled away. It was then that she realized that the driver had been waiting for her, and her heart beat suddenly with a nervous insistence. The turn of a head, dark brows under a soft felt hat, the unmistakable set of a lean jaw, all these were proof enough of Stuart, but her tingling nerves had been aware of his presence even as the car had passed her back there on the drive. She wanted to run. She did not want to meet him like this, so desperately unprepared and tired after a long, exacting day!

He leaned over, opening the off-side door for her to get in, and she saw those fine hands she had watched earlier in the day grasp the wheel again with a tightened grip.

"I thought I couldn't have been mistaken," he said. "Hop in, and I'll give you a lift home."

Cool, suave, impersonal, it was not the voice she remembered. Stuart had changed so much in so short a time.

"Thank you." She tried to keep her own voice quite steady. "I wondered if you recognized me this morning in the theatre."

She had not meant to say that, but she accepted the fact that she had uttered the most dominant thought in her mind in a moment of stress and could not retract it now Stuart started the car before he answered her.

"It was easy enough," he said. "Eyes don't change a great deal, even after four eventful years."

She had not expected him to refer so directly to the past, not as he had done, without the slightest vestige of emotion, and the coldness she had experienced all day took final possession of her heart. What was there to say to him?

"They've been eventful years for you. Everyone is talking about your success, Stuart. You have done so very well."

He steered the car in among the tea-time traffic.

"And you?" he asked. "When did you leave the hospital?"

"Three years ago."

"I thought you would have stayed there. Do you find it—more profitable at Conyers?"

If she were to tell him the truth she would have to confess that she had left the City General because of its memories, because she had been unable to go on working there when he had gone. It had been the scene of their love affair, that short, brief passion of a distant day.

"When we moved out to Heppleton, Conyers was nearer for me. There were other reasons, but that was the chief one."

"And you're happy at Conyers?"

He asked the question formally, as if it were expected of him, and a small spark of anger kindled in her eyes.

"Perfectly happy," she answered defensively. "I am doing the sort of work I love."

"We both seem to be lucky in that respect." He kept his eyes fixed on the road ahead, but Jane had the impression that he saw each small, nervous movement of her hands and the tensed way she continued to sit upright in the seat beside him. "Matron told me that this morning was your first day in the theatre. You stood up to it very well."

They were on safer ground here and she admitted to nervousness.

"At first I was quite certain I should disgrace myself. I felt that I wouldn't know one instrument from another, and then I was relieved to discover that I didn't have to pass you anything——"

Had that sounded like an admission of some other type of nervousness, the strain of their meeting, confession of her continuing love? She stole a look at his face, but the dark profile told her nothing. All emotion remained submerged beneath the conventional, professional mask which Stuart knew so well how to wear to advantage.

"It will all come naturally enough in time," he said. "I felt much the same when I first started to operate on my own. There was that desperate moment when the mind becomes a blank, when nothing registers, and then it is forgotten. The interest of the job is all that matters. You have Matron's confidence, and that means quite a lot."

Had he asked Agnes Lawdon about her, discussing her future if not the past? Jane could not think so. He seemed to have buried himself behind that calm professional mask, the eminent surgeon to the exclusion of all else. Was this what four years had made of him, four years when bitterness had eaten deep and disillusionment had left its scar?

"Will you be at Conyers permanently?" she asked as they neared Heppleton, with its rows of neat cottages and the tall maypole on its village green. "Do you mean to settle in Norchester?"

"Settling has rather a stagnant sound. I still feel that I have a great deal to learn. No," he concluded without taking his eyes from the way ahead even for an instant, "I don't suppose I shall be much longer than a few months at Conyers. Then I hope to go abroad again."

She felt the coldness in him, accentuating the furtherance of his career before everything else, as if that could be all that concerned him now, but surely rumor said otherwise? There was Della Cortonwell.

An ugly thought, pregnant and sharp with jealousy, suggested that Della would further that career, too— Della, who was Sir Gervaise Cortonwell's only child. 'A doctor, if he is wise as well as ambitious, marries in the right quarter, even in these days!' Was she always to be haunted by Matron's cynical reflection? *In the right quarter!* The Cortonwell's were undoubtedly the right quarter for Stuart, and she was convinced that he knew it.

Pride, fierce and stinging, gripped her by the throat, forcing back the hurt she felt.

"I dare say you will settle out there, Stuart," she said. "You were always most interested in clinical work."

Whatever she said, apparently, brought them back to the past.

"First love—last love!" He smiled cynically. "I've been true to that, after my fashion. But what of you? Have the past few years treated you kindly enough?"

She had been unprepared for the intimacy of such a question, but pride kept her head high and her eyes clear. "I've had my work," she said. "That in itself was interesting."

"And it brought you fulfilment?" There was a faintly derisive note in his voice. "It gave you complete satisfaction?"

"Yes," she told him with spirit, "it must have done. I have no regrets."

She thought of Hazel and Linda Jane and knew that what she said was true, if only in part, but somehow her voice hadn't been quite convincing enough. It had shaken a little and she had lowered her gaze to her gloved hands clasped over the worn leather handbag in her lap. As he slowed the car at Heppleton's only pedestrian crossing, Stuart turned his head to look at her. He was the old Stuart again, kindly, thoughtful, the lines about his mouth erased, but almost before the change in his expression had registered on her tired brain the mask was down again and he was the rising young consultant, attentive, interested, but remote.

"We go round here," Jane said as they moved on, "but you needn't turn the car off the main road. If you pull up I'll get down at the end of the lane."

She saw him look about him, at the row of shabby houses and the children playing noisily on the pavement, arguing over turns on a battered tricycle.

"Don't bother to come any farther," she repeated, and her voice was hard.

"What about your mother, Jane?" he asked.

"She died—three years ago. Not long after I went to Conyers."

"And your sister? She was married, wasn't she? I don't think I ever met her."

"She's widowed now." Jane's face had lost most of its color. "We live together." She got out of the car and bent to the open window. "Thanks for bringing me this far."

She turned away. The bonnet looked ridiculously long and shining, out of place in their plebeian neighborhood, part of the background Stuart had deliberately built up for himself in those four years since their parting. It shut him away from her as effectively as the shining plate glass of the windscreen closed him in now.

He leaned over the wheel to say evenly:

"*Au revoir*, Jane. In the nature of things, we are bound to meet again."

She turned swiftly away, almost running the short distance between the end of the lane and the gate which Hazel had barred to keep Linda Jane in the garden. Fumbling with the patent latch, she was aware of Stuart's car still standing on the main road, aware of him sitting there behind the impenetrable glass barrier watching her

41

retreat. She saw him take a case from his inside pocket and light a cigarette. The match flared and he cupped it loosely in his hands before he raised his head and exhaled a satisfying cloud of smoke.

She had watched the action hundreds of times and it stabbed deeply. The latch responded to her efforts and she let the gate slam to behind her. Before she had reached the front door the car at the end of the lane moved noiselessly away.

Her throat parched, every nerve in her body taut, she thrust her key into the lock. Hazel was in the hall, carrying Linda Jane up to bed.

"I'm going up pick-a-back!" that bright young sprite announced unnecessarily. "Watch me, Auntie Jane!"

It was Hazel that Jane watched, however, Hazel mounting the stairs with absolute confidence now, her small daughter perched securely on her back. So many things had happened in four eventful years.

Hazel took a long time to come down. She had left Jane's meal on the end of the dining room table, salad and some pressed meat and small, home-made tarts. Obviously her own tea had been shared with Linda earlier, and when she came into the room Jane noticed that she had changed her blue print overall for a tweed skirt and coat. Her eyes were shining with a quiet happiness.

"Jane," she said, "could I be a selfish pig and ask you to baby-sit again? I know you must be tired, but Lindy's generally a lamb once she's been put to bed."

Linda's behavior was anything but lamb-like at the moment. With the peculiar sixth sense of childhood, she was fully aware of something unusual afoot and was asserting her claim to her mother's attention in her own peculiar way.

"Mummy! I want a drink. Please can I have 'nother drink, 'cos I'm thirsty?"

When there was no immediate reponse from a normally doting and attentive parent, there was a brief pause, followed by a series of sleepy yells.

"She isn't generally like this," Hazel apologised, glancing uneasily at the clock in the corner. It was evident that she did not notice Jane's own distraught state. "I did so want to go, but——"

Jane thrust her out of the door.

"Go, Hazel! Go quickly. You'll be late!"

She heard the garden gate clang behind her relieved sister and turned to mount the stairs. She ought to be glad.

She *was* glad, but somehow she wished that the knowledge that Hazel was in love again hadn't come tonight.

Linda capitulated swiftly to the offer of one of Jane's tarts and a bed-time story, and Jane made fresh tea when she got downstairs again. She washed up, thinking of Hazel. Young, hopeful, radiant again. Hazel had a right to happiness, the sort of happiness she had lost when George had died, and it could mean added security for Linda Jane. She wanted them both to be happy, and they would share it with her, as they had shared so much in the past.

Brief, foolish thought! Hazel came back shortly after eight o'clock, bringing Eric Bridgewater with her.

"I thought you wouldn't mind me bringing Eric in to supper," she said, limping through to the kitchen to prowl in the larder for something to feed the man, and Jane was left confronting Eric and liking what she saw.

He was big and fair and obviously easy-going, with his affection for Hazel an open book shining in his honest brown eyes. Like a faithful spaniel, Jane thought, whose mistress's every wish is his command, although there was more of the tenacity of the bulldog in his determination not to let Hazel out of his sight. There was a certain possessiveness in his voice, too, which suggested that he might have one or two desires of his own.

He met Jane with just a hint of defensiveness, as if he was prepared to do battle should she attempt to stand in his way, but Jane knew that Hazel's decision was already made. She would marry Eric Bridgewater, and that quickly.

"Jane," she said when she came back into the room with a tray, "Eric and I are going to be married."

Jane's delight was instantaneous, sweeping aside selfishness and doubt. This was right for Hazel, right for Linda, too. They would have someone to care for them, a man to stand between them and the outside world. She felt no resentment at the thought of Eric Bridgewater coming to live at Heppleton with them. The house was amply big enough. It had really been too big for them after her mother had died, but Hazel had been reluctant to let it go.

Jane drank a companionable cup of tea with them while they ate their supper. Eric was pleasant, cheerful in a hearty sort of way that suited Hazel after all these years of depression. She had never been made to live alone, and a man's adoration was essential to her. She blossomed under it like an unfolding rose, watching Eric dispatch the last

43

of her succulent pastries and sighing quite audibly with content.

"You're a satisfying sort of person to cook for, Eric," she said. "You're not hidebound by a lot of likes and dislikes!"

"I've always been partial to a bit of home cooking!" he acknowledged readily. "My mother used to turn out stuff like this."

Fair enough, Jane thought. Satisfaction on both sides.

Rather pointedly, Hazel chose to do the washing up alone.

"You did the tea things, Jane. Sit and talk to Eric!"

It was Eric who did the talking. No sooner had the kitchen door closed upon his beloved than he rose and offered Jane a cigarette from the packet in his pocket. When she refused it he lit one for himself, rather nervously, she thought. His voice was quite steady, however, when he said:

"I know you won't mind this, Jane—I know how fond you are of Hazel and young Lindy—so you won't grudge Hazel a home of her own, I'm sure." He paused, drawing hard on the cigarette, forcing an added firmness into his voice as he went on: "It's all rather a surprise, I guess—rather sudden, perhaps. What will you do about the house?"

Jane stared at him.

"The house?" she repeated stupidly.

"Hazel and I will want our own place."

Of course! It was only natural with two people in love. Jane crushed down the rising pain in her heart.

"I'll have to think about the house," she said. "It's—too big for one person, but I kept it on because—because it held so many memories."

She crossed to the fire, stirring the laggard coals into new life.

"When will Hazel and you be married?" she asked.

"Pretty soon. There's no point in waiting, really." He was more confident now, once he had got that awkward bit over. It seemed that Jane wasn't greatly concerned about living alone. He didn't quite know what to make of her, that taut upper lip and the clear grey-green eyes meeting his squarely when she might have been accepting defeat. "It'll be a quiet affair, of course. I've no people." He went on outlining his plans, unconscious of any cruelty. "Hazel and I will have our own place, somewhere in the country, I guess. It doesn't matter where I live. I travel

44

about a great deal, but Hazel and young Lindy can come with me most days. It will be good for her to get about. She'll have a woman to do the rough work in the house."

When, eventually, they were alone, Hazel appeared sensitive about their fully matured plans.

"If Eric hadn't wanted to live out of town you could have come with us, Jane," she began.

"No, Hazel—good gracious, no!" Jane was quick to protest. "It's the most natural thing in the world that Eric should want you to himself once you're married. I'll be all right. I'll have to give up the house, of course. The rent's too heavy for one person, and we can share the furniture. I'll look out for a flat somewhere."

Hazel did little things to please her after that, so that the hurt they had inflicted should not go too deep. She felt guilty, but sometimes she consoled herself with the reflection that her own unexpected romance was not the only reason for Jane's sudden reticence.

Jane plunged back into work. There was plenty of it at Conyers. They were hopelessly understaffed, as usual. Two of the Irish nurses had left after a 'few words' with Matron. They were more independent these days, knowing their value in the general shortage. Quite often she helped in the rooms when the theatre was not in use.

It was a week before she met Stuart Hemmingway again. Clarrie Parr was on leave and she had taken her duty on the downstairs corridor, where bells rang incessantly. She saw the tally go down on number seven as she prepared the mid-morning trays and she picked up Della Cortonwell's diet chart with a quickened heartbeat. Nothing special. Marmite, biscuits and cream cheese. It was all ready.

She walked briskly along the corridor, tapping lightly on the door of number seven before she entered.

The room was full of flowers. Their heady perfume was the first impression she got as she entered, but her eyes went instinctively to the girl in the bed. Della Cortonwell looked as if she might be taller than average and she was very slim. She had hollows at the base of her throat and there were deep shadows beneath her amber colored eyes. Otherwise, she was strikingly beautiful. Her hair was a deep chestnut brown, her skin pale by contrast, and her red lips were firm and exquisitely moulded. There was a determination about the lift of her head that Jane liked, although she told herself that it was probably immaterial what she thought about her unexpected patient.

45

"Good morning!" She put the tray down on the bedside table and felt for the bed rest. "I heard your bell. I'm deputizing for Nurse Parr."

Della gave her a long, searching look.

"Why haven't I seen you before?"

"Normally I'm in the theatre, on the floor above."

Della's interest deepened, the amber eyes darkening a little.

"That's Stuart's sphere, I suppose. Was he operating yesterday?" She laughed suddenly. "Of course! I should learn to call him Mr. Hemmingway!"

"We've been concentrating on tonsils and the odd appendix this week." Jane's heart was beating with ridiculous energy. "There hasn't been anything big."

"Big enough for Stuart, do you mean? I suppose he's gone beyond tonsils." Della studied her tray uninterestedly. "How long do they expect me to thrive on this hateful mess?" she demanded.

"If you don't like it you can have something else, but it really is very nourishing."

Della made a wry face.

"And that's the point, isn't it?" Suddenly her voice was harsh. "The unequal battle against the insidious disease."

Jane said cheerfully: "There are times when we all need to rest, when we've overdone things a little."

"At twenty-five!" The lovely mouth twisted bitterly. "Can you imagine anything more ghastly than having to 'take care' at every step because they've suddenly discovered that one lung is doing the work of two?"

The amber eyes, clear and alert, were steady on Jane's, disdaining the soft answer, challenging her to speak truthfully.

"No," Jane admitted. "But you're not being terribly fair, are you? This is one disease where a cure can be almost certain these days, but you have to give it a chance to work. So much advance has been made in the past decade that nothing is impossible. Mr. Hemmingway is an authority on the subject. You are in safe hands."

"I know." Della looked ashamed of her sudden outburst. "He wants me to go to Switzerland, but I won't."

Jane removed the offending Marmite, proffering the biscuits, which met with as little enthusiasm.

"Why won't you go?" she asked.

A flood of color suffused Della's pale cheeks.

"I couldn't. There are—reasons. I don't want to leave Norchester. Surely Stuart can do something for me here?"

46

She was clinging to Stuart's strength, to his ability to help her, and possibly to the comforting knowledge of his love.

Jane turned abruptly to the window, making a pretense of drawing back the curtains, rearranging the chrysanthemums in the tall vase on the sill until she was in absolute control of her emotions.

Della was not what she had expected. She was not small and soft and delicately appealing, the sort of person to stimulate a man's protective instinct, but she probably had a greater attraction for Stuart for that very reason. Della knew where she was going. Strength of will lay behind that high, narrow forehead and in the fold of the red lips, and there was purpose, too, in the unwavering look of the strange, light eyes. Della Cortonwell was a personality not easily assigned to any particular niche, with her direct approach and baffling suggestion of reserve. Jane knew instinctively that her present illness had come upon her with all the paralyzing quality of shock, a thing undreamed of and, therefore, the more resented. It was something to which she would never become resigned.

Jane had turned back to the bed when Stuart came in. He put his head round the door after a first brief knock, and then he came into the room and crossed to his patient's side. Jane saw Della's face light up, her eyes grow warm and deep in the instant.

"Well, how do we feel this morning?" he asked with a mixture of professional reserve and a tenderness Jane remembered only too well. He took Della's wrist between his fingers. "Sleep well?" he asked.

"As well as could be expected, Doctor!" Della mocked. "Stuart, you've got to get me out of here. I'm not really as ill as all this!"

"And have you running all over the town, and heaven knows what else besides?" he queried, keeping his gaze fixed on his watch.

"I promise you I won't run—not if you say not to!"

"I'd have to have someone to keep a check on you." He released her wrist and smiled into her stubborn face. "No, Della, you're safer here."

"Because I refuse to do as you say and go to Switzerland?"

He sat down on the bed with his back to Jane.

"Because what I propose would be the best way, the surest way for your recovery."

Della put her fingers over the wrist he had released, as if to protect it. She was no longer looking at Stuart.

"You've got a strongly sadistic streak somewhere," she accused. "You know quite well why I don't want to go."

He got up from the bed and crossed to the dressing-table, idly examining the chart Jane had left there.

"You needn't go back to St. Moritz," he said evenly.

"I'm not suggesting that."

"It would be all the same." Della's eyes were still resentful. "I'm not going," she said.

He raised his shoulders in the faintest suggestion of a shrug and turned to Jane.

"How goes the theatre work?" he asked. "You look tired."

His eyes searched hers, gravely, professionally. There was nothing else.

"I'm beginning to gain the confidence you promised I should," she said. "I had none at first."

"I'm surprised at that," he said immediately. "Time was when you had plenty of confidence, Jane."

Della's eyes searched first Jane's face and then Stuart's. Jane was very pale.

"I had no idea you two knew each other," she said.

"We're both fledglings of the City General," Stuart answered, the indifference of his tone stinging Jane, as it was probably meant to do. "We—lost touch for a year or two, though. I had no idea Sister Calvert was at Conyers."

Or Conyers might have been deprived of your valuable services, Jane thought. Oh, Stuart! this is too paltry. If you want to hurt me there are so many other ways. Yet, indifference was the final, the most dreaded barb, and he knew how to use it with the finesse of an expert. It could of course, be quite genuine.

She turned sharply from the thought, but it remained. It had been pursuing her for days. When she had stood listening to his retreating footsteps walking out of her life that night four years ago she had lived in the hope that he would return, that this was not the end. It never could be, she had reasoned, between them, but the days had passed and there had been no word. They had drifted into weeks, to months, and, finally to years. Stuart had accepted her decision as irrevocable. It was he who had considered it final, not she. She had expected faithfulness beyond the limit of man's frailty.

The whole argument was unfair, of course! It was she who had refused to leave England and take her chance with him in a student's job abroad. That had evoked bitterness, the bitter, accusing harshness of his first blind reaction to her refusal of him. He had accepted the post and gone off without further explanation and she had heard nothing from him since.

"I'll take this cup away, Miss Cortonwell, and bring you something else."

She wanted to escape, to get away from that look on Della's face and Stuart's tall, angular confidence. He was master of the situation, the man at one with his profession whose confidence was expected of him. It was part of his stock in trade, but it was new to her. There had been a time when she had shared his uncertainty, his youthful groping with the future, but now it seemed that he needed nothing, neither tenderness nor encouragement nor the help of love. There was a hardness about him that emanated from within. She could not think that it had been put on as an armor.

Tom Sark was in the corridor when she reached it.

"Hullo!" he said. "I'd no idea you were down on Millionaires' Row. I thought you were exclusively theatre these days?"

"I can't sit twiddling my thumbs waiting for emergencies to crop up." Her answer had been sharper than she had intended and she was instantly sorry. "Have you finished for the day?" she asked.

"Not me! 'A doctor's work is never done'!" He quoted Matron with a grin. "Anyway, you've been avoiding me these past few days. Why?"

"I've been very busy."

"You're always busy. We all are, but we must get some sort of relaxation or we'll develop into very dull boys!" He looked at her keenly. "You appear to be in need of relaxation right now, so I shall prescribe a 'cuppa' at the Linden Café and a visit to the flicks. Doctor's orders!"

"I'm standing in for Clarrie Parr," Jane hedged, "and I'll be on call even if I do get the afternoon off."

They had reached the green baize door leading to the kitchens and she put her back against it and slid through, relieved that she had managed to evade him without undue argument, but she had not taken Tom's natural persistence into sufficient account. He was still there when she reappeared with Della's beaker of warm milk.

"Look here, Jane," he declared; "it's no use trying to put me off like that. I'm a persistent devil when I try,

49

and I'm certainly trying now. We've got to have time off, and we've got to have it together. To hell with Conyers' rules!"

Jane walked briskly along the corridor, her head up, a purposeful gleam in her eyes.

"It's no use, Tom. If Matron gets to know we'll both be on the carpet."

His face reddened.

"She's not going to interfere in my affairs," he declared. "Not any more. I'm not one of her nursing staff."

"But I am," Jane pointed out. "Please, Tom, don't make it difficult. I—I'm serious about this."

"The devil you are! So am I." He put a detaining hand on her arm as a door opened ahead of them. "It's not like you to lie down to this sort of thing, Jane. See you later!"

He wheeled and went off in the direction of the doctors' common-room, leaving Jane to face Stuart Hemmingway outside Della's door.

It would have been impossible for Stuart to have pretended that he had not seen the incident with Tom. He scorned pretense at any time, and he was regarding her now with a sardonic expression which deepened the color of his eyes until they were almost black.

"What have we here?" he asked, lifting the beaker from the tray and sniffing curiously. "Nothing obnoxious, I hope?"

His care for Della came first, of course. Jane felt her hands tighten on the tray as her breathing quickened.

"Miss Cortonwell didn't want the Marmite you ordered. It appears to upset her."

"A good many things appear to be upsetting Della at present," he mused, "but I think we'll have to humor her over the Marmite. She isn't really a difficult person, but at times you will have to exert your authority."

"I'm not really Miss Cortonwell's nurse," she told him. "Nurse Parr is in charge down here."

"Pity," he said, as if the fact had only just occurred to him. "Of course, you're in the theatre. Is it a permanent posting, or are you very much on trial?"

"Very much on trial, I should think."

He glanced at her keenly.

"It's what you wanted?"

"Yes." She looked away from him and a wretched sort of pride goaded her to say: "I don't think I disgraced myself the other day. Matron was apparently quite satisfied—or so she told me."

"Compliments from Matron are never anything but genuine, I should imagine," he said. "She approves of you, Jane. You should go far." Satire deepened his tone and the lines about his handsome mouth were etched more deeply. "Beware of the romance angle, though," he warned. "She has an interest in young Sark's career, I understand."

He moved slightly, opening Della's door to let her pass through, but he did not follow her into the room. Della looked up indifferently, waving the tray aside.

"I don't want that," she said. "Sit down and talk to me."

Jane stood at the side of the bed.

"My only excuse for being here would be to make sure that you drank your milk."

"If Matron comes along, do you mean?" Della laughed. "Good heavens, the woman must be a veritable sergeant-major! Don't you ever relax?"

"Off duty—quite a bit," Jane smiled. There was something about Della which she had to like. "But at the present moment we're hopelessly understaffed and there's very little free time in consequence."

Della's finely pencilled brows drew together in a quick frown.

"Stuart told me about you being in the theatre. I expect you like it much better than lackeying in the corridors?"

Jane wondered what Stuart had said, in what way he had discussed her with Della. Had he mentioned the past, or had he skimmed that part over, confessing nothing more than the fact that they were old acquaintances? Her heart twisted with the thought of his indifference and the studied hardness about him whenever they confronted one another, and she contrasted it jealously with his manner to Della, yet she could not honestly dislike the girl who lay propped among her pillows watching her with steady, heavy-lidded eyes. The torture of her love was her own undoing, for she knew that she could continue to see those contrasts daily and be powerless to change them. I've had time, she thought—time to school myself against loving like this!

Della began to drink the milk, turning the warmed beaker round and round in her thin hands, a little, musing smile playing about her lips.

"Tell me, Jane, what made you take up nursing?" she asked.

"It was what I wanted to do."

"A calling?"

"If you like. Sometimes I think one could never do it with any success otherwise."

"The mop-and-bucket part?"

"Partly that."

"Would you say that your life was complete, now that you've got what you wanted by way of a career?"

A slow, painful color stained Jane's cheeks.

"Do we ever get—all we want from life?" she challenged.

Della raised herself on the bed, leaning forward with such a look of intensity in her pale eyes that Jane felt suddenly anxious.

"No," she said, "we don't. It's forbidden by an all-powerful Providence, or what-have-you. It would not be good for us to have all we wanted from life, presumably, not even such little things as happiness or abundant health!"

Jane saw it then, the pitiful, groping desire under the bitterness, the tortured indecision with which Della Cortonwell faced the future. The lung infection might or might not be serious, but for anyone like Stuart it would be madness to take a chance.

The sudden revelation clutched her by the throat, sending the blinding tears into her eyes, and she turned sharply from the bed.

"You'll come again?" Della asked urgently. "You're so restful, Jane. I can't stand arrogant, healthful specimens like Nurse Parr always about. They make me green with envy and retard the cure!"

She had re-encased herself in her former armor of cynicism, but that one brief glimpse of the frightened soul underneath had been enough for Jane. Della was not nearly so sure of herself as she would like everyone to believe. Deep down in the secret places of her heart she was vulnerable, as vulnerable as Jane herself.

CHAPTER THREE

THREE DAYS PASSED in which Jane continued to work like a Trojan. The theatre work was heavy, especially the important hour of preparing and checking before the operation itself. Norman Fash, the gynaecologist, was easy to work for, passing over minor errors with his vaguely tolerant smile, and she began to gain confidence by slow degrees.

If Stuart visited Della—and she heard that he did—he and Jane did not encounter one another, even in the corridors. He might have passed completely out of her life again but for the fact that his name was on everybody's lips and there was the certainty that he would operate again very soon.

When she glanced down the lists each morning Jane read the surgeons' names with a mixture or relief and disappointment, and then, one morning it was there.

"Miss Cowrie. Room twenty-four. Mr. Hemmingway."

The color rose to her cheeks and receded, leaving her abnormally pale. Stella Oakroyd had so much confidence in her now that she was allowing her to pass the better known instruments to the surgeons—scalpels, tweezers, retractors—but suddenly it seemed that she had no experience, no confidence. Stuart's familiar name had blotted all that out once more and her nerves were on edge again, her blood pounding madly through her veins. The operation would leave her stripped of her hardly won calm, an easy target for the barbed shafts of Stuart's continuing bitterness.

The final settling up between Hazel and herself had come sooner than she had expected, too. Eric had decided on an early marriage so that they could be in their own home before Christmas, and to Jane's silent consternation he was preparing to remove her sister and Linda to some considerable distance. He could work quite well, he maintained, from either side of his district, and he had found a house outside Nottingham.

Jane had tried not to mind, and Hazel was too starry-eyed to consider possible loneliness. She would have Eric and Linda Jane. Her world was, in effect, complete.

She did not remember to ask Jane what she planned to do when they finally gave up the tenancy of the Heppleton house, and Jane, fighting a growing and rather terrifying apathy about the future, said that she would get a flat somewhere as soon as they were settled.

"Will you store a few pieces of furniture for me, Hazel?" she asked. "They could go with your things and you could send them back when I needed them."

"And in the meantime?" Hazel had asked quiltily.

"I'll get a room at Conyers."

"An attic bedroom!"

"They're all right," Jane had assured her. "They have the loveliest view between the Cathedral spires."

"You'll have more work put on your shoulders, that's all," Hazel had been quick to object, although she had no alternative arrangement to suggest. "Matron will be only too pleased to have you on call all the time!"

"It's my job in life," Jane had reminded her without her usual buoyancy. "It's what I can do."

And work blots out memory occasionally, she thought.

When she made her way to the operating theatre she felt tired. It was something so unusual that she would not let herself admit it and began her preparations immediately. The conversation with Hazel was two days old, but it still lingered in her mind and she thought that perhaps it would be best to ask for a room at Conyers. If she was to become a regular theatre sister Matron would prefer her to live in.

Tom Sark put his fair head round the door at quarter to nine.

"I know I'm playing second fiddle to a few swabs and a hank of sutures," he observed, "but how much longer am I to wait for an answer to that dinner invitation of mine?"

Jane went on stacking swabs, turning only when she had closed the sterilizer door.

"See what I mean?" he grinned. "Swabs, instruments, diathermy! All in order for the great Mr. Hemmingway. 'Yes, Doctor Sark, what can I do for *you*?' "

Jane laughed. His mockery was only slightly barbed and he was looking at her with a speculative light in his blue eyes.

"I've been busy at home," she explained briskly. "I'm —moving into the top storey."

"Here—at Conyers?" He evidently could not believe it. "But why? You'll get twice as much work to do, Janey, old girl, and twice as little time to yourself."

"And twice as many opportunities of seeing you! Just think of it!"

"It has its possibilities," he agreed. "I might even move in myself."

"You've heard, of course, that resident physicians are

barred? The male of the species can be too much of a distraction."

"Surely not to Matron! Anyway, she might be persuaded to make an exception of me."

"The decision doesn't rest with Matron," Jane pointed out. "It would be entirely one for the Board."

"And the Board is sitting tightly under Matron's firm little thumb," he declared. "Even the all-powerful Norman Fash daren't cross her too often."

Jane frowned.

"One woman ought not to have so much power."

He laughed, perching himself negligently on the end of the wash basins.

"It's no use, Jane! You're not cut out to uphold causes. You're just not the militant type! Has anyone ever told you before how sweetly feminine you look in that starched napkin you wear round your head, or am I the first?"

Someone had told her that the first time she had worn the 'starched napkin' and she was waiting for him now! Jane's heart turned over with longing and regret. Oh, Stuart! Stuart! How shall I ever learn to forget you? How am I to put you out of my life deliberately and for all time?

She moved away from Tom, over to the scrubbed bench, and began to count out masks, seeing them suddenly through a mist of tears which made her burningly angry and ashamed. What sort of nurse was she that she let her own affairs dominate her will like this? Stuart would come and she must present a calm, resolute front to him. He had dismissed the past, brushing it aside as of no moment, and she must do the same. Repeated emotionalism would only leave its mark on her for him to see. Those deep grey eyes missed so little.

Tom wandered round the ante-room, picking up this and that and laying it down without interest.

"I'd never be any use at carving people up," he said gloomily. "Someone else will have to gather the laurels in that direction. Hemmingway is doing rather well, isn't he?" he added tentatively, half turning to survey her under lowered brows. "He had all the cards stacked in his favor, of course."

"I don't think so." Jane had turned slowly, her level eyes on his, her cheeks faintly colored with her rising impatience. "Nobody has *all* the cards stacked for them, Tom. Most of us have to work for what we finally achieve. It's—rather belittling to suggest otherwise."

He looked at her for a minute uncertainly and then he laughed, coming up behind her to pinion her arms close to her side.

"If you were half as efficient a nurse as you imagine yourself to be, Janey," he said, "you would imprison that topknot of auburn curls under your coif. As it is, they're more than somewhat exasperating, and, coupled with the flush and the anger, they're irresistible."

For one desperate second she fancied that he was about to kiss her and she froze in cold horror at the thought. Not here! Not in the ante-room of the operating theatre, with her tasks only half completed because he had already distracted her. Her eyes widened and she saw him look up and glance over her head. In the next instant she was free.

Stuart Hemmingway walked through from the theatre, closely followed by Matron. He held one half of the swinging door open and Jane could see the theatre through the round port-hole of the other one—the hooded lamp, the oxygen cylinders, the high, tiled walls with their green patterned dado and the fan-like air-conditioner revolving at the window. It all seemed unreal, like a stage set for some tense drama, and she felt Matron's eyes upon her, scorching in their contempt.

She could not look at Stuart, but she knew that he had removed his coat and was waiting for someone to help him with his gown. It was her allotted task, but she could not move to perform it, knowing so well the expression she expected to see in his eyes. Cynicism, and some of Matron's contempt, perhaps.

"Do you mind, Sister?"

He indicated the waiting gown and mask, and when she was forced to look at him, at last, she read neither cynicism nor contempt in his eyes. Only a cold and furious anger.

Of course, he thought that she had encouraged Tom! He would view the incident as nothing but a clandestine affair played out in the worst of taste. She bit her lips, trying to keep the stinging tears out of her eyes as he said in an assured matter-of-fact way:

"We will be over three hours on this particular job. Do you think you feel up to it? You look decidedly peaky."

"I'll manage," she said, keeping her voice calm. "I've got a constitution like a horse."

"And eyes like a hurt fawn! Never mind, Jane, doctors are not all impervious to a woman's blandishments. You're sure to win in the end."

His words struck her with the force of a blow. Not only

had he accused her of encouraging Tom, but he believed that the initiative had been hers. Anger welled up in her from the very depths of despair.

"You must think that I have no more to do than trade on people's emotions," she accused him shakily, "but it isn't true! I—I——!"

He turned casually and held out his gown.

"Suitable explanations rarely present themselves in an emergency," he said briefly, "and proffered advice has its own reward, apparently."

He was referring to his cynical warning that afternoon in the downstairs corridor when he had first seen her with Tom and there was no way of telling him how wrong he had been, even then.

Matron had come over to check the list and there were still last-minute items to set out. With a sense of relief Jane saw Stella Oakroyd come through from the theatre with the anaesthetist, who had stopped at the pantry for the inevitable cup of tea.

"All fixed up?" Stella asked encouragingly.

"I've only the blood plasma to fetch," Jane said as she made her escape from the room.

She almost ran along the corridor to the small office tucked away at its far end where the blood was kept, wondering who was on duty and if she could hide her agitation before she got there.

Tom Sark looked up from the bench beside the window when she opened the door. He had been peering through a small microscope at some cultures and he moved to make room for her beside him.

"Look here, Jane!" he said. "Come and look at these bugs."

"There isn't time." Jane knew how irritable that had sounded, but she couldn't help herself. But for Tom, all this need never have happened. "Can you get me a bottle of blood—A group, please."

He looked up at her lazily.

"What's the hurry?" he asked.

"It just happens to be rather urgent," she told him coldly. "I'm in the theatre."

"Oh, I see! The great Hemmingway mustn't be kept waiting, you mean!" He shrugged carelessly. "Help yourself. The blood's in the 'frig."

Jane hesitated.

"Hadn't you better check up?" she suggested.

Tom applied himself to the microscope with exaggerated care.

"I'll enter it later," he said. "Better not keep the Great One waiting."

There was resentment and envy in his tone, the jealousy of a lesser nature for the brilliant surgeon who was rapidly making his mark in the world, but Jane could not take time to think of these things.

"Which shelf?" she asked, moving quickly to the refrigerator. "You know the case-history, of course?"

"Everyone knows the case-history," he returned almost aggressively. "No one but the great Mr. Hemmingway himself could operate with any hope of success at this stage! Top shelf, right-hand side."

There was a dull red color in his cheeks and he did not rise from the desk. He kept his eye glued to the microscope, as if the conversation had ceased to interest him and only his 'bugs' held his attention.

"Some day, Jane, I'll get you interested in these little fellows," he said lightly. "So many things show up clearly under a miscroscope."

"So many unpleasant things," she agreed acidly, wondering in the next instant why she had been so harsh. Tom was comparatively harmless.

He turned, looked up from the bench, and laughed.

"All right—you win!" he said. "There's no harm in being wedded to your profession, but don't let us be enemies, Janey!"

She hurried back along the corridor without answering him, her breath coming quickly between her set teeth, the high color of angry impatience still in her cheeks, but she slowed her pace before she reached the theatre door.

Stuart was still in the ante-room, waiting with his mask ready. He looked down at her, noting the flush and the depths of expression in her anger-darkened eyes, but he did not speak, and for the first time Jane was aware of the strain of these meetings, the constant sense of doing battle with something in him that would not yield. He was stronger than she was, less likely to crack even if their coming together like this did affect him, which she thought unlikely.

The impervious set of his jaw as she tied his mask only served to confirm her belief. It was like iron, the whole man cast in iron.

Perhaps that was the sort of control he needed to do his job thoroughly, but he needn't let it bite into his soul. She reached up to adjust the tapes of his mask, her fingers just brushing his smooth hair. This nearness was shattering. She was losing her grip. Four years ago she had known how to keep the clamor of emotion under control, but now she was shaken by the very thought of him. She had become time's fool, but she must not show it.

"If you are ready, Sister?"

Coolly, his voice steadied her, but she was forced to grip the end of the towel rail for a second for extra physical support. Instantly he was at her side, not touching her, holding her with his eyes steadily, mockingly on hers.

"What is it?" he asked. "I can't believe that you are not level-headed enough to accept all this as a job of work."

Too shaken by his nearness to offer any logical reply, Jane shook her head.

"I'll be all right," she said. "Everything is all right as soon as we start."

He looked at her again, keenly this time, his eyes probing the surface, but he had given her time to prepare her defences. She was even able to smile with a modicum of assurance as he moved away.

"Sister Oakroyd calls them 'theatre jitters,' and we all get them, apparently," she said.

He did not answer, waiting in silence while the patient was wheeled in and lifted to the table.

Jane fixed her eyes on the anaesthetist's steady movements, and as soon as Stuart had made the first incision her nervousness had gone. She had forgotten everything but the task in hand.

The operation was a deep abdominal, the woman on the table thin, emaciated and very pale. After an hour in the gruelling heat the beads of perspiration were standing out on Stuart's brow, and Jane moved automatically to wipe them away. He did not look at her. He did not look at anyone. He worked more silently than his colleagues, only flinging out a brief request now and then for retractor scalpel or swab, which was met almost before he had made his requirements known. Stella Oakroyd's efficiency was something which Jane envied, despairing of ever being able to emulate, even after years, but it gave her confidence now, which was what she needed most.

She stood beside the suction, watching the diathermy with a concentration as intent as Stuart's own, but once or twice she saw him look up sharply and meet the anaesthetist's eyes. They watched the rubber bulb above the patient's head for a second or two, and once Jane saw it almost deflated and caught her breath. It filled again in the next instant, but she was conscious of doubt in Stuart now. It was almost two hours since the woman had been wheeled in and he was no more than half way through. He worked steadily, but when the breathing flagged again he said briefly:

"We'll need a transfusion. Better give it now, I think."

Jane stepped to the apparatus, adjusting it for height when she had wheeled it into place. It was a job she had done many times before and she performed it now with the swift, sure movements of one accustomed to the task. The anaesthetist moved towards the trolley and lifted the bottle of plasma, checking it against the chart, and she heard a swift, impatient exclamation of disgust.

"This is wrong," he said briefly. "The woman's group is A."

Hastily she crossed to his side.

"Yes, I—I thought I had brought A——"

She could feel Stuart's gaze fixed upon her flushed face and her eyes were drawn to his by some cruel demand.

"It is your job to be sure," he said curtly. "Get more— and quickly. You can't afford to make mistakes of that kind."

As if the woman's life depended upon it—as if her own life might well depend upon it, too—Jane fled from the theatre back along the corridor to the open door of the office. Her face was white now, her limbs trembling as she pushed open the door.

"What! Back so soon?" Tom asked. "Don't tell me the bugs hold more attraction than Mr. Hemmingway!"

She thrust the bottle at him.

"This is wrong," she almost shouted. "There's been a ghastly mistake. Be quick, Tom! They're waiting."

"The unforgivable sin!" he mocked, crossing to the refrigerator to bring out another bottle and replace the unwanted plasma on its correct shelf. "Sorry," he apologized, "if it's urgent. Come back and see the bugs another day!"

There was a sense of urgency about her return flight along the corridor for which she could not account. It took more than an hour for blood to act, so that her hurry was meaningless, but for all that her hands were trembling and there were small beads of perspiration on her upper lip when she opened the theatre door.

The room was very still. The old-fashioned sterilizer which Matron wanted replaced sputtered somewhere behind her, but that was all. Paralyzing fear closed in Jane's throat as her eyes went instinctively to the deflated balloon above the anaesthetist's chair and she realized that the woman on the table was dead.

Pale and exhausted, the anaesthetist himself appeared to droop at the head of the table, and Stella Oakroyd was wheeling the useless oxygen cylinders away. Stuart, too, seemed momentarily paralyzed, and then, with a swift, impervious gesture, he signalled Stella back to the table and lifted a small lancet from the tray. The light glanced across it as he made the first incision under the patient's heart.

Jane stood where she was with the blood plasma still clutched in her hands, rooted to the spot in wonder and admiration as he gently manipulated the silent heart, massaging it with those long, slender fingers.

He worked without any sign of emotion for twenty minutes and then she knew that the battle had been lost.

Tight-lipped, he sutured up and turned away. Defeat lay grimly upon him, on the sealed mouth and hard, expressionless eyes. Nobody spoke. Jane felt the minutes, like weights, pressing relentlessly against her temples, and then Stella Oakroyd crossed to her side and took the plasma bottle from her.

"It's too late," she said unnecessarily. "Finish up in here."

Jane's whole body began to tremble. She had seen death before, but not like this. The whole theatre seemed to be hazed in a thickening mist, but she knew that she must not faint. Stuart passed her, seemingly without seeing her. He had lost a life.

It's dreadful, she thought, to go out like that—so swiftly, like a blown candle.

They wheeled the body away, Stella and the ward orderly but she still stood there, staring at the floor. In these first moments she wondered if the blood transfusion would have made any difference, blaming herself wildly for the mistake that had been made. I can't bear it, she thought. I'm not cut out for the suddenness of this sort of thing—its utter ruthlessness.

She closed her eyes, seeing a man's sure, strong hands at work, the tall, stooped figure under the merciless heat of the great, shadowless lamp, and suddenly she reached forward and switched it off. A sickening sense of having failed Stuart in some way assailed her, and she realized that failure had no place on his horizon. Swaying slightly where she stood, she felt a hand fall firmly on her shoulder.

"Pull yourself together, Jane," a kindly voice advised, but it seemed that she was looking at Stuart through an obscuring mist of pain. "It was one of those unfortunate sets of circumstances which we stumble upon all too frequently in our profession. The trouble had gone much deeper than I guessed. Nobody can really be held responsible."

Yes, there had been kindness in his voice, but there had been remoteness, too, and in spite of the kindness she was remembering the look in his eyes when he had faced her across the table and commanded her not to make mistakes. Would the correct blood transfusion in the first place have bridged the gap between life and death? She shuddered away from the answer. It might have done!

Might! Might! At least it would have given Stuart a chance to fight on equal terms with the Dark Enemy.

Uncertainty would not let her go, although all her training and experience pointed to the time element. There was no swift result from transfusion.

Automatically, she bent down to pick up the discarded swabs. So much to do; so much already done! How old would the woman be? Forty at most, she guessed. Forty, and unmarried. She could visualize the chart she had made out the day before. 'Mary Cowrie, spinster, aged forty-one. . . .' The woman could not have been completely alone in the world. Jane remembered a sister, a tired woman with fear in her eyes.

Perspiration beaded her upper lip, and it seemed that a greyness had taken the place of the sunshine in the walled courtyard outside. If there had been any way of saving her, she thought, Stuart would have done it. She had been given the greatest skill, but she had gone out so quickly!

The scene in the operating theatre seemed imprinted on the greyness beyond the window and she knew that her nerve had gone. I'm no use, she thought, averting her eyes from the narrow table as she turned. I never shall be—after this.

Shivering, she switched off the remaining lights and went through the swing doors, hearing the soft swish of them closing behind her with a strange finality.

There was still work to be done in the ante-room and she turned to it automatically, and not until the floor was swabbed over and the towels stacked beside the sterilizer did she look at her watch. It was one o'clock.

The food trolleys were being trundled along the corridor from the lift, punctual to the minute, but the thought of food was suddenly revolting. The door opened and the anaesthetist put his grey head into the room.

"Don't take all this too much to heart," he advised at sight of her pale face and darkly-shadowed eyes. "We did everything we possibly could, you know. The heart was very weak. It didn't even respond to massage. Hemmingway tried everything in that last desperate effort—coromine, oxygen, massage—the whole bag of tricks. He fights to the very last ditch."

She tried to smile. Somehow, she could not bring herself to ask him if the transfusion would have made any difference.

"Go and get yourself a strong cup of tea," he advised. "It will do you a world of good. I'm sorry I spoke so harshly about the blood," he added, "but Hemmingway abhors carelessness, even in details. Even though it wasn't really needed, after all, he would consider it important."

Was he trying to reassure her, to wipe out the consciousness of something that was irrevocable?

She went to her room, because she couldn't face the others in the dining room, where death was a commonplace.

By two o'clock Matron had sent for her. Jane's feet began to drag as she walked along the corridor and she felt empty inside.

Matron was sitting in her usual position at the desk near the window, with her back to the light so that it fell directly on her visitor's face, head up, body stiffly erect commanding brown eyes on the victim across the room. Today, however, there was more than criticism in the look she gave Jane; there was something stony about it, as if her mind was already made up about her course of action, her determination about the future unshakably strong.

"I think, Sister," she began, "that you will not be surprised at what I am about to say. A mistake has been made in the operating theatre and it is my duty to sift it to the bottom." She looked down at the pad of notes lying before her. "Can you tell me who checked out the first bottle of plasma this morning, the one you had to change during the course of the operation?"

Jane moistened dry lips. There was nothing for it but the truth, and probably Matron already had the information, anyway.

"Doctor Sark."

The dark eyes opposite looked straight through her.

"You realize, of course, what you are saying?"

"Yes, Matron."

The brown eyes did not waver.

"Would it interest you to know that the blood was never booked out?" Agnes Lawdon demanded.

Jane felt her heart contract, but there was no reason for her to appear dismayed.

"Doctor Sark gave me the plasma," she reiterated steadily.

"And you saw him initial the bank book?"

"No."

The quiet, damaging monosyllable echoed through the room like the first whisper of defeat, which indeed it was. Matron raised her grey eyebrows a fraction of an inch, but her face was still almost expressionless.

"That would be the correct procedure," she observed impartially. "Any withdrawal from the safe must be notified. In that way there can be no room for error."

"I did notify it," Jane protested. "I asked Doctor Sark for the plasma. If I didn't check it, perhaps that was my fault, but I did ask for group A."

Matron's slight movement was just perceptible. She leaned a fraction of an inch nearer across the desk.

"I am going to suggest to you, Sister, that Doctor Sark was not in the office at all when you took that blood," she said.

The measured tones were those of suggestion, and Jane stared at her incredulously as she added with increased deliberation:

"Furthermore, I suggest that you also exchanged the plasma on your own initiative when you were sent out of the theatre by Mr. Hemmingway. That morning I had given Doctor Sark some slides—cultures he wished to study under the microscope. I put it to you, Sister, that he was downstairs returning those slides when you went for the plasma and you had left your final preparations in the theatre too late to wait for his return and helped yourself."

"No!" Jane gasped. "No—that isn't true! Doctor Sark had the microscope set up in the office. He was studying the cultures when I went in."

"Are you trying to suggest that a doctor so forgot his duty as to hand you the wrong blood plasma?" Agnes Lawdon demanded icily. "Who took the bottle out of the refrigerator?"

"I did, but——"

Suddenly Jane recognized the futility of all argument. There was cold fury in Matron's voice, and she had a sudden vision of two accusing brown eyes fixed on hers over Stuart Hemmingway's broad shoulders as Matron had followed him into the theatre and Tom Sark had released her and gone his way.

It was useless, she thought. Denial would gain her nothing until Tom came forward with the truth. She had expected to be questioned, but Agnes Lawdon was fair-minded enough to thresh everything out to the final detail. That was true, wasn't it? She looked across at the tightened expression on the older woman's face and thought that Agnes Lawdon's mouth looked curiously contorted for a moment, as if a mask had been ruthlessly pulled away, but in the next instant the older woman was saying coldly:

"You are evidently not willing to be truthful, Sister. I feel that it amounts to that, but my duty is with discipline. I cannot let this mistake pass unchallenged."

Jane was staring at her now, seeing her and not seeing her, conscious of defeat with an overwhelming sense of its inevitability.

"I had not expected you to try to shield yourself in this way," the icy voice went on. "When a mistake has been made the only honorable thing to do is to own up to it."

"But I don't feel that I have made a mistake—not in the way you mean." Jane was herself again, determined to hold her own. "I asked Doctor Sark for the blood and was given what he considered was the right plasma. I understood that he would sign for it after I had gone."

The cold fury in the older woman's eyes was replaced by a look of steely determination.

"I must tell you, Sister, that there was no signature against either withdrawal," she said with studied calm, icy in its intent. "Apparently you took both bottles without authority, on your own initiative."

Once again Jane became acutely aware of suggestion, of pressure being added to an argument.

"Doctor Sark may have forgotten——"

"Are you not the one who has forgotten, Sister?" There was a leashed intensity about the tall, spare figure as Agnes Lawdon rose to her feet and bent forward across the desk, fixing Jane with those authoritative brown eyes. Her ears were apparently closed to all reasoning. "Doctor Sark is a busy person. I am not going to insult him by trying to verify these wild statements of yours because I am quite sure he is not given to mistakes of such a nature. His training would be all against it. Besides," she added with deliberate emphasis, "a doctor's career can never be sacrificed to that of a nurse, however much in the right she may think herself to be. The two are simply incomparable. I'm afraid I consider you wholly responsible for a reprehensible mistake, Sister. Conyers is a private Home and our reputation could be endangered by the result of such a mistake as you have made this morning. I have no alternative but to ask you to let me have your resignation."

Jane drew back aghast. She had expected a reprimand, but not this.

"You can't mean it!" she cried. "You couldn't be so—cruel, forcing me to face such a responsibility when I have told you the truth."

Agnes Lawdon straightened to her full, commanding height. Jane had never realized how tall she was before, nor how ruthless.

"Whatever you feel, the facts remain. You cannot, without evidence, shift the blame on to Doctor Sark." She leaned forward again, her hands clenched tightly on the polished wood of the desk until the knuckles showed white through the taut, dry skin. "What is your future compared with that of a rising young doctor?" she demanded. "Unless Mr. Hemmingway is entirely satisfied that the blood transfusion would not have helped at all, this will all come out at the inquest. It is for him to decide."

"But the woman's heart failed," Jane protested. "Even if transfusion had been given right away, it would have proved useless. It takes all of an hour to work."

Her mind was quite clear now. She was not so much reassuring herself as stating a fact in her own defence, but she saw that Matron was no longer prepared to listen. The operation was not the real issue. It was Tom Sark and that meeting at Crale, and Tom again in the ante-room before the operation began. Matron was acting according to code, but somehow Jane knew that she was also shielding Tom.

'*What is your future compared with that of a rising young doctor?*'

The coldly incisive words cut into Jane's heart and she knew that she was going to accept them. There was no other way, because once before she had failed a man when his career had been at stake. Accepting it, she dared not think of Stuart or of how nearly his career had been wrecked because of her. But for his own force of character, he might not have gone to Zurich at all.

"You may go now, Sister." The coldly precise voice sounded far above her head. "You will not be needed in the theatre again." Jane clenched her hands to keep them from trembling as she turned away, but before she reached the door she swung round to face the woman on the far side of the desk.

"I can't expect you to believe me now," she said, "but what I have told you is the truth—every word of it." In spite of her effort at command, her pale lips quivered. "Have you never made a mistake, ma'am—never in all your life?"

The question did not seem to reach Matron, for the hard face remained in its set lines, but suddenly the eyes wavered and weakened. It was only for an instant, however, and if Agnes Lawdon had looked into the past in that split second of remembering, she was as swiftly in control of the situation again.

"Discussion remains useless, Sister, and singularly unpleasant in the circumstances," she observed. "It cannot alter facts. A serious mistake has been made, and I shall not permit you to tarnish Doctor Sark's reputation to save your own. Your respective careers are not to be considered in the same breath."

Yes, Jane thought briefly, that was it. Scapegoat!

She left the room, stunned but fully aware that there was nothing more to be said on the subject. Strangely enough, and in a matter of hours, she was beginning to convince herself that Matron was right. Her career was not to be compared with that of a doctor. If blame were to be fastened on Tom Sark the incident might yet have to go before the Board of Governors and Jane could see it damaging his future out of all proportion to its seriousness. Frayed nerves and a desperate tiredness began to dim the lucidity of reasonable argument until she reached the stage where any sacrifice she might make could be measured against the past. Four years ago she had failed Stuart, or so he had thought. His career had hung in the balance then, but he had chosen what was, after all, the right road. When she closed her eyes his bitterly accusing words came back to her: 'You couldn't love anyone like that—giving everything! You'd have to make sure of the future first, wouldn't you?'

There had been no room for explanation. Stuart had hardly demanded it, standing there with bitterness and disappointment in his eyes, the fiercely accusing bitterness of youth, with disillusionment treading fast upon its heels. It had lasted with him, too. The man still carried the marks of it, although first love had long since passed.

Something struggled in her, wanting to refute that, but cold logic reasoned that love entwined with bitterness could not last. Stuart had put her completely out of his heart even if fate had brought her back into his life, and this new hardness in him was of her own making.

There was a problem, too, at Heppleton, the problem of how to break her news to Hazel. Her sister's happiness was so obvious, and in less than a month Hazel would be starting a new life, but if she was not to go back to Conyers there would have to be some sort of explanation of the position. Matron would terminate her contract within a week, and before that happened she must make her decision about the future.

Hazel's wedding preparations were so well ahead that she even considered the possibility of not telling her at all until a chance remark from Eric Bridgewater decided her.

"Everything's set!" he observed with complete satisfaction, coming into the house as if he owned that, too. "Nothing can alter your decision now, Hay. You'd have me to reckon with if you so much as tried!'

Jane supposed that was how it should be, but the next few days at Conyers were agony for her. There seemed nobody in whom she might confide. She tried to appear normal and must have succeeded up to a point, because the news of her dismissal did not leak out right away. For once the corridor grape-vine appeared to be out of action. The excitement was mostly centred on Della Cortonwell and the fact that she had refused, point blank, to remain at Conyers a moment longer. Stuart, it was rumored, had reasoned with her, but all to no avail. Life in the confined and regulated atmosphere of a nursing home irked Della beyond endurance and she would have no more of it. She was going home.

"The girl's a fool of course," Matron said dispassionately, but Jane did not think that Della was a fool. She thought that she could understand the desperate motivating force which drove Della to appear normal, to take up the threads of life again so that Stuart might continue to love her.

Jane saw Stuart twice during those unhappy days, on his way to the operating theatre, but he passed her without a word, acknowledging her with the briefest of nods, as if he was too preoccupied with other, more important matters to remember the incident which had altered her whole life. To her complete surprise and absolute relief she was not called as a witness at the inquest. Stuart, it seemed, had given a complete and satisfactory account of the circumstances leading to the woman's death and there was no question of censure.

On the Friday Tom Sark sought her out deliberately. She had been conscious of avoiding Tom, but when he came to the nurses' pantry where she was alone, she was forced to stay and listen to what he had to say.

"Look here, Jane," he began impetuously, "what's all this about you leaving us? Matron mumbled something about it this morning when I asked if you were still in the theatre."

Jane had the distinct feeling that Tom suspected something and could not exactly put a name to it, but nothing would be gained now by letting him discover the truth. She felt that she could not go on working at Conyers, in any case, because the strain of seeing Stuart day after day was likely to become too great.

"It's quite true," she said as calmly as possible. "I am leaving."

"What's happened?" he demanded. "Got a better berth somewhere else?"

His manner suggested that he might not be averse to such a possibility and he did not quite meet her eyes. Did he know about the blood transfusion? The instant's suspicion was followed by shattering disappointment, crowding in to choke further utterance. Did he know about it and was keeping silent? She looked at him and felt empty, drained of all emotion. What had she really expected of him? That he should rush to her aid, confessing his own negligence in the matter? Well, he hadn't done that. He had saved his own skin, and Stuart had decided that there was no need to mention the transfusion at the inquest, so the matter would rest there. Everything had hinged upon Stuart's decision, but she knew that he would do only what was right. How far he towered above the common herd! Her heart caught at the thought of him. Was this to be her everlasting regret, the knowledge of the might-have-beens?

In a clumsy sort of way Tom tried to make amends. When she told him she had no other job, he said:

"Don't worry too much, Janey. Things will straighten out. They always do."

He ran her home and Hazel asked him to stay for tea. When they went through to the kitchen to prepare it, leaving him to amuse Linda Jane on the sitting-room hearthrug, Hazel said:

"Is there anything wrong, Jane? You look like death. Has something come unstuck at Conyers?"

Jane was at the sink, filling the kettle.

"I've given up my job," she said.

"Oh, Jane—why?"

"I—I needed a change."

"But you were so happy at Conyers!"

Jane laughed, a dry, almost harsh sound. Yes, she had been happy at Conyers. She had considered it her job for life.

"It's—not because of me?" Hazel asked hesitantly. "Because I'm going away to be married?"

"Good gracious, no!" Why did everyone think the world revolved about their own actions! "It has nothing to do with you or Eric, Hazel. It's just that—one can be too long in a job I guess."

"But what are you going to *do*?"

Jane squared her shoulders.

"Private nursing, I suppose. I've no doubt that Matron will give me a suitable reference."

Hazel was disturbed. She showed it during the meal and afterwards when she insisted on putting Linda to bed right away so that Jane could talk matters over with Tom.

There didn't seem to be a great deal to talk about, however. Jane carried the dishes into the kitchen and ran the water and Tom stood watching her gloomily.

"You could, of course, marry me" he suggested tentatively. "Does this make a difference, Jane?"

"I'd be a strange sort of person if it did, marrying you on the rebound from a disappointment over my career," she said.

"I suppose that's reserved for love—the rebound, I mean?" He came over to stand beside her. "Change your mind, Janey, there's a good girl! I can't give you the earth—I may never be able to do that—but at least we could get along together."

For an instant she wondered if that might be the solution to all her problems, and then she shook her head.

"It wouldn't work, Tom. You're only at the beginning of your career."

He laughed roughly, turning her to face him.

"That sounded just like Matron! 'A doctor has to look

to the future. He has to think carefully about his career!' You don't really believe that, Janey?" he protested. "You know that love counts."

"Yes," she whispered. "I wasn't trying to deny that."

Love, she knew, counted most of all. It should conquer all things. *Amor omnia vincit!* Stuart had laughed at that, quoting it derisively when they had stumbled upon it in the past. He had suggested that 'ambition' would have been the better word. And now she was thrusting love aside for a second time, when she needed it most. She could not think, however, that Tom's laughing challenge was the sort of love she really wanted.

The front door bell rang as she went back into the dining room, but Hazel was coming downstairs with Linda's empty beaker in her hand so Jane let her answer it, deciding that it must be Eric.

A second or two later Hazel put a rather flushed face round the dining room door to say:

"There's someone to see you, Jane. I think it's Doctor Hemmingway."

The color rushed to Jane's cheeks and every pulse in her body seemed to be throbbing convulsively. Tom said coldly:

"I'd better make myself scarce, I suppose. It's not every day one is honored by a visit from a famous surgeon. Be careful of that armored heart of yours, Janey! These brilliant men are generally the ruthless type when it comes to getting what they want."

A slightly bewildered Hazel saw him to the door. Perhaps I've done the wrong thing, she thought, but I think Jane knew Doctor Hemmingway years ago. Yes, I'm sure she did, and I think she liked him! Hazel wasn't very sure whether her sister liked Doctor Sark or not.

Jane found Stuart standing on the sitting-room hearthrug, much as Tom had stood only a few minutes before in the room across the hall—the more homely room! There was nothing unconventional about Stuart's attitude, nothing of easy familiarity. He looked restrained and very much as if he had come on business.

"I'm sorry to butt in like this," he said. "I saw young Sark's car at your gate, but I'd like to have your answer to a proposal I have to make right away. I may not have time to come back again."

The sound of Tom's car pulling away from the gate filled the silence.

"Doctor Sark is on duty at seven," Jane said almost stiffly. "He does the last round with Matron."

Strange, she thought, that she had no connection with Conyers now. After tomorrow, she was a free agent, the future her own to do with as she pleased. The irony of the thought made her smile.

"I've heard that you are leaving Conyers," Stuart said briefly. "Are you going anywhere else?"

He was watching her closely and she lowered her eyes as she answered him.

"Not at the moment. My sister is being married shortly. I shall settle up here before taking another job."

"Jane," he said unexpectedly, "would any other job be quite the same?"

The question hit below the belt and a lump rose into her throat, but she managed to crush emotion down as she faced him determinedly.

"I shall have to earn my living," she told him. "Apparently I am not cut out for theatre work."

Once again she was conscious of that brief, searching look.

"But you are a nurse," he said. "Which takes me back to the object of my visit. In the course of the next few weeks a—patient of mine is going to Switzerland."

"Della!" Jane thought, her eyes flying straight to his.

"I'm particularly interested in this case," he said deliberately. "Nothing must stand in the way of a complete recovery. I can't pretend that it will be an easy task superintending Della's daily life. She's wilful and she has always had her own way. There is, too, the complication that you are practically of an age, but I feel that it would simplify matters all round if you would agree to go."

She drew a deep breath.

"You're offering me a job," she said. "Have you heard why I am leaving Conyers?"

His mouth tightened perceptibly and she saw a glint like anger in his grey eyes.

"That doesn't come into the question," he said. "I am offering you another kind of job."

"Because you are sorry for me, Stuart!" she flashed. "You needn't be, you know."

She could have bitten out her tongue immediately she had uttered the foolish challenge because it had pulled their relationship down to the personal, which she felt he had been trying to avoid.

72

"On the contrary," he said slowly, "this was Della's idea. It had absolutely nothing to do with me."

Absolutely nothing! She should have known that. Pity hadn't touched him. Nothing could touch him. His answer had shut a door in her face. Humiliated, she tried to laugh.

"It's too fantastic," she said unsteadily. "Besides, I have no training for that kind of work."

"Specialized training wouldn't be necessary." She felt even then the determination behind his words which would eventually carry the day. "Your ordinary experience would be all you need. Della would be under expert supervision from the clinic." He produced a long silver cigarette case inlaid with gold which slid open on the pressure of his thumb. "I've been trying to persuade her to go to Zurich for some time," he continued, "and she has agreed on condition that I will not force her into a sanatorium and let her take a nurse-companion of her own choosing."

He passed the silver case, but Jane shook her head, grappling with the full significance of what he was offering. As he lit his own cigarette she said slowly:

"How long would we be away?"

He shrugged.

"Six months—a year, perhaps. It would depend upon Della's progress. The point is that she must go now, before the winter sets in here in earnest. She mustn't be allowed to face a succession of damp November days."

He stood quite still, waiting for her answer, and quite suddenly she knew that he was willing her to accept this strange proposition. He had made it quite plain, of course, that it was Della Cortonwell's offer, that he had no part in it, but she wondered forlornly if he preferred it this way, if there had been some measure of strain for him, too, working under the same roof at Conyers.

Yet, Conyers lay behind her. Twenty times a day she had to remind herself of the fact. Assuredly Stuart wanted to forget the past, so might not this be the easiest way, to put the best part of a continent between them?

"I've mentioned you to Sir Gervaise Cortonwell, and so has Della. She left Conyers this afternoon, by the way." His tone held disapproval and anxiety, Jane thought painfully. "Quite frankly, the nursing home environment irked her."

"I guessed that," Jane said. "She's sensitive about her present condition, though she tries to hide it. It's quite

73

easy to understand when she has always been such an active person. There's bound to be some revolt, especially when she sees—the things she cares about passing beyond her grasp."

He looked up, meeting her eyes, and she saw that his own were intent and steely with purpose.

"They mustn't elude her," he said briefly. "She must come to lead a full and happy life again. It can be done, and I mean to spare nothing to achieve that end."

The hint of ruthlessness in his voice brought back Tom Sark's cynical warning, and she found herself wondering just how much he would be prepared to sacrifice for Della's future happiness.

"What about your family?" he asked, taking it for granted that she would accept. "I always thought you had a keen sense of family, Jane. You don't mind leaving England?"

"No," she said, "that wouldn't matter now."

He said musingly:

"It mattered at one time, but that was years ago." Every coldly detached syllable cut deep, as they were meant to do. "Do I take it that you have made up your mind, or are there still—considerations that will keep you in England?"

She met his cynical smile with a sudden proud lift of her head.

"Why shouldn't I take this job?" she said, her forced indifference as effective as his had been. "Matron will give me a reference, I dare say, and Sir Gervaise will pay me well. I've never been abroad before. It will be a wonderful experience."

He looked at her keenly.

"And you have no regrets?"

"None whatever!"

"He stubbed out the remainder of his cigarette and stood up to face her.

"It looks like a clean sweep, Jane," he said. "I confess that I think you have done the right thing."

Probably he meant about Conyers, and she wondered what Matron had told him, but she knew that he would not discuss her dismissal now. He had offered her this job and she had accepted it, and there the matter would end. When she set out for Switzerland with Della Cortonwell she would never see him again, or, at least, not for a very long time, and perhaps that was what he wanted.

His closed, set face told her nothing.

"I shall make all the necessary arrangements for your journey," he said, as if Della was already his own dear responsibility. "You won't, of course, be going to the clinic. We hope that the privacy of my friend's chalet in the mountains will prove more congenial. Doktor Frey will make you welcome, and I hope you will be happy."

"You went to Zurich four years ago," she mentioned, thinking of his career and not remembering until the words had been uttered why he had gone, but if the memory held its own particular sting there was nothing in his expression to show it.

"Yes," he agreed coolly. "I have never regretted that step. It was the beginning of my real work, what, for want of a better word, I might call my mission in life. I studied under Doktor Frey and he taught me all I know. There is, of course, always something new to learn—new methods, new treatments to study, results, sometimes, beyond our wildest dreams."

The earnestness in his deep voice was surely the heart-cry of the lover, despairing, yet clinging to the miracle that his colleague's skill might bring about. Jane knew a little of the hazards of pulmonary tuberculosis, the recurring tragedies, the long-drawn-out cures and the ever-present doubt. Doubt and hope alternating, hope that science had assaulted the final citadel of disease.

She knew little of Della Cortonwell's case, however. Only what had been discussed at Conyers, but she had gathered that the trouble was in no way hereditary, and that was encouraging. It had been brought on by a severe chill while Della had been in Iceland on a skiing holiday and the continuing disregard of what Della had termed her "smoker's cough." Under the circumstances, there could be hope of a complete cure. Pity struggled in Jane's heart, pity and a deep and sincere understanding of the other girl's feelings.

"On no account must we let her see that we feel sorry for her." It was as if Stuart had read her thoughts and disapproved of them. "There's no need for pity at this stage. If she recovers she will have everything in the world she wants."

Including your love! Jane turned away from his searching gaze, biting her lip to stem the cry of protest that rose from her heart. She must refuse this job, she thought wildly. She couldn't go on with it! To be always with the woman he had come to love in her stead would be unending torture. Why should I do it? something cried

75

in her. Why should I grind my heart out for Della's sake?

"I'm relying on you to see this through, Jane," he said, and she remembered that once, long ago, he had relied upon her, in vain.

'*I relied on you in this!*' he had cried from the depths of his dawning bitterness. '*I relied on you and you are failing me—now when I need you most!*'

Yes, she had appeared to fail him then, but now it did not matter so much. He was no longer the ardent boy who cherished her love above all else, but a man grown cynical about such things to whom disillusionment is to be taken in life's stride and thrust into the shadows, making one harder, perhaps, but wiser.

"What's the matter?" he asked. "You're not regretting your bargain already, surely?"

"I—feel that it might be better if you employed someone else," Jane said in a stifled whisper.

"That's out of the question," he answered decisively. "If it is any help, you can remember that you are Della's choice, not mine."

She straightened, angrily ashamed that she had forced him to repeat his indifference.

"Very well," she said, "I'll go. Will you let me know when Sir Gervaise would like to see me?"

"He'll want to meet you almost immediately, I should think." He began to fasten his coat, pulling on his gloves as she moved with him to the door. "You'd like to be here, I suppose, for your sister's wedding?"

"Yes. I should like that."

She watched him drive away, still slightly stunned by the impact of their meeting, still not quite able to believe that it had changed her whole future in less than half an hour.

CHAPTER FOUR

ERIC BRIDGEWATER felt that the whole idea was a godsend. It was his attitude of ill-concealed relief which kept Jane to her promise more than anything else during the week which followed Stuart's visit when everyone was so busy with their own affairs that she was left with plenty of time to think. Eric considered her an obstacle; there was no doubt about that. He was fully aware of Hazel's concern about her sister, the odd little feeling of guilt which was the only cloud on Hazel's bright new horizon, and Jane at several hundred miles distance as the crow flies seemed to be the answer as far as Eric could see.

If his vision was limited Jane did not blame him for it. She continued to help with the wedding preparations and at the end of the second week of her enforced unemployment she went to meet Sir Gervaise Cortonwell.

Stuart had telephoned early that morning and it was Stuart who came to pick her up and take her out to Friar's Cour, the rambling, grey stone mansion on the edge of the town with its splendid views northwards to the spur of the Malvern Hills and eastwards towards the Cotswolds.

She had protested when he had made the suggestion, but he had swept all argument aside with a brief:

"We're expected there together. It may be the only opportunity I shall find to give you the details of your journey."

"Why, oh, why, did she give him so many opportunities to deliver the direct rebuff! She sat beside him in the car, trying not to remember the past, reminding herself that all this would be over in a very short space of time—the constant meetings, the ache of loneliness that his barbed indifference brought to her wilful heart, the planning and his thought for Della and their future together.

She dared not look at him as they drove along or she might find herself wishing that they could drive like this for ever, yet what use was 'for ever' when love had died? The lean, angular profile she could see reflected in the windscreen might have been carved from stone for all the help he gave her, and at last she felt impelled to say:

"They may not like me. Sir Gervaise may have different views about my age, for instance."

"If that's all the trouble," he answered, "you can rest assured. My recommendation added to Della's was all that Sir Gervaise needed. For a moment," he added, "I thought that the wrench with Norchester and romance was proving too great."

Angry, painful color flew to her cheeks.

"Wrenches have to be made, and you said yourself that it might not be for long," she reminded him.

"A year, perhaps. You don't think that it is too long to wait for young Sark to make his mark in the world?"

Her color faded at the implication in his studied remark, but it did not seem to need an answer. He had put his foot down hard on the accelerator and they were speeding recklessly through the countryside in the one desire to reach Friar's Cour and Della Cortonwell in the shortest possible time. Jane saw it all so plainly, and the fact that she might or might not be in love with Tom Sark did not seem to concern him now.

They reached the impressive iron gates of the Cour and turned into the tree-shaded avenue leading to the house. Stuart drove with the easy confidence of familiarity, bringing the car up expertly within a few feet of the main doorway.

"Well," he said, "this is about the last phase. From now on, you will be in Sir Gervaise's expert hands."

She read relief into the remark and hated him for it. She was doing as he wished, falling in with his desire to put distance between them. What more did he want of her?

The anger passed and she followed him up the circular steps to the open door, where Sir Gervaise was waiting.

He was a tall man in his late fifties, with a rather autocratic bearing, a fine head and long, sensitive hands, and he studied Jane for a full second before he spoke.

"I'm glad you've been able to come, Miss Calvert," he said. "I feel that this little ceremony was necessary before you and that headstrong daughter of mine went off into the blue, even on Stuart's recommendation!"

He gave Stuart an appraising glance, calculated to reduce any sting which might inadvertently have been conveyed by his words, but Jane followed him across the hall with a subtle ruthlessness forming in her mind. If she did not appear suitable, she would be dismissed on the spot, Stuart or no Stuart. She was quite sure of that. Why, then, was Stuart so sure that she would succeed?

He looked at her and smiled, cynically, perhaps, because he knew what she was thinking?

"There's no need to panic," he said beneath his breath. "The job's already yours. If it isn't, there will always be Doctor Sark!"

These barbed references to Tom were unforgivable. Surely if he knew the truth about the blood transfusion he would not go on coupling her name with Tom's!

Sir Gervaise ushered them into a long, high-ceilinged room where Della was waiting. She had been lying on a *chaise-longue* near the fire, reading, but she stood facing them now, the book in her hand, her strange eyes going directly to Stuart's face as he led Jane forward.

"Stuart! Jane! I'm so glad you've come! It means, of course, that you have finally made up your mind to go to Switzerland?"

"I think that will depend upon your father's verdict," Jane said shyly. "After all, his must be the final decision."

"Oh, Pop's resigned to anything so long as I obey Stuart and give Zurich a trial!" Behind the pale eyes, Della's expression was suddenly blank, as if a wall had been erected to hide her deeper emotions. Switzerland, Jane guessed, was the last place in the world to which Della Cortonwell wanted to go, but Stuart had overruled all her objections. "Stuart is one of these people who must be obeyed to the letter; otherwise, he'll wash his hands of you!"

"And we can't have that happening," Sir Gervaise said briskly. He came across the room to where Jane stood, offering her his arm. "Miss Calvert, shall we lead the way in to lunch?"

Jane took his arm. It was all rather formal, she thought, but no doubt Sir Gervaise liked it that way. He was courteous and kind during the meal, pulling up just short of friendship, which was the correct thing to do when interviewing a nurse-companion for his daughter, she supposed. He left Jane in no doubt about their relationship, and she did not think that he knew anything about her former friendship with Stuart.

It would not have mattered very much if he had known, she thought as she accepted her coffee cup from Della. All that was over and done with now.

Stuart supplied them with the details of their journey.

"Doktor Frey will meet you at Zurich and take you to Oberzach," he said, but Della was quick to protest.

"There's really no need for that, Stuart. I know the way like the back of my hand."

"All the same," he returned firmly, "you'll be met."

"I see," she answered bitterly. "I may not be able to stand the journey. That's it, isn't it?"

"Not necessarily." His voice was completely emotionless, his eyes steady and compelling on the wide amber eyes across the table. "If you take things easily and don't rush around in your usual impetuous manner, Del, there's no reason why you shouldn't live almost a normal life at Oberzach."

"Almost!" she scoffed. "Half measures all the time, Stuart. It's all you have to offer, isn't it?"

"For the present, yes." He would not evade the truth, even to please her. "In a good many ways it's up to you, Del."

"And Miss Calvert, of course!" Della's smile in Jane's direction was a mixture of antagonism and affection. She wished quite frankly that she had no need for a nurse-companion, but she was willing to put up with Jane. "She'll be the good, steady watch-dog, guaranteed to keep me from straying very far!"

"I hope you're not going to look at it in that way," Jane said, conscious of Stuart's swift glance in her direction. "It would be much easier to co-operate, you know. It would make things more pleasant all round."

"That would be the sensible approach," Sir Gervaise agreed, smiling a little. "Stuart isn't putting you under lock and key, my dear," he told Della, rising as she got to her feet with flushed cheeks and brightly defiant eyes. "He's quite sure about this cure, and you know that it means a great deal to all of us."

His swift glance in the younger man's direction included Stuart in his statement, but Stuart made no sign of having noticed it. He was watching his patient, studying Della intently and frowning at some inner thought. Almost immediately, he shot up his sleeve and looked at his watch, saying that they must get back to Norchester.

"I have an appointment at three," he explained.

"We'll see you this evening, though?" Della asked eagerly. "You did promise."

"Stuart never goes back on a promise," her father told her authoritatively, "and he doesn't need to be on the end of a telephone these days, so we can be quite sure of an uninterrupted meal!"

There has been satisfaction in his voice, a rather arrogant pride that his protégé was doing so well. Stuart, the consultant, would be a far more interesting person at Sir Gervaise's dinner table than Stuart, the general practitioner, would have been.

Anger stirred hotly at the thought, and then Jane was

criticizing herself for the swift censure. These people were employing her and she owed them a certain loyalty.

She came away from Friar's Cour, however, with a distinct impression. Sir Gervaise Cortonwell was determined to procure Stuart for a son-in-law, and Della's present state of health was irking him as much as it did Della herself.

Jane settled into the car beside Stuart for the journey back to Norchester with a sinking heart, and for a considerable time they remained silent. He drove looking straight ahead, and then he said, as if he had reached some impasse in his troubled thoughts:

"This has got to come right, Jane—this business of Della's health. She's not the sort of person who could live her life by halves, and I wouldn't want her to. It's a damnable business all round!" he added vehemently. "Thank God, though, it's not hereditary and we can work on it with a reasonable prospect of success. It's Della herself who is going to give us most trouble, I'm afraid, and that must be dealt with from the beginning—firmly and delicately. She'll shy off like a colt if she believes she's being browbeaten in any way."

"She's sensitive about it all," Jane said. "Do you really think I'm the right sort of person to go with her?"

He turned from his contemplation of the road for an instant to look at her.

"Why not? Your career has always meant a good deal to you, and Sir Gervaise and Della are apparently satisfied."

That was the main thing, then—Della's satisfaction, the care of Della and her eventual happiness which was linked so closely with his own!

Jane felt her hands trembling and she clasped them more firmly over her bag.

"I owe a great deal to Sir Gervaise," Stuart said as the rooftops and spires of Norchester came into view. "You know about that, of course. My career would not have been possible but for his help."

"And your own ability," she reminded him jealously. "You have done very well in a short time, Stuart."

His handsome mouth twisted in a wry smile.

"Success," he admitted, "can be encouraging, but is it everything?"

"It means a lot to you."

"I suppose it does." His eyes had hardened and the momentary friendliness went out of his voice. "Prestige

81

and the constant shuffling for position! It's a demanding game, isn't it?"

"But, apparently, worth while."

The underlying sting in her remark did not leave any trace. He was invulnerable, utterly impervious to hurt.

"It's always necessary to find a get out in life, Jane," he said with measured impartiality. "When an avenue apparently leads nowhere, we must look for the most likely side-track. Exploring it often proves quite enlightening."

"And one is quite often surprised to find—compensation at the end of it?" she suggested in a voice which she hoped sounded as cool as his own.

"The word doesn't appeal," he told her immediately. "Compensation always struck me as a second-grade sort of affair."

"Yet it could hold—kindness and tolerance, perhaps," she said. "Some people are forced to accept compensation of one kind or another in life. Perhaps it's one sort of 'get-out,' and at least it doesn't leave one quite so—vulnerable."

Her eyes were fixed on the cream circle of the steering-wheel and she saw his fingers tighten over it till the knuckles stood out white against his tanned skin.

"I should not consider you vulnerable," he said, "unless the past year or two has completely changed you."

"We are both so desperately changed, then!" Jane cried, struggling with the sob in her heart. "You are hardly the person I knew——"

He steered the car expertly among the first of Norchester's traffic.

"Did you expect that?" he asked. "A woman's recurring cry for faithfulness when she has been in the wrong will never cease to amaze me, Jane. What do you hope for? The lamb-like quality of the adolescent male evaporates rapidly in the light of disillusionment, you know."

"We were old enough to fall in love!"

"And young enough to part in a frenzy of reproach and bitterness," he said. "Why rake over the grey ash? We both appear to have got what we wanted out of life—or almost so."

His tone was almost impartial, making a plain and unemotional statement of facts, and Jane felt her throbbing pulses subside, her heart grow cold. Why had she forced this issue between them with that impassioned cry of hers? Why hadn't she allowed the past to remain dead and buried, as he wanted it to be?

She dared not look at him. The sight of his compressed lips and indifferent eyes would be unbearable now. She was glad—glad that she would soon be leaving Norchester—leaving England, even if it was to go with Della whom he had come to love with a grown man's deeper passion. 'The lamb-like quality of the adolescent male evaporates rapidly in the light of disillusionment'. His words screamed at her, underlining the old bitterness, but the voice in which they had been uttered suggested the new ruthlessness in the man which even Della had come to recognize and respect. Stuart had thought that her love wasn't great enough to share the struggle of beginnings four years ago, and now he could send her out to Switzerland with Della without a qualm, to the very scene of his determined success. The irony of it, the unconscious cruelty, silenced her more effectively than his studied indifference, and she was glad when he set her down at Heppleton and drove on towards the town.

CHAPTER FIVE

HAZEL AND ERIC BRIDGEWATER were married a week later in the church at Heppleton and Jane took a rather bewildered Linda to the sea for the duration of their short honeymoon.

During that week she did her best to adjust her thoughts to the future, accepting her changed circumstances without bitterness. She had chosen the south Devonshire coast rather than the nearer Weston-super-Mare or even favorite Porlock because she did not want to be easily accessible from Norchester. She did not want Tom Sark to seek her out because of a feeling of indebtedness. Matron had evidently made no secret of the reason for her dismissal. Jane had met Clarrie Parr in the High Street, and even Clarrie had been emphatic about that.

"We all think it is a pretty poor show, especially since we know who was on duty in the office that morning," Clarrie had said. "Tom Sark is letting you take the rap for him, and Matron is shielding him for some obscure reason of her own. Come to think of it, though, he always has been her particular white-haired boy!"

Tom had tried to get in touch with her. He had telephoned the house twice and Hazel had taken a message for Jane. He wanted to see her. Would she telephone Conyers? But Jane did not want any further contact with Conyers before she left for Switzerland. She told herself, too, that she did not want anything more to do with Tom. The best that could be said for him was that he was weak and irresponsible.

She took Linda Jane back to Norchester at the end of their holiday with a mind no clearer about the future than it had been on the day of her first meeting with Sir Gervaise Cortonwell at Friar's Cour. Her confusion was understandable, for the simple reason that events had moved so quickly, carrying her with them with all the impetuosity of swift destiny. She felt that the road she was taking now had lain before her long ago, as it had in very truth, but she knew that she would travel it with a sadly chastened heart.

Her approach to the journey was much the same as Della's. It was a road they both had to travel, with not even an inner excitement to make it an adventure.

Jane did not know how long it would take her to forget Stuart, even when she did not see him day after day, for her pulses still increased their beat at the thought of his nearness and her heart leapt at the very mention of his name.

'How can I forget you? Even for the least division of an
  hour
Could I be so beguiled as to be blind to my most grievous
  loss?'

Words stumbled upon long ago rose now to mock her, a simple passage so pregnant with meaning for her that she shut them out of her mind with tears in her eyes.

A week before they left England she went to Friar's Cour at Sir Gervaise's invitation. She would stay there, he had decided, and get to know Della thoroughly before they set out for Zurich.

Jane wondered if she would ever get to know Della as thoroughly as all that. There were barriers of reserve and bitter hopelessness behind which Della chose to remain, and nothing Jane could do would alter the fact. Della was gay, nonchalant, ready with the witty quip, but far beneath the surface raillery ran the dark current of uncertainty which threatened to sweep her away.

Jane was wise enough to see that it would be impossible to force a confidence, and during that first week she did establish some sort of contact. An understanding was perhaps the better word, for it seemed to Jane that her patient had wrung from her a mute agreement not to probe. Confidences there might be, but the time for them was not yet.

By moving out to Friar's Cour, Jane had successfully avoided a meeting with Tom Sark. It had been quite deliberate, and even on the eve of their departure she did not think that Tom knew where she was. He had evidently not connected her in any way with Stuart or the Cortonwells.

Della had suggested a farewell dinner for that evening and would not be gainsaid.

"It will upset me much more if I *don't* have it," she declared when her father had raised the possibility of undue strain and excitement so near their departure. "And Stuart will be on hand to keep an eye on his patient!"

Jane should have been prepared for the fact that Stuart would be one of Della's guests—probably her most important guest—but the tell-tale color stained her cheeks at the sound of his name and she caught Della looking at her with a frown between her brows.

"How well did you know Stuart before he went to Switzerland?" Della asked, studiedly casual as they mounted the wide staircase together. "You never speak about him, yet he told me once that you were old acquaintances."

The blood drained slowly out of Jane's cheeks and she was glad that the main lights had not been switched on so that Della could not see the sudden trembling of her lips.

"That's about—how it was," she managed. "Old acquaintances. When Stuart first qualified he was at the City General and I was a probationer there. One is very raw at that stage."

And you hurt each other in some way, Della guessed. A man doesn't go rigid and stubborn with animosity unless a hurt has gone deeper than he will admit. But she left the matter there. Once before she had attempted to probe into Stuart's past, receiving the snub she had undoubtedly deserved, and it had taught her a lesson. All the same, she mused, there was more to this 'old acquaintance' business than met the eye. People weren't touchy about old acquaintances, but they might be about old love affairs.

Jane took longer over her dressing than she should have done, recognizing her reluctance about meeting Stuart, the recoil in her when it came to saying goodbye.

He was standing before the fireplace in the hall when she finally went down, tall, suave, apparently unconcerned that the time had come for parting with Della, and she recognized his iron control as something which he had forced upon himself in the past few years.

The rustle of her stiffened cocktail frock brought his eyes swiftly up to her and she stood for a moment looking down at him, as if the answer to the future was written on his dark, closed face. His eyes continued to hold hers as she moved slowly down the last few stairs, but the guttering candles in their high sconces gave them unfathomable depth, etching the shadows more strongly along the line of his angular jaw and about the firmly compressed lips.

His scrutiny told her nothing, his acceptance of her less.

"If there's any last-minute advice I can give you," he suggested, "let me know."

"About Della?" The control in her voice was surprising, even in her own ears. "No, I think we understand each other quite well."

He smiled ironically.

"Woman to woman! Does it answer better that way?

You know I would never presume to offer you advice on your own future."

"You've done that in a way," she countered. "You offered me this job."

He did not contradict her this time nor stress the fact that she was entirely the Cortonwells' choice. Instead, he looked down into the fire, thrusting at a blazing log with the toe of his immaculate evening shoe.

"I'm sorry about the blood-transfusion business, Jane," he said unexpectedly. "It was unfortunate that it should have happened that way. I understand you stood between young Sark and a severe reprimand from the Governors."

Jane's nails dug into the soft flesh of her palms in an effort at control as he continued to watch her, his searching gaze steady on her quivering mouth.

"You were in love with him, of course." His words came, weighted with conviction, impossible to deny. "His career meant a lot to you."

No more than yours did once, she wanted to cry, but was silent in a moment given only once in a lifetime, the moment that slips so silently from us to be pursued for ever by the senseless plea for another one.

Before she could make even one gesture of protest Della had hailed them from the stairs, Della, tall and ethereal-looking in deepest black, the auburn lights in her hair like flame under the candles, her amber eyes denying the chill that lay close against her heart.

After that Jane had no chance to speak to Stuart alone, even if she had been able to think what to say to him. He believed her to be in love with Tom Sark and probably that would be a relief to him. They had both found compensation for the past.

She had recoiled before the word, but in the next instant she was forcing herself to accept it. Second best, recompense—it could go by so many names, but something in her heart kept whispering ironically, payment in full!

She had not cast Stuart's love aside lightly. She had not wanted to let him go. . . .

What was the use? The past had taken him from her and she was face to face with the present, staring his love for Della straight in the eyes. You've got to learn about taking things on the chin, Jane! You've got to learn, slowly and painfully.

Stuart was at the airport to see them off. He stood beside Sir Gervaise when the last farewells had been said,

87

when Della had clung to his arm and asked him how long it would be before she saw him again.

"I need your particular brand of courage, Stuart," she had told him unashamedly. "You're always so reliable in an emergency."

"There aren't going to be any emergencies," he assured her in the kindest way possible. "If there are, I shall get through to you somehow, but don't forget that you're going to the man who taught me all I know."

'I'll get through to you somehow!' The words burned themselves steadily into Jane's mind as she stood, in turn, with her hand in his. It was a lover's promise.

"I'm counting on you, Jane," he said quietly. "At the moment I can't get across there myself, but you'll have all the support you are likely to need from Doktor Frey."

Professionally businesslike, his grey eyes searched hers with a hint of demand in them which she could not understand. Payment in full?

Was she doing this for Stuart? Was she going because he wanted it?

The engines revved, blotting out thought for a moment, and she took her place beside Della in the 'plane. I wish we needn't wait, she thought. I wish this parting could be clean-cut and swift. Yet her eyes clung to the tall figure on the tarmac standing so stiffly erect beside the man to whom he owed so much.

When they moved at last, Stuart did not wave. He stood bareheaded in the cold November sunlight, watching the 'plane rise before he turned abruptly away to wait for Sir Gervaise beside the latter's car.

High above the Channel Della spoke for the first time.

"Have we been wise to come away, Jane, cutting adrift like this, going out to—God knows what?" she demanded.

"It's the only way, Della, for you."

"And you?"

"I don't count," Jane said briskly and with conviction. "You've got to come back well and strong again. That's all Stuart asks of us."

Della's lips twisted in a wry smile.

"You make it all sound so easy," she said. "It's part of your stock-in-trade, of course. Stuart's, too!"

"We won't talk about it just now," Jane advised. "I've a feeling that Doktor Frey will give you all the confidence you need once we get to Zurich."

"More than Stuart could, perhaps," Della mused.

Yes, Jane thought, more than Stuart could. Love

might cast doubt, seeing the wish as father to the thought, the desirable conviction. Della would see Stuart's heart struggling with his brilliant, incisive mind and hope would be dulled in her.

Over France they met dense cloud and even when they rose above it visibility was none too good.

"Snow!" Della said despondently, and then two bright red spots burned high and clear in her cheeks and her pale eyes glittered. "Why shouldn't I live my life as I always have done—what's left of it?" she demanded bitterly.

"There can be years of full living ahead if only you'll take things quietly at first," Jane persuaded gently. "Being a rebel won't do any good, not in this case, Della."

Argument ended there. Della shut herself away behind the façade of conventional remark and they touched down at Zurich with a flurry of snow in their faces.

Out on the wide airstrip blurred figures were hurrying to and fro, a gangway was wheeled into place, and the first passengers got down and ran for shelter.

In the waiting room, with the blissful warmth of central heating thawing their numbed limbs, they looked about them for their guide, and almost immediately a small, thick-set figure in a black greatcoat came towards them.

"It is Miss Cortonwell I am to meet," he announced. "You will excuse me if I have made a mistake, yes?"

Della assured him that there was no need for apology and introduced Jane. Albert Frey studied her with frank and unembarrassing curiosity.

"So!" he said. "You are both very young—of an equal age! That is good. My friend, Doktor Hemmingway, rarely makes a mistake. He is so sure, always, of what he will do."

He glanced at them for corroboration and Della encouraged him with a nod.

"You seem to know Stuart very well," she said.

"First of all," Doktor Frey said, his keen blue eyes unobtrusively on his patient, "we must go somewhere to eat. Is it that you have not been in Zurich before?"

Jane shook her head.

"I have never been out of England until now."

Della had not answered the doctor's question, and Jane remembered her saying that she knew Zurich 'like the back of my hand.'

The Doctor led them to his car, bundling them in out of the snow, which was now falling thickly. It obscured everything, but once they had reached the town Jane sat forward in her seat, peering out at the lofty buildings and wide squares as they passed until they turned into a main thoroughfare where linked trams clattered by in nerve-racking insecurity. People were hurrying along the pavements with downbent heads and obscuring umbrellas, but she would have loved to be out in the snow under that white flurry of gigantic flakes which was rapidly clothing the pavements and monuments in a mantle of purest white.

They pulled up at their hotel, where the doctor had ordered a meal. Jane knew that she was going to like the little professor with his bushy grey brows and eyes which gazed mildly at a hastening world. Kindly tolerance seemed to be the keynote of his personality and his smile was gentle and soothing. It seemed strange that this small, almost insignificant man should have influenced Stuart so much and still left him hard and dominating.

Before very long she was to realize that Stuart had also left his mark on Doktor Frey.

"Never have I known such an apt pupil!" the little professor declared. "Doktor Hemmingway will do very great things in our world of medicine one day and I shall be proud to say that I taught him all I knew. But first of all, he must come back to Zurich so that he can learn of my new treatment. He have made me that promise, and he is not a man who will ever break his word."

Jane's heartbeats quickened as she wondered what arrangements Stuart had made for his return to Switzerland, but she could not question the professor with Della there.

From the moment the 'plane had touched down on Swiss soil Della had wrapped herself in a new armor of reserve, seeming to accept each step they took warily, and once or twice Jane saw her glance round the busy dining room as if she expected to see someone she knew.

"If you will accept my advice," Doktor Frey said, including Jane in the critically professional look which he masked with his engaging smile, "You will retire to your rooms early. The weather we have today is not suitable to see our beautiful city of Zurich, but tomorrow it may be of a happier kind. Then we will look into the shop windows, as the ladies always wish to do, before we go on to Ober-zach."

Della stretched indifferently.

"I've brought all I shall need with me from England,"

she said, "but there's no reason why you shouldn't go window-shopping, Jane. I've seen Zurich before."

The indifference had been pointed, and Jane could not shake her from her decision even when they awoke the following morning to a world bathed in the clear gold of Alpine sunlight with a backcloth of fire-flushed mountains rising behind a city that looked truly magical.

Jane had not been prepared for Zurich, nor had she experienced anything to compare with the kind and generous spirit of the Swiss. Doktor Frey was sorry that Della would not join their shopping expedition, but thought that she was wise to rest in her room, as she had suggested.

He motored Jane round the town, pointing out monuments and churches with the same zest that he brought to bear on his description of the native craftsmanship which adorned the shop windows in the Bahnhofstrasse, and finally he brought her back to the Hotel Sandalp for lunch.

Della greeted them with a tolerant smile behind which Jane could detect that same hint of wariness which she had no iced the evening before.

"What's in the Jelmoli carrier-bag?" she asked, feigning an interest in their purchases which Jane felt was only partially sincere. "A woolly cardigan made in Scotland?"

"No!" Jane laughed. "I've been completely mad and bought myself the flimsiest of hand-made blouses. I couldn't resist it, but I don't suppose I shall ever have the opportunity of wearing it."

"No," Della said icily. "Sanatoria are hardly the places for diaphanous apparel."

Jane flushed, instantly ashamed of her momentary preoccupation with the tinsel of life, but it was impossible to apologize to Della in the circumstances. She was probably hating herself pretty strongly for having given vent to her bitterness in such a way and it was no use underlining the fact that they were not in Switzerland for any ordinary holiday.

"I was awfully tempted to buy a musical chalet, or one of the little urchins who whistle a gay tune underneath a lamp-post," she said instead. "All this is so new to me, Della! I don't quite believe that I'm really here yet!"

Della regarded her curiously for a few minutes.

"Yes," she reflected, "I suppose it's like that the first time—a wonderful adventure. The cities are attractive, of course, but they never quite become the fire in your blood that you experience when you go into the mountains."

Her voice was distant, her gaze far-off, as if her amber eyes might penetrate the barrier of walls and sophistication and see beyond them the distant white world of the mountain country she loved.

"Of course, we're going there," she said, "but with a difference."

In the silence which followed Jane saw two men rise from an alcove table near the door and stride towards them. They were dressed in black vorlage trousers thrust into heavy ski boots and the deep tan of the mountains lay on their skins like smooth gold. Della sat staring at them in undisguised dismay. They were tall and young and virile, with the gleam of perfect health in their blue eyes and the vigor of a climbing race stamped clearly on their long, clean limbs.

"Hello!" Della's breath seemed to run out in a small gasp which was checked almost instantly. "I didn't expect to see anyone I knew with the first snow in the mountains and a clear sky overhead!"

Both men bowed and laughed at her sally. They were amazingly alike. The same height, the same sapphire blue eyes that, like Della's of a moment before, demolished barriers and looked towards the great peaks which were their spiritual home. Politely they turned towards Jane with almost identical movements.

"Meet Hans and Martin Kirchhofer, Jane." Della's introduction was mechanical, her hands clenced tightly by her side. "They are, without doubt, the most intrepid climbers this side of St. Moritz!"

Hans smiled, but Jane noticed that Martin's mouth did not relax. Or was it the other way round? Already she had to confess herself confused by such a close likeness and realized that the brothers must be twins.

One of them asked Della politely how long she would stay in Zurich.

"You are, of course, going straight to Davos?" he suggested.

Every vestige of color drained out of Della's face and it was Doktor Frey who answered for her.

"First of all Miss Cortonwell will stay at Oberzach as my guest. Perhaps, later, she will come to Davos."

It was said with the jealous intent of someone guarding an old and valued friend, and Jane found herself thanking him inwardly for the kindly gesture.

"Perhaps you will stay the night in Zurich?" Hans

Kirchhofer asked. "If that is so, we would be delighted for you to join our table this evening for dinner."

"No," Della said, averting her frozen gaze from his friendly smile. "We are going on—this afternoon—now, as a matter of fact. I do not wish to stay in Zurich another night."

The decision might have sounded petulant if Jane had not been fully aware of the strain under which Della was laboring, and she thought that she had discovered its cause. Swiftly she glanced at Doktor Frey, but the little professor rose to the occasion without prompting.

"That is indeed so," he agreed pleasantly. "One night we have in Zurich, and then we go on. It is best that way. Soon there will be more snow and the roads will be difficult. We can return here some other time."

"But surely," Hans protested, "you cannot reach Oberzach now before nightfall?"

"It is a full moon," the professor returned, unperturbed, "and I have an excellent French car."

Martin Kirchhofer had barely spoken. He stood slightly aloof, looking at Della with faintly reproachful eyes.

"We'll meet again, of course," Della said with sudden gaiety. "It's too early for St. Moritz, Hans, and Davos just isn't on the map before Christmas!"

"You have changed, my friend!" Hans smiled back. "At one time anywhere was 'on the map' when the snow had fallen! Is it that the spell of our mountains has lost its hold upon you?"

"It may be that." Della's eyes were hard. "The reason being that I am not Swiss, my friend."

Her voice seemed to crack on the final words and Jane's heart contracted in sudden distress. All this meant so much to Della, the free life, the conquering of mountains, a communing on the high peaks with the great forces of nature which man could never really hope to overcome.

Yet, so many attempted it—Della among them.

The Kirchhofers took their leave and Jane found herself being spirited away from Zurich by the force of Della's determination to leave the city well and truly behind them, but she knew that the Kirchhofer brothers were also on their way into the mountains.

Doktor Frey drove out along the silver length of Zurichsee with a slight frown between his grey brows, although he kept up for Jane's benefit, a running commentary on the places of interest which they passed, which left nothing to be desired. They drove south, and then in an easterly direction on a road clinging to the white mountain wall, with all about them the white peaks glittering in pink-flushed magnificence and here and there the ice-blue glimpse of a glacier shining like a drawn sword in the dying sun.

Jane found that she did not want to speak. The grandeur and awe-inspiring majesty of the eternal snows gripped her by the throat, silencing utterance. Everywhere she looked the great massif of the Alps crowded the horizon, closing them into a new world of sun and snow. Lakes appeared and disappeared far beneath them, sapphires in a strange wild setting, reflecting an inverted world of white and gold. The great spur of the churfirsten thrust out at them, cold where the sun had left it and ice blue in the deep cols, and then they were dropping down to a little, sheltered town on the edge of a lake and Doktor Frey drew up for tea.

"This is about our nearest link with civilization," he smiled. "Oberzach we reach by the mountain road. We have a small tourist hotel there, but it is not much patronized by English people. They prefer to go farther south, to Klosters or Davos, and, of course, St. Moritz."

Jane heard Della draw a deep breath, which might have been relief. Oberzach and its isolation would suit her very well.

Darkness fell swiftly as the sun sank behind the peaks, but here and there a sudden flush would appear, pink on purest white, as an isolated mountain was caught in a noose of light. Doktor Frey drove swiftly now. They were beginning to feel the cold and the glitter of frost lay like spilled diamonds on the winding track. Della had not shown any signs of fatigue until now, but strain began to be evident in the way she sat forward in her seat, her hands clasped together, her body rigid, as if the end of their journey suggested dread.

The moon came up, standing poised above the mountain rim and shedding a silver radiance on the valley which opened out before them. Clustered lights on the way ahead warned Jane that they were nearing a village, but the professor passed it without slackening speed. There appeared to be a narrow main street flanked by small chalets and an occasional shop, and farther on, in the shadow of the mountain wall, the outline of a large house came into view. It was low and rambling and many-eaved, and a light burned companionably outside the stout pine door.

"We have arrived!" Albert Frey announced, bringing

the car to a halt. "I hope you will be very comfortable here."

A small, stout woman in a black dress came to meet them. She had the doctor's shrewd blue eyes and skin like parchment, which made her look older than she really was. Beside her, Jane's clear, fresh complexion looked almost pale.

"This is my sister, Hilde," the professor said. "She will show you where you are to sleep."

"I am pleased to welcome you," Hilde Frey told them in her careful English. "Any friend of Doctor Hemmingway is also a friend of my brother and myself."

It was said with such sincerity and natural dignity that there could be no doubting Stuart's place in their affections, the pride they felt in having known him and assisted him with his career, and Jane followed the homely, black-clad figure of Hilde Frey up the carpetless staircase with the old, familiar hammering in her heart, the old tell-tale flush in her cheeks. It was as if Stuart himself had come home with them.

Della's room was nearest, a large, airy apartment at the top of the staircase with a balcony overlooking the white mountain wall and almost touching it, or so it seemed in the uncertain light. She stood looking about her at the austere simplicity of uncarpeted boards and light pine furniture before she tossed her travelling hat down on the bed and turned to take her dressing-case from the maid who had followed them up.

"It's all quite normal," she said. "Thanks to Stuart, I suppose. He knew I could never have survived the hospital atmosphere."

Hilde was waiting to escort Jane to her room.

"My brother does not believe in uniforms," she said as they walked along the corridor. "It is not necessary for Miss Cortonwell to consider herself a complete invalid, and she will progress better here than she would in the sanatorium, although it is not unpleasant there. She does not yet accept her trouble philosophically, I see."

"There's so much at stake," Jane answered. "She's been the virile type all her life, apparently."

"You do not know her well?" The blue eyes looked surprised.

"I only met her a few weeks ago when Doctor Hemmingway employed me as her companion."

"But you are a nurse?"

"Oh, yes. I think that was necessary."

"It will be so, perhaps." The blue eyes were studying Jane more closely now. "We have given you the room which Doctor Hemmingway liked best. He stayed here with us for some time when he first came to work at the sanatorium."

The room they entered was smaller than Della's but it was at the end of the house and had windows on two sides, looking down the valley and out to the silvered mountains. Moonlight lay whitely across the polished boards before Hilde switched on the light, and in that split second Jane could imagine Stuart standing there, tall, broad-shouldered and dominant, his mocking eyes full on hers as she took possession of his room.

Was she never to escape from the memory of him? Her fingers trembled as she unlocked the shabby old suitcase which had travelled with her since her student days and she remembered that it might have come to Switzerland with her four years ago, to this silent valley, even to this very room!

Before she changed out of her travelling suit she switched off the lights and opened the long windows leading to her balcony, stepping out into the night air with a feeling of release. All about her the world was crystal-clear and the snow made a silence that could almost be felt. Peak upon silver peak rose above her, and far beneath the gleam of water shimmered on the valley floor. She felt, suddenly, as if she had come home.

CHAPTER SIX

FOR THE FIRST few weeks at Oberzach Della continued to preserve a dismaying silence. She obeyed all the rules, but Jane was aware of tension, of the subdued spirit threatening to rise to the surface at any moment.

They led the normal life of the village, which made it necessary for Jane to learn to go about on skis.

The first time she saw Della smile was at her amazing contortions on the slopes above the last chalet which formed a beginner's paradise of shallow hollows and gentle, undulating ground easy enough to negotiate without a great deal of skill.

"I'll never be able to get about on these things!" she lamented, struggling to her feet once more. "Who invented them, anyway?"

"The Norwegians, I believe, but that's not quite the point!" Della was still laughing. "The thing is that they are absolutely essential if we ever want to leave the valley on foot."

Her eyes had gone to the mountains with a look in them that was not very hard to define. Longing and defeat struggled with the desire for mastery and the knowledge of her own physical weakness. Her activities had been confined to the nearby slopes and the village street, but her thoughts were constantly among the shining peaks.

Jane wondered how long they would be at Oberzach before there was some sign of improvement in her condition, and then she realized that there was improvement, a slight lessening of the persistent cough, a more natural color in Della's cheeks, the visits to Doctor Frey at the clinic fewer and farther between.

Her heart quickened at the thought, but she had already been warned against over-optimism.

"Such a little thing can undermine all we have achieved," Doktor Frey had said. "Progress is necessarily slow."

They read a lot, and Jane embroidered a tablecloth for Hilde with an English herbaceous border down either side, but there was no real intimacy between them. Della had withdrawn behind the emotionless barrier which she had raised again after that one revealing outburst at Friar's Cour, and even when they walked beside the frozen river and deep among the silent pines there was apparently no impulse to repeat it.

They became known in the village, the two young

English ladies who did not go at all to the hotel, even when there was company there at the weekends. Jane did not care to dance if Della would not join her, and she watched the winter sports enthusiasts from a distance, mostly from the vantage-point of her own balcony while Della lay asleep, or feigning sleep in the room along the corridor. Once, when she was almost sure that she recognized Hans and Martin Kirchhofer coming up the incline, their tall figures bent over their ski sticks, she went to the rail to wave to them but drew back swiftly, as if at some warning sign from the darkened room along the way.

Christmas came, and with it a host of entertainment. A tree was set up in the hotel grounds and hung with colored lights and the sound of sleigh bells was everywhere. Doktor Frey said that a little variety would do them the world of good.

"Always on the eve of Christmas my sister and I dine in the hotel and watch the dancing," he explained. "Many people come out from Zurich for the celebrations and sometimes we have visitors from further afield." His eyes were sparkling, as if this would be a special occasion for him, too. "At Christmas there are so many surprises and secret packages about that I feel myself returning to my youth!"

Jane and Della had done their Christmas shopping locally and a dancing bear had been sent off to England with Linda Jane's name on it, tied up with some beautifully embroidered lingerie for Hazel and a pipe for Eric. Sir Gervaise paid Jane well, but she found very little use for her money at Oberzach until now.

"Wrap up well," Doktor Frey cautioned when he brought the sleigh round to the terrace steps on Christmas eve. "You must not catch cold."

It was his only reference to Della's health, that and his advice that full evening dress would be better left for a later date.

Jane had brought out a full-skirted cocktail frock with a gold thread woven into the material which almost made her glitter, and Della had chosen the inevitable black, a wonderful, bead-embroidered dinner gown with long, wide sleeves, which had come originally from Paris.

They put on their coats, tied fine woollen scarves about their heads, and packed into the sleigh. It was the most wonderful Christmas scene Jane had ever witnessed, with jewel-bright stars overhead and glittering snow everywhere and the sound of joyous sleigh bells echoing back from the mountains. Why was it, then, that there seemed to be something missing, the rich kernel of living, the deep, absorbing sweetness of happiness and love?

She thrust the question aside, looking forward to the evening ahead. The hotel was very full. Guests had gathered from the surrounding towns and there was not a vacant table anywhere. They left their coats in the care of the concierge and stepped out of their snow-boots. Lights had been switched on everywhere and the little hotel looked very gay. Two of the young doctors from the sanatorium farther up the valley and some of the nurses made up their party and they were crossing the polished floor to their alcove table when the occupants of another table rose with one movement and bowed. Hans and Martin Kirchhofer had come to the mountains for Christmas.

"We must ask your friends to join us when the dancing begins," Doktor Frey suggested with an encouraging smile in the brothers' direction. "They are also known to me and are nice boys. Their father held the ski-jump record for many years and Hans was unbeaten in the slalom at one time."

Della's eyes were stony.

"They may be waiting for a party," she said, giving the professor no encouragement. "They rarely go out on their own, and they won't have come up to the mountains just to dance, even at Christmas. I had no idea the hotel would be so busy or so popular."

It was plain that she shrank from meeting old acquaintances of the days when she had been one of just such a party and Jane felt that she could sympathize with her feeling of inadequacy. Della was impatient; she was demanding a quick cure, an unconditional return to the life she loved.

When the meal was over the tables were quickly cleared by a cheerful staff who seemed indefatigable in their efforts to ensure that Christmas should go with a swing, and the guests gathered round the walls to watch a group of dancers in national costume perform in the cleared space. It was all local talent, and the lively Swiss orchestra set Jane's feet tapping on the polished floor. When they began to dance, she did not lack partners and she was whirled round to the fast new rhythm of a Continental one-step until she was flushed and breathless. Her partner was one of the young doctors from the clinic and her eyes shone as brightly as the lights on the Christmas tree outside on the moonlit terrace. There seemed to be a strange new madness in her veins, and when the Kirchhofer brothers rose from their seats and joined them she welcomed them warmly.

Della danced once with Hans, but Jane danced every number, sitting out only when a game was in progress or when someone got up to sing. It was her first real party for a very long time, and she was determined to make the most of it.

Half way through the evening Doktor Frey was called to the telephone. He came back with a deepened smile and a decided twinkle in his eyes, sitting down beside Jane as she returned from the dance floor.

"I told you that Christmas was a time for secrets and surprises!" he said. "I have just received a very pleasant surprise which you will share with me in a few minutes!"

"You're making me terribly curious," Jane declared. "What can it possibly be?"

"Someone from home, perhaps," Martin Kirchhofer suggested. "Do you not expect a friend to join you for the holidays?"

"No—no, there is no one," Jane was saying when she looked up and saw Stuart Hemmingway standing in the larch-draped doorway.

His eyes held hers as he came across the room and she seemed to have lost all power of movement as she stood beside the young Swiss mountaineer waiting for him to reach them.

"Hello, Jane!" he said. "This looks slightly different from Norchester, even at Christmas. How is our patient?"

His grey eyes had gone to Della and Jane saw the gleam of satisfaction in them as he noticed the signs of improvement.

"I—Doktor Frey is very pleased with her progress."

Jane felt that her answer had sounded stilted and unnatural, but every pulse in her body seemed to be throbbing with excitement at his coming. She wanted to gain time, wanted to put even the distance of the room between them so that she might reconstruct her sadly crumbled defences and be able to meet him on an equal footing.

She thrust her arm through Martin's and drew him on to the floor. While they danced she could see Stuart greeting Della and the professor, and she could almost hear Della's swift cry of delight. How wonderfully satisfying it must be to know that the man you loved had crossed half a continent to be with you, even if it were only for a few hours!

The music seemed to go on indefinitely, but at last Martin was leading her back to the doctor's table. Stuart got up to give her his chair.

"You appear to be indefatigable," he observed. "It would be unwise, though, to let the Swiss admiration society go to your head."

"They are the kindest people I know," Jane flashed, "and the men are at least polite!"

"I retire defeated!" He sat down beside her in the chair Della had vacated to dance with Martin's brother. "How have you achieved the miracle? Doktor Frey tells me that Della has behaved like the proverbial lamb."

"Leading has been the secret, I think." Jane was on surer ground now, meeting him on a professional level. "Della can be led, you know."

"So far," he said. "It surprises me that there hasn't been a break in the routine, though, a sudden feminine divergence from the uphill path."

"You expected it, of course! You have so little faith in a woman's staying powers."

She wished immediately that she had not said that because it brought their personal relationship into the conversation like a challenge.

"Do you blame me?" he asked mildly. "I have yet to experience my first proof that woman can be the more faithful animal."

She flushed scarlet, biting her lip on an angry retort.

"Did you expect me, Jane?" he asked after a moment's pause.

"How could I expect you? Apparently you arrived like a bolt out of the blue."

"And with, apparently, as unpleasant a shock! Doktor Frey knew that I intended to come, either at Christmas or shortly afterwards."

"Why?"

"To check up."

She knew that she need not have asked the question. His professional sense of responsibility alone would have brought him to Zurich to see such an important patient as Della, and he must be well pleased with what he saw.

"Doktor Frey called you a secret surprise. Was the secret your idea?"

"Not entirely. I asked him not to upset Della by

mentioning it too long beforehand because she might have thought that I was anxious about her condition."

"It has improved so much. I think she is almost out of the wood now."

He did not answer and she turned in her chair to look at him. His grey eyes were fixed on Della's tall figure circling the floor in Hans Kirchhofer's arms and there was an expression in their depths that was as hard as flint. She saw the jutting line of his jaw suddenly exaggerated as his teeth fastened fast on the stem of his pipe. Was he jealous, she wondered, or was that one of the emotions he knew nothing about, like pity and tenderness and the impulse to forgive?

Surprisingly, he asked her to dance. Most of the others were already on the floor and the professor and his sister were gossiping volubly at another table.

"There's no way out, Jane," he added dryly.

"I had no idea that you had learned to dance," she explained her momentary hesitation. "Once you considered it a great waste of time."

The past again, cropping up so naturally in her thoughts that she was constantly being betrayed into referring to it.

"I was taught out here," he confessed, leading her on to the crowded floor. "That's why I ventured to suggest that I could amuse you for the few minutes that are left until midnight."

His arm went round her, strong and lightly supporting, and the heady quality of the whole evening was renewed a thousandfold as they moved to the music. Bitter-sweet memories came crowding in and the tune they danced to was a tune they had listened to many times in the distant past. Oh, Stuart! Oh, Stuart! Her whole body was trembling at his touch and she knew that he must feel it and wonder.

Before the dance had finished he guided her to the edge of the floor and drew her hand imperiously through his arm.

"Enough of that," he said. "Come out on the terrace and get a breath of air. This place is stifling." He pushed open the double glass doors, standing aside for her to pass through before him. "If you are very quiet," he said, drawing her towards the verandah rail, "you will hear the Christmas bells sounding down the valley. They ring them at Ober Gletscher on the last stroke of midnight."

Jane's breath caught on a sound that was half a sob. She might have heard those bells, listened to them in his

102

arms that first Christmastide when he had come to Ober-zach to study under Doktor Frey.

Her fingers gripped hard on the icy rail. The outside world was very still, the dance music shut away behind the plate glass of the long double windows, and beyond them the chains of little lights winked on the Christmas tree, making it a brilliant pool of diffused color at the far end of the verandah. The children would come down to receive their presents from it in the morning and another day of secrets and surprises would begin!

Stuart stood behind her, wrapped in an uncompromising silence, but the night held too much magic for that to make any difference. It was enough, for the moment, that he was here.

"What about the ski jaunts, Jane?" he asked eventually, knocking out the contents of his pipe against the rail and thrusting it into his jacket pocket. "How has Della been reacting to the nursery slopes?"

He had thrust Della between them, and she recognized her own madness as she tried to answer him with true professional detachment.

"She loathes it, of course. Can you blame her?"

"No. The amazing thing is that it is working at all, especially with so many of her old cronies in the offing."

"The Kirchhofers have just come," Jane explained. "We met them for the first time this evening." There was no real point in mentioning that first meeting in Zurich. "They may not be staying very long, and we don't come often to the hotel. This has been a special occasion."

"You're liking it here," he said. "Is it—compensation for all you may be missing in Norchester?"

"My life would have been very lonely in Norchester."

"Not, surely, with young Sark about," he returned sardonically. "I hear he has turned over several new leaves, by the way. Matron was loud in his praise at the last Board meeting."

"It all sounds very encouraging," Jane said stiffly, glad that he could not see her face clearly in the uncertain moonlight.

"It ought to be. Your magnanimous sacrifice is proving the foundation stone of his career!"

Before she could reply the first bells were chiming out across the snow, and Christmas Day had come to the silent valley. They stood quite still, listening as the distant carillons took up the sound, a paean of happiness reaching them out of the night.

Someone opened the doors behind them and a gust of laughter flooded out on the beam of yellow light.

"*Joyeux Noel!*"

"*Mit herzlichen Grussen!*"

"A Merry Christmas!"

The hotel guests were raising glasses, toasting each other, embracing laughingly in the aperture as they heard the bells. Jane raised her eyes to Stuart's.

"Merry Christmas!" he said, and kissed her full on the lips.

Della came out, followed by the professor and the rest of his guests. They formed a group round Stuart and Jane to listen to the bells and the merry little doctor kissed all the ladies in turn, decorously, on either cheek.

Della turned swiftly into the room.

"The fun's just beginning," she declared. "I've been to many of these affairs, and they go on till the dawn. After that you luge home behind the sleighs!"

Jane wondered if Della had seen that swift, mocking embrace out there on the terrace? There was a high color in her cheeks and the light of rebellion in her eyes, and Jane knew sudden anger with Stuart. How ruthless he could be! How deliberately hurtful. Surely, if he loved Della he must realize how she felt!

She danced the final waltz with Martin Kirchhofer, who told her that he and his brother would spend the next few days in the mountains before they went south to St. Moritz. Something in her responded to the sheer physical perfection of the man and she realized how Della must feel when she listened to him talking of his plans. It was her world, too, that he was setting out to conquer, the world she knew so well, which had captured her wayward heart so long ago and still held it deeply in thrall.

When the music ceased Stuart found their coats and boots for them. He helped Della into hers while the doctor fastened Jane's.

"Your evening has been a pleasant one?" Albert Frey enquired courteously.

Stuart's kiss was still stinging Jane's lips, but she told her host that she had enjoyed the evening very much, and in many ways it was true enough. There was only the bewilderment that Stuart should have stooped to such a shabby trick.

He rode back in the sleigh with them, sitting between her and Della under the bearskin rug, while the doctor and his sister travelled in front. Della was very quiet, tired by the long evening, no doubt, but Jane was quick to notice a certain amount of tension too. It had been apparent even before Stuart had put in his appearance, but his coming had certainly not lessened it in any way.

When they reached the doctor's house they drank steaming, milky chocolate round the tiled stove in the living room, and as soon as it was finished Stuart ordered Della to bed.

"But that's ridiculous!" she protested instantly. "It's not quite one o'clock yet."

"The fact remains that it is long after nine, which is your regular bedtime."

"You're treating me like a child, Stuart!" she protested. "It's Christmas!"

"And a good child would consider herself privileged to stay up till one," he reminded her with a firmness of purpose which she could not fail to recognize. "Be reasonable, Della. Every hour is precious at this stage."

"They're precious for you, too, aren't they?" she suggested. "Full, waking hours to do with as you wish!"

He took her lightly by the arm.

"Yes, I know, my dear," he said with amazing gentleness, "but it's no use arguing that way. We've got to make certain of this cure, Della, because of the future. It means so much to both of us."

For a moment she looked as if she might still resist and then she drew her arm away and ran towards the stairs without a backward glance.

"Goodnight, everyone!" she called.

"Go with her Jane," Stuart said at Jane's elbow. "She may need you."

Della was at her own door when Jane reached the head of the stairs.

"You needn't come in," she said in a stifled whisper. "I can manage."

Jane hesitated for a split second before she followed her into the darkened room. It was a full minute before Della switched on the light. She stood with her hand raised to the wall, breathing hard, and then the little click of the switch broke the silence and flooded the room in brilliant light. It was almost more than Jane could do to restrain a sharp cry of concern as she looked into the ashen face with its large, darkly-shadowed eyes staring out beneath the finely marked brows. Despair and rebellion fought for supremacy in Della's expression, and her hands were tightly clenched as they fell to her side.

"You're tired," Jane said. "We all are. It's been a long, exhausting day."

"You don't need to say that just because you're sorry," Della cried fiercely. "*You're* not exhausted. You're not very nearly at the end of your tether. You're happy, Jane. One can see it, shining out of your eyes, even though you try to hide it!"

Jane turned to take down the silk dressing-gown hanging behind the door.

"I've danced a lot and I've met people I liked," she confessed. "It's all so new to me, Della, but I can still feel tired."

"Happily tired!" Della returned accusingly. "Tomorrow you'll be full of vim again while I remain deflated. You can go with the others into the mountains. You're free to go. Even with your limited experience you could still join a sky party and go so far with them!"

"All that will come again for you, too," Jane promised.

Della wheeled round, her nostrils distended, a white pressure line clearly defined about her mouth.

"You think so, but I know better than that," she said. "Did you see Stuart's face tonight—the doctor suppressing his verdict for the sensitive patient's sake? What chance have I of happiness?" she demanded harshly. "The sort of happiness I want. What chance have I with a—life sentence like this hanging over my head?"

She wheeled round to the window, pacing the room restlessly.

"I can read a man's eyes as readily as the next one," she declared. "The doubt in them, the shock to his affections and the hardening determination. I ought to have been prepared for it, of course!"

Her laughter was suddenly brittle, and Jane found herself blaming Stuart, recognizing the ruthlessness of the doctor in him when faced with such a situation but unable to account for the man's rejection of his own hopes. Was he ruthless all through, cold and dispassionate now that the first bitterness of disillusionment had been checked?

When she finally left Della, she could not sleep. She watched the grey dawn filtering over the peaks, the first blue staining the eastern skyline, and suddenly, below her on the shadowed terrace, a man's figure moved into the light. He crushed out the stub of a cigarette before he turned back into the house, and Jane saw the dark stain of several more lying against the snow. It was Stuart.

CHAPTER SEVEN

DELLA WAS SMOKING against Stuart's orders. It was the one defiant gesture she needed now that she had agreed to obey him implicitly again.

Jane looked about the untidy bedroom, drawing the wooden shutters in a little to dim the bright rays of the early morning sunshine.

"I'm not getting up," Della announced. "Christmas morning bores me."

Fundamentally, Jane knew the statement to be quite untrue. Della was fighting sentiment to prove to herself how little she cared about it, but Jane was not deceived.

"What about the presents you bought?" she asked. "I've tied them all up neatly and put them on the family's respective breakfast plates. I managed to slip down before Hilde was astir, which I think must be a record!"

It was no use mentioning the fact that she had slept so badly that five o'clock on Christmas morning had seen her awake again, restless and cold in spite of the great down-filled bolster which covered the wooden-canopied bed.

"What did you do about Stuart?" Della asked curiously, flicking the ash from her cigarette on to the polished floor while her pale eyes searched Jane's across the room.

"I'm afraid I—haven't done anything." Jane's color was high and the battle of the evening before seemed joined again. "He came so unexpectedly," she pointed out.

"True, Della agreed. "But we can't leave him present-less on Christmas morning. It would hardly be charitable. We'll split Daddy's birthday present between us, and I can buy the old man something else next week when the shops open. It will still be in plenty of time."

"I'd rather not, Della—if you don't mind." Jane knew that her refusal must sound churlish, to say the least of it, and she was also surprised that Della had not sent her own gift to Stuart at Norchester. "It's different for you, but—I'd rather not," she ended lamely.

"Why is it different for me?" Della demanded. "You told me that Stuart and you were old acquaintances. Doesn't that justify a Christmas present?" She leaned over to pull out one of her dressing-table drawers. "I'll be utterly magnanimous and let you give him the silk scarf while I take the rap for the wrong kind of pipe!"

There appeared to be no rancor in her at Stuart's actions of the evening before, but perhaps she was hiding that, too, trying to persuade herself that she could take every knock on the chin.

"I don't really think Stuart will expect a present—not from me," Jane protested. "It would only embarrass him."

"I don't see why," Della said stubbornly, laying the rejected gift on the table beside her bed. "He's sure to have bought you something."

"I don't think so," Jane said, turning away.

There might perhaps be a present from Hazel and Linda Jane, but the wildest of imginations could not conjure up a reason for Stuart bringing her any sort of gift. In spite of herself, her heart sank at the thought and the day seemed a little less fair.

"Jane," Della said, "did you quarrel with Stuart at one time?"

Jane had reached the door and she was glad that the length of the room stretched between them. She said with forced indifference:

"Not really. Stuart came to Switzerland and—well, that was that. He didn't take any leave, and I only met him again when he came to Conyers last October."

There was a prolonged silence before Della remarked:

"It doesn't seem just three months since we met that day. Stuart must have known how right you would be for me."

If Jane ever wondered why Stuart had brought them together she was quick to acknowledge that it was the action of the doctor rather than the man in love. He knew how right she would be for Della, and that was all that really mattered. The past, her own feelings, his possible reaction, all these were counted out. Della was a case history to him now and she had become necessary to help bring about the desired cure. Could anything be more diabolically cold-blooded and cruel?

She went downstairs to find him sitting alone in the lounge. Doktor Frey had brought a little fir tree indoors in their honor, festooning it with tinsel and fairy-lights. It reminded Jane vividly of the tree on the hotel terrace and Stuart's mocking salute.

"Good morning," he said, glancing up at the clock. "Is Della sleeping off the effects of last night?"

"No. She's awake, but she doesn't feel like coming down this morning."

"What is it?" he asked, coolly. "A mood?"

Della's impassioned outburst of a few hours ago was too fresh in Jane's memory to permit of lightness. She saw

Stuart's broad shoulders silhouetted against the long oblong of the window, his body virile and strong in the dark vorlage trousers and fitting wind-cheater and she heard the despair in a girl's quivering voice. 'I can read a man's eyes as readily as the next one, the doubt in them, the shock to his affections and the hardening determination!'

Her own heart twisting with pain, she turned to Stuart bitterly.

"Have you no pity?" she demanded. "Can't you see how Della feels about all this? The despair and desperate agony of not being like other people—the utter inadequacy of her life as she is living it now?"

"Della has the chance to be like other people if she will take it," he said evenly. "I've stood out against her going up to the clinic, but I must and will be obeyed down here."

"She has obeyed you! She's stuck to all the rules," Jane cried. "It was only last night when she saw all these people dancing and leading a full life that she rebelled. Perhaps—your coming so unexpectedly had something to do with it, too," she added in a choked whisper.

He chose to ignore her last remark.

"Della's chief trouble is lack of patience," he said. "Any cure must be immediate or she will toss it over her shoulder and live for today." His mouth hardened perceptibly. "I have to fight Della and fight her trouble, too. I repeat, Jane, there can be no room in this situation for sentiment or leniency, and very little room for pity. Della will only use it to her own advantage when she decides to kick over the traces."

"You're actually expecting that!" she accused him. "How much you've changed! You're not capable of leniency or love——"

He gave her an odd, probing look.

"I was capable of loving you once," he said unemotionally, "and I was foolish enough to believe that you returned that love. I'm four years older now, Jane, and four years wiser."

She stood transfixed, desperately unhappy, not knowing what she could say to him, wishing passionately that he would leave her alone now that he had told her in so many words that his love was dead. In spite of his affection for Della, in spite of all he owed to Sir Gervaise and Sir Gervaise's obvious desire to capture him for a son-in-law, hope had been long in dying. It had flickered in her heart in spite of everything, but the cold breath of his indifference had just blown it out.

"Things have changed," he said slowly, "for you as well as for me."

Statement or questions? She did not know and would not try to guess.

He moved towards the stairs.

"I'll go up and see our patient," he said. "Will you ask one of the maids to send her up a tray?"

He must care about Della—surely he must! Jane turned blindly in the direction of the kitchens to give the order for the tray, and then she made her way to the dining room, where Hilde Frey was waiting for her.

The post had arrived and letters and packages were piled neatly beside each plate. The continental breakfast had been abandoned and there was an array of silver chafing dishes waiting on the sideboard, yet Jane felt that she could not eat. Her own place was not quite so bare as she had expected when she sat down at the table with a small slice of omelette on her plate. Several packages, wrapped in tissue paper and tied with gay ribbons, lay on the snowy cloth, and her eyes filled with grateful tears as they met Hilde's.

"May I wish you a Merry Christmas again, Fraulein?" she asked. "This is all very kind of you!"

"Do not look at it entirely in that way," Hilde answered. "It is a great joy to us to have Doktor Hemmingway with us like this for Christmas, and I do not think he would have come back so soon if it was not that you are here." She smiled mischievously, looking far younger than her fifty-odd years. "It is true, is it not, because you blush so prettily! What a pity it is that blushing has gone out of fashion with so many young ladies nowadays! Yes," she went on happily, "we are glad to have you in our home. The spirit of Christmas sits coldly in a house where there are no young people, and my brother and I always try to draw youth to us at this season of the year. Later, we shall all go up to the clinic to help with the celebrations up there."

Jane wondered what Della would think about such a suggestion, but she thought that Stuart would wish her to go if only to see what other people more greatly afflicted than herself did about their lives.

Doctor Frey came in, beaming and rubbing his plump hands together.

"We had Stuart with us last Christmas, too," he said

when he had greeted Jane. "Three Christmastides in all, and now we have him for a fourth!" He laid an affectionate arm about his sister's stooped shoulders. "It is good, Hilde, is it not?"

"I have been telling Miss Calvert so." Hilde looked up as Stuart came into the room with two tissue-wrapped parcels in his hand. "Ah, we are almost all here now. My brother, he is like a child and can scarcely bear to wait before he will open his presents!"

"We *are* all here," Stuart said, and Jane could not tell from his expression what he thought about Della's 'mood'. "Della doesn't feel like making the trip downstairs this morning. She appears to be tired by last night's activities."

A quick look was exchanged between the two men, a reassuring look on Stuart's part, for the little doctor pulled out Jane's chair for her and bowed her into it.

A maid brought in the coffee as they opened their parcels, putting the percolator at her mistress's elbow and smiling brightly at their preoccupation.

"Well, Erna," Hilde asked, "what has St. Nicholas brought you this morning?"

"A new blouse, ma'am!" The little maid's eyes were shining. "And a skirt to dance in!"

"Always the dance!" Hilde sighed. "Ah! what it is to be young!"

Jane looked across the table at her, thinking that people like Hilde Frey never grew old because they were so young in spirit.

"You are not opening your parcels!" Hilde reprimanded. "We are all as anxious to see one another's as we are to see our own! It is always so, is it not, at home with you in England?"

It had been like that once, Jane thought, caught in a wave of sudden homesickness as she remembered Linda Jane and Hazel opening the parcels in a small girl's stocking on Christmas morning. How far away they seemed, bound by new loyalties and new happiness!

She opened her first parcel with trembling fingers. It was the one that had come by post and contained a box of handkerchiefs from Linda Jane with little horseshoes and black cats in the corners.

"Someone appears to think that you are going to need a lot of luck in this job," Stuart observed over her shoulder. "I wonder why black cats are supposed to be lucky."

"Possibly because there's no doubt about them. They're black—definite, reliable."

111

"Like black sheep?" he suggested.

"We're merely being silly!"

Why were they bickering like that on Christmas Day? His attitude to Della had hurt her, but he had gone up to Della and, apparently, all was now forgiven. At least he had come downstairs with Della's gifts in his hand!

She turned back to the table to open another parcel, producing a beautifully embroidered dressing-gown which was her present from Della. Tears gathered behind her eyes. Della gave the sort of thing she liked herself, the rich, luxurious present dear to every girl's heart.

A third and fourth package contained a monogrammed horn spoon from the doctor and a small musical chalet from Hilde. Jane set the little tune tinkling by opening the lid and there were tears glinting in her eyes as she faced the Freys across the table.

"It's terribly kind of you," she said. "I don't really deserve all this——"

"Apparently we think you do!"

Stuart was still standing behind her chair and she could not see his face, but she felt that he was waiting for her to open her last parcel.

The paper wrapping contained a long jeweller's box inside which lay a beautiful linked bracelet, the work of local craftsmen, which she had seen and admired many times but knew she could never afford. On the accompanying card was the brief message: "Merry Christmas—Stuart.'

For a moment she could not speak. Why had he done this? She could only see it as some quixotic jest, or, at best, consolation for having to spend Christmas so far away from home. Pain blurred her vision for a moment. What had she expected? A love gift?

He bent over her shoulder and took the bracelet from its velvet bed.

"They assured me that it could be altered if it didn't fit," he said calmly. "Shall we try?"

"I—you shouldn't have done this, Stuart!"

"Why not—for old acquaintance' sake?" He snapped the clasp into place about her wrist. "You can thank me prettily when you find time."

She did not know what to say to him. Words would not come, but mercifully the Freys were busily examining their own presents and did not see her distress. She had no gift for Stuart. but surely he would understand about that?

Hilde had bought him a carved wood tobacco jar and

the doctor had filled it with his favorite brand of tobacco. There was no doubt about his pleasure in their gift.

"It will go nicely with Della's pipe," he said, taking out the yellow meerschaum and eyeing it critically. "I am completely Swiss again!"

He had not opened the second parcel, but when breakfast was over he came to stand beside Jane at the window.

"Do I thank you for the scarf, or do I owe Della for the thoughtful little gesture?" he asked.

Jane flushed scarlet.

"She gave it to me with the pipe," he continued relentlessly. "Said it was from you, and I gathered that you were too shy to pass it on personally."

"It was Della's idea," Jane murmured. "We didn't know you were coming."

"True," he agreed. "Well, thanks all the same, Jane. I've never had a present by proxy before."

The telephone bell shrilled before Jane could reply and he turned to his hostess.

"I'll get it, Hilde," he offered. "It will probably be for me. I rang the clinic earlier."

He went out, and Jane stood quite still by the window, her eyes on the sharp rim of the mountain, her fingers tight over the unexpected gift he had clasped about her wrist.

"If Della remains in bed you must come up to the clinic with me this morning," Albert Frey suggested. "It is a wonderful day up there, when all trouble is submerged in celebration of our Lord's Birth. They are a grand people, these isolated ones! They have discovered how to make the best of life."

"I'd love to come with you," Jane said. She had never visited the sanatorium, mainly because of Della's distaste for the idea, but she knew that she would find it interesting from a professional point of view. There was the possibility that she would see Doktor Frey at work later on, but today would be special in its own right.

When Stuart came back into the room he looked directly at her with a tenseness about his jaw which had not been there five minutes ago.

"The call is for you, Jane," he said briefly. "It's from Doctor Sark. Apparently he is at Arosa—not so very far distant as the crow flies."

Jane's first reaction was a sick sort of disappointment. The day which had started off so warmly had suddenly gone cold, but she remembered that her call was waiting, that somewhere near at hand Tom Sark sat at the end of the line conscious of surprising her with his unexpected presence in Switzerland.

"Hello!" he said gaily when she lifted the receiver. "Guess who?"

"I've already been told." It was impossible to keep the flatness out of her voice, impossible not to let Tom feel that he was intruding. "You gave your name, you know."

"I didn't give it so much as had it demanded of me!" he declared. "Your host appears to be somewhat of a dragon, Jane, defending you against all comers!"

"That—wasn't Doktor Frey, but—it doesn't matter," Jane said unsteadily. "You're out on holiday, I suppose?"

"Partly—and partly to look for you! Don't grudge me the holiday. I haven't had one in years."

"Arosa is rather wonderful, I believe," Jane said politely. "How long have you been there, Tom?"

"Just long enough to learn how to keep my feet on a pair of skis. I'm coming up to see you!"

"Oh—no! I—we're living here privately, you know." Jane caught her breath, wondering how she was to explain the position, yet not quite sure which position she was trying to explain because Stuart's presence in Oberzach dominated the situation so much. "We're Doktor Frey's guests. It's a very quiet place—isolated, in fact. There would be nothing here, for you, Tom."

"Think not? You're forgetting that you are there, aren't you? Seriously, Jane, I've got to see you. You've been deliberately avoiding me ever since that damned inquest business with Hemmingway."

"Mr. Hemmingway is here."

Jane didn't know why she had made the statement, unless it was that she felt suddenly defenceless.

"What ho! Opposition, eh?" Tom's laughter held just the slightest suggestion of annoyance. "I knew he had left Conyers, of course, but I had no idea we would meet again so soon."

"I don't know how long Stuart will be here," Jane parried. "It isn't really a holiday resort."

"Never mind! You can't put me off with that excuse. I know there's a hotel of sorts. I looked you up in the telephone directory, by the way. Wonderful institution that, after you've mastered the continental system!"

Jane's limbs were trembling. She did not want Tom to come to Oberzach, but there seemed no way of stopping him. She had told him that she was Doktor Frey's guest, but he had lost no time in pointing out that he could go to the hotel.

"This sounds like a rather unflattering silence, Janey!" he accused. "And telephone calls eat into one's already depleted currency in this part of the world. However, I've got quite a scheme about that, and I feel that your Doktor Frey may be useful!"

Jane opened her mouth to protest, but in that instant Tom had rung off with a breezy "Expect me sometime soon!" and she was left standing with the dead instrument in her hand. Slowly she replaced the receiver and turned back towards the dining room, where Stuart met her in the doorway.

"Everything set?" he inquired sardonically. "This should make Christmas for you, Jane. Life is full of surprises!"

She stood where he left her until Doctor Frey came out of his office with an armful of parcels and his habitual smile.

"Are we ready to start?" he asked pleasantly. "Hilde will look after Miss Cortonwell until you come back. Perhaps it is best that she should rest a little this morning."

"I must go up and see her." Jane would have liked to get away by herself, but she had promised the doctor to accompany him to the clinic and she could not disappoint him.

Della was completely offhand about the morning's plans.

"Of course, Jane, you go!" she said. "It will interest you professionally, I dare say, but I have no desire to see how the disinherited pine out their lives even under the ideal conditions of Doktor Frey's clinic. It just wouldn't interest me."

Della had decided to fight out her own battle and today Jane felt that she could not reach her.

"I've had some news," she said, fastening her blue wind-cheater. "Doctor Sark is at Arosa. You remember Tom Sark from Conyers?"

"Matron's white-haired boy!" Della looked up at her keenly. "I had no idea that he was a winter sports enthusiast."

"He isn't." Jane fastened the ear flaps of her fur-lined cap. "He has just learned to ski."

"Is he coming here?"

"Yes. He means to put up at the hotel."

Della laughed.

"How popular we are!" She took up her manicure set

115

and began to file her nails with the usual pretense at indifference. "What did Stuart give you for Christmas?"

Surprised that Della should have expected Stuart to be so lavish with his goodwill, however seasonal it might be, Jane did not know what to say. She held out her arm with the carved bracelet clasped about her wrist.

"A nice little bauble!" Della observed. "Probably cost him a packet, too, but Stuart needn't worry about a thing like that. He left a great deal of his former earnings in the Swiss banks, knowing that he would return."

Jane wondered if Stuart had known how soon he would come back when he had sent them out to Zurich, but Della was not in the most communicative of moods, so she left the subject there.

"I'll get up for dinner," Della said. "Stuart will be back then."

Albert Frey had brought the sleigh round to the terrace door and his sister was stacking it high with parcels. They live for the clinic, Jane thought. It is their lives' work.

Hilde thrust a basket into her hands.

"These are for the little ones," she explained. "Tell them I shall be up in time to hear them sing."

Jane had not realized that there were children at the sanatorium and her heart contracted at the thought.

"I wish I had something to take to them——"

"You will take yourself! A visitor is the most welcome gift they receive, for some of these little ones have no parents of their own. They are orphans from the debacle in Europe. We do what we can for them, and when you have seen them you will know what gratitude means."

As she got into the sleigh beside the doctor Jane's heart was very full. She thought of Linda Jane at home in England and of those orphaned children she was going to see and felt ashamed at the extent of her own self-pity, for her childhood had been sheltered and rich in love.

Stuart had gone on ahead of them. He had set out on skis, but they did not pass him on the twisting valley road. The ski trails cut across the fields, down over the hidden meadows where the cattle grazed in the summer months, while the road dipped and curved, clinging precariously to the rock face in places or spanning a deep ravine by an inadequate-looking wooden bridge.

The sleigh glided evenly over the ice-bound surface, and presently they entered a wooded stretch where the sun lay dappled on the snow and the pines cast long shadows. The air was like wine at that altitude, crystal-clear and invigorating now that Jane had become acclimatized to it, and she breathed it in with keen appreciation. No wonder it held healing in its wings!

They drove on, climbing steadily until they came to a cluster of chalets set on a hill. The valley behind them was obscure, lost beyond a great bastion of jutting rock, and it seemed as if they had entered some secret province, shut away from the busy world outside and entirely at peace.

"These are the doctors' quarters," Albert Frey explained, pointing to the tiered chalets. "We are a small, self-supporting community up here, with our own dairy and our own workshops. Many of my patients are first-class craftsmen and it does them good to remain employed."

Beyond the chalets a long, low-built house squatted at the foot of a towering peak. It appeared, at first sight, to be made entirely of glass until Jane saw that it was surrounded by a vast glassed-in verandah on to which all the rooms on the lower floor opened. On the top storey were the usual wooden balconies of the average Swiss house, but they, too, were glassed in, forming a private division to each room. The patients at the clinic were evidently not forced to lead a communal life if they did not wish to do so. The question of companionship was entirely up to them.

"I love your chalets on the hill," Jane said, looking back towards the little wooden houses silhouetted against the snow. "They look like a miniature village, Doktor Frey."

He drew the sleigh to a standstill beneath the last of the little houses, and Jane saw that, like most Swiss dwellings, they were entirely unfenced, but the gnarled boles of apple trees standing knee-deep in snow suggested that they boasted shady gardens in the spring and a reasonable harvest when autumn came.

"All our chalets are occupied, with the exception of one," he said, indicating a distant homestead with his whip. "It belongs to Stuart, although he never uses it now. My sister and I got it ready for him coming to Oberzach four years ago, thinking that he was to bring a bride with him, but the girl let him down. He came alone and lived up there for many months with his disappointment, but he worked, too—savagely, determinedly. How bitter he was at that time! How much passion and hatred we can expend on our disillusionments in our extreme youth! Even Stuart was no better than his fellows in that respect. He was harsh and unforgiving, and nothing would induce him to forgive the girl he had lost; but it also seemed that he could not forget her easily."

Jane felt as if a strangling hand had gripped her by the throat. The doctor's words pounded against her heart and she stared up at the closely-shuttered chalet as if she looked in at a vault. The grave of love! 'It seemed that he could not forget her easily!' That phase had passed now. Stuart had forgotten, but it seemed that he still could not forgive.

"Doktor Frey," she said unsteadily. "I was that girl. Stuart could not have told you, and now I am wondering if I had any right to come here."

There was a deep pause in which the doctor laid his whip along the horses' silken flanks and they drew away with a jangling of harness-bells.

"So!" he said. "My sister wondered which one it was! When Stuart wrote to me we knew that he must have a special interest in this patient he asked us to take, and Hilde can always find the seeds of romance somewhere. This time, however, it is not so."

Jane felt that she could not explain how deeply interested Stuart really was in Della, quite apart from the fact that she was his patient. The Frey's would soon discover that for themselves. She could not, however, have gone on pretending that Stuart's past was a blank to her, not after the many little kindnesses which the doctor and his sister had shown her. If Hilde and Albert considered the situation strange, it would be up to Stuart to explain it to them in his own way, for all she could tell them was the simple truth.

"You will see how Stuart has worked during these past four years," the professor said, his manner completely unchanged as he led her up the clinic steps. To all intents and purposes it looked nothing more than a comfortable, residential hotel, and Jane felt that Della need not have been afraid to come to it. "It was here that he laid the foundations of the great work he has yet to do."

They went from room to room, and Jane was introduced to the patients; people from all walks of life, who were also the doctor's friends. An aura of tense excitement prevailed, and the women were all attired in their prettiest dresses. Some of them had put artificial flowers in their hair or diamanté clips at their throats, and they chattered incessantly. It was all so natural that Jane almost forgot she was in a hospital at all. These people had accepted the limitations of their lives and were reasonably content with what they had. Here and there a group of four were gathered round a table playing canasta, and in the long, pine-panelled games room a set of table-tennis was in robust progress, the dark shadow hovering in the background held completely at bay.

When the luncheon bell rang Stuart came through from the children's clinic to join them.

"He'll take you to see the babies afterwards," the professor said. "They are Stuart's especial interest."

Jane could never have guessed that Stuart could be so kind. There was not a patient there who did not frankly worship him, and he had a word for them all. He sat at the luncheon table with Jane on one side and a Madame Cliquot on the other, the little Frenchwoman hanging on his every phrase. He had been to Paris? But how wonderful! Had he managed to visit her sister at Le Mans? Ah, well! perhaps he would have more time to make the journey when he passed that way again. Doctors were notoriously busy people, but her sister would be charmed to have him!

When the meal was over the presents were cut from the tree and Jane was asked to present them. It was all very informal and very gay. Doktor Frey came away with a great many gifts he had not expected, and Jane could see that he was deeply touched by his patients' generosity, which he accepted as a mark of their love and esteem.

They each took their individual leave of him when they went for their afternoon rest, and Jane followed Stuart to the children's wing. The noise here was terrific. Lunch had been served early and the afternoon routine had dissolved into chaos. It was Christmas Day, and not even the smallest child could be induced to sleep for any length of time. Hilde had arrived, having negotiated the journey from Oberzach on skis, as Stuart had done, but she had not managed to persuade Della to accompany her.

The children called her 'Auntie Hilde,' laughing uproariously at the comic stories she told, and then they sang, shyly, at first, because Jane was a stranger in their midst, and then joyously, because Stuart encouraged them.

The presents were taken from yet another tree and tired three-year-olds clasped teddy bears and wonderful dolls and toy engines to their grubby little pinafores as they were shepherded off to bed.

"It's almost six o'clock," Stuart said. "Have you enjoyed your afternoon?"

Tears stood bright in Jane's eyes.

"How I envy you!" she said. "No wonder you have made this your life's work."

The thought rose unbidden that it might have been hers, also, standing like an unsheathed sword between them for a moment before he turned away.

"When do we have to expect Doctor Sark?" he asked abruptly.

"I don't know. He said he was coming. That was all."

He did not answer, and they went out to the sleigh, where the Freys were waiting for them.

"Would you like to ski down, Jane?" Hilde asked. "It would be good practice for you. It's practically all down-hill and Stuart will take care of you."

Jane hesitated, wondering what Stuart thought of the arrangement. She would have given anything to ski down through this enchanted night with him as her guide, and they could be sure of a moon. The sky was very clear. He looked across at her, saw her momentary hesitation, and said:

"Why not? Doctor Sark couldn't possibly have made Oberzach by this time."

Jane hated these sardonic references to Tom, but she accepted the loan of Hilde's skis in silence. Hilde and she were almost of a height and Stuart buckled the skis on for her as the sleigh pulled away.

"We'll follow the trail," he said. "The road is rather dangerous."

Jane discovered that the ski trail led up behind the chalets, and they covered the ground slowly at first because of her inexperience of uphill work. She was still uncertain when the ground dropped away steeply beneath her feet, but Stuart kept close to her side and she regained confidence enough to smile at him in the moonlight.

It was then that it happened. With no very definite movement, she had gone over on one ski and plunged head-long down the slope.

Shaken and almost buried in icy snow, she lay there until he reached her, convinced of a dozen sprains, at least, to say nothing of a broken leg.

"All right! You're not hurt." His sensitive fingers were going over her limbs with professional care. "Damn these new-type bindings!" He swore under his breath, "I never did have faith in them. That's all that happened. This one gave way." Relief was struggling with anger and anxiety in his deep voice. "We'll have to go back, at least as far as one of the chalets, to see if we can get this thing mended."

"I shouldn't have come," Jane whispered remorsefully, shaken and shivering with cold after her plunge into the snow. "What a fool you must think me!"

"It could have happened to anyone," he assured her. "It means walking back without your skis. Do you think you can manage it?"

"I can always try."

As they approached the chalets she could see that they were all unoccupied. The Swiss doctors and their wives were all up at the clinic half a mile away and the chalets remained unlit. Jane felt desperately cold, and already she was growing tired. Stuart stood on the ski trail to consider the situation, and then he said grimly:

"There's only one thing for it. Come on!"

He led the way in a determined silence to the last chalet of all, the dark, closely-shuttered building which Albert Frey had pointed out as his own.

Jane held her breath. It seemed impossible that he was taking her there, that fate should have thrust this upon them. Stuart was tight-lipped and uncommunicative, and he did not tell her that the chalet belonged to him.

They reached the door and he brought out a bunch of keys, fitting one into the lock. Jane could see a wrought-iron lantern hanging at the side of the door and a chain bell pull, and then he was ushering her into a long, narrow hall.

It was very dark, and she had to grope her way, following him till he flicked on his cigarette lighter and fumbled for a switch. They went ahead again, still in darkness, with only the faint beams of moonlight coming in at the open door behind them. Jane could feel smooth wood panelling under her fingers as she ran her hand along the wall, and then, ahead of her, a light was switched on and Stuart stood aside at the entrance to a spacious room.

Closely shuttered windows occupied two of the walls and a third was almost entirely taken up by a beautifully tiled stove behind which a wooden stairway led to a gallery and the bedrooms above. There was no soft furnishing, however, such as a woman would have provided. The tables and chairs were all austere and serviceable and dust lay thick on them and on the long pine bench beneath the shuttered windows.

This should have been her home, she thought, and madly, cruelly she was clothing it with the curtains which would have brightened it and the cushions to give comfort on the long, hard, window seat.

"Well," said Stuart behind her, "this is it. In the ordinary way, I don't suppose you would ever have seen it."

He turned to the stove without further explanation, opening the small door at its base to peer inside, and Jane shivered involuntarily. He looked up and met her eyes.

"You're cold," he said. "I'll try to find some wood and light a fire. You can sit above the stove and brew cocoa while I mend your ski."

When he had gone she gazed about her, through the partition in the remaining wall which folded back to reveal a dining-alcove which had probably never been in use. She could imagine Stuart eating all his meals, bachelor-fashion, beside the stove.

He came back with an armful of log chippings and some old magazines, and soon the warmth of crackling timber was easing the silence between them. He also found a sealed tin of coffee and produced sugar from another tin while she measured the coffee into a pan.

"We're quite modern," he said. "There's an electric cooker in the kitchen."

The sardonic note had crept back into his voice and he was watching her with faint mockery in his grey eyes, yet behind the mockery lay a deeper emotion, hard to define. Jane felt incapable of thought, unable to account for anything he might say. Perhaps he thought that she had failed him all these years ago because she believed the mountains of Switzerland to be primitive and cruel.

A gradual warmth began to steal through her veins as she stretched her hands to the fire and some of her old assurance came back. It had deserted her most basely as soon as Stuart had opened the chalet door, but now she had had time to compose herself.

When she had made the coffee he brought two beakers and they drank it huddled over the stove before he went to look at the broken ski.

Jane sat on, nursing the warm beaker between her hands and wondering how she should feel sitting here in the chalet that would have been her home during those past four eventful years. She could imagine it so well in the spring with its blue shutters flung wide and all the windows open to the sunshine. There would be a breeze wafting in the scent of pine from the giant cones which the valley peoples laced along their window sills, and butterflies flitting up from the grass beneath the orchard trees. There would be the hum of a saw in the distance, cutting through the pine logs that would be stacked high about the outer walls when autumn came and the sound of bells coming down from the high pastures beyond the clinic. There would be Stuart's work, too, going on placidly, day by day.

She closed her eyes, unable to think of anything more peaceful, yet it must all remain a dream. It had come so near, the thought of it too bitter-sweet to endure for long.

When Stuart came back with the mended ski she was kneeling before the stove pushing small logs on to the flames. She looked up at him, conscious of sudden tension, aware of an emotion she could not name which hovered on the brink of panic. There was no kindness in his face, and his eyes were as cold as steel as he came towards her.

"You should have come here as a bride," he said harshly. "As my wife. In those days I felt myself cheated of something worth while. I've wondered since if I could have been wrong."

His eyes held her as securely as if his strong hands had fastened over her wrists.

"No, Stuart—no!" she pleaded.

For a moment longer he continued to look at her and then he turned away.

"Don't worry! I'm not that sort of a savage." He flung open the inner door. "I brought you here to prove something to myself, but I'm not sure if I have entirely succeeded. Men can be everlasting fools!"

Something rose in Jane to choke back utterance. The past, the truth—what did it matter now? She got to her feet and followed him to the door, watching as he bent to close the stove and see that it was safe before they left, much as he might have done if they had, indeed, been man and wife.

Outside, the sky was full of stars. They seemed so near that she could have touched them, but they shone out of her reach, like happiness and love.

Stuart scarcely spoke as they negotiated the distance between the chalets and Oberzach, and she felt humiliated and crushed and willing to die.

Dinner that night was a fiasco. They all tried too hard, endeavoring to capture a festive spirit that was no longer there. Hans Kirchhofer and his brother had been invited up from the hotel, but even their bright company did little to lessen the tension which bound Della as well as Stuart and Jane. After the holiday, Martin Kirchhofer said, there would be plenty of room at the hotel. He had turned out to be quieter than his twin, more thoughtful perhaps. There were times when his thoughts seemed to be far away in a world of his own, a white world of slaloms and ski-jumping and long trail runs into the wilds.

That Della was there with him in spirit was not very difficult to see, and two days later, when Stuart announced that he must go to Geneva for a week, he sought Jane out with a warning.

"I'm not too happy about these old associations," he said candidly. "The Kirchhofers and their like are mountaineers, of course, and they live for climbing. They have, too, enough money to make it possible all the year round. If it won't be too much of an effort to tear yourself away from Doctor Sark's company occasionally, keep an eye on Della for me."

Jane met the mocking gaze with an angry challenge in her eyes.

"I don't think I've ever neglected my duty, Stuart—not even for love." Her voice had sunk to a whisper and all the color fled from her cheeks. "You needn't remind me of my duty to Della, but I can tell you that you might be kinder to her."

He looked down at her, faintly surprised.

"In what way?"

"You—she's in love with you. Can't you see what your—rejection of her is likely to mean?"

He stood for a moment, searching her distressed face, and then he laughed.

"My dear Jane," he said, "love has you by the ears! It can even distort your vision, you know, so beware!"

He was gone with that, callously assured that he was doing right, Jane thought in bitter disappointment.

Surprisingly, Della did not seem unduly depressed by his sudden departure for Geneva. She appeared to consider herself more free, less under his unchallengeable domination, but her preoccupation with the thought of the mountain trails still remained.

One morning when a party of climbers came up from the village with alpenstocks and icepicks across their rucksacks, she watched them pass with the flame of unquenchable envy in her pale eyes and a hardening expression about her mouth.

"I'm well enough," she said. "I could easily go."

It was the first time she had openly confessed her desire and Jane was glad that the issue had come out into the open, at last.

"It's so soon, Della," she cautioned. "If you would only wait a little longer till you were really well——"

"Wait! Wait!" Della was on her feet, cheeks flushed, eyes blazing. "You're like Stuart! All you ever think about is your precious cures. You don't care that I'm being crushed with shame every time I meet these people, that they can only look my way with pity in their eyes!"

"Are you sure they look at it in that way?" Jane asked quietly.

"Why shouldn't they? All men are a little resentful of the woman who can meet them out there on the snowfields on their own level." Her eyes travelled longingly to the high peaks, sudden purpose in their depths. "But I'll show them," she declared. "One day I'll show them, if it kills me!"

"Della, you mustn't!" Jane cried desperately. "What good would it do? We've come such a long way in these past few months. Don't undo everything Stuart and Doktor Frey have done for you by this sudden foolishness."

"Stuart?" Della laughed, bitterness still the predominating emotion in her deep voice. "How much do you think Stuart really cares—or anyone else? He owes it to my father to see me through this, but it will just be another cure as far as he is concerned. Stuart's like that. As hard as nails. He won't give way—"

"Della! it's because he can't. Don't you see?" Jane was imploring now. "If you take a risk at this stage it might prove—fatal. Stuart knows that. Promise me you'll do nothing rash. Promise me you'll wait till Stuart gets back."

"And then I can be as rash as I please!" Della laughed with a swift return to her former indifference. "We both know Stuart far too well to believe that, Jane!"

Two days before Stuart was due to return Doktor Frey went to Zurich for the day. The Kirchhofer brothers had invited them to the hotel the evening before for dinner and Jane had been frankly relieved to find that Tom had not yet put in an appearance there. The dinner party had consisted of eight people, Doktor Frey and Hilde, Della and Jane, the two Kirchhofers and a married couple whom Della already knew. The talk had turned inevitably to the local ski runs and the glacier conditions up in the passes, but Della had contributed very little to the conversation, contenting herself with a sly dig at Jane by asking if she intended to join the climbers.

"They're willing to take any risk, short of calculated murder," she had added.

"Not with a complete greenhorn!" Jane had countered, and Hans Kirchhofer had laughed and said that he considered she was doing very well for a beginner.

Doktor Frey left Oberzach early in the morning. There was much movement in the house, and Jane thought that Hilde must have been up to see her brother off. When she looked at her watch it was not quite six o'clock and still dark, so she pulled the down bolster up under her chin and snuggled beneath its comforting warmth. In spite of central heating, the house was often chilly in the early morning.

She must have slept for two hours, because the children were skiing merrily down the valley road when she crossed to her window and the baker's sleigh was already at the terrace steps.

"I expect Della will breakfast in her room later," Hilde said when she reached the dining room. "She prefers to spend the morning there, and it is always good when she agrees to rest. You and I will have a cosy chat over our rolls and jam, and you will tell me how to make your English hot-pot, of which I hear so much from Stuart when he is with us! He will tell me always that Swiss cooking is superb, but there are some things in England which cannot be imitated!"

They spent the greater part of the morning together, and when Hilde buckled on her skis to go to the grocery store with the weekly order Jane went in search of Della for the first time, hoping that she had managed to sleep in the interval and felt refreshed.

Della's room was empty.

Even before she began her search, Jane knew where Della had gone. The innocent questions of the evening before; those few minutes alone with Hans Kirchhofer in the foyer of the hotel; the voices down on the terrace so early in the morning all pointed to the one fact that Della had gone to the beckoning heights.

For one bewildering moment Jane knew sheer panic. She was alone in the house. There was nobody to help her or give her advice, and she had no idea how far the ski runners had gone or when they had left.

Even if their rendezvous had been the hotel, they would be hours ahead of any pursuit.

The idea that she must go after Della to dissuade her from this mad adventure at any price had been fixed in her mind from the moment of her patient's disappearance and she did not stop now to examine it. To go down to the village would be wasting precious time. The skiers could only have taken the single trail up the valley as far as the chalets above the clinic, and she knew her way to the clinic.

With trembling fingers and her breath driving hard between her lips, she buckled on her own skis, almost sobbing when the bindings slipped again and again under her unpractised touch, but she was equipped, at least, and she dug her sticks into the snow with a fierce determination in her heart.

"It is madness, Fraulein!" Hilde's maid said as she watched her go. "You will never catch them up. They run like the wind!"

Jane thought that she could get to the clinic, at least, hoping that Della might not have gone any farther than that.

It was an easy enough task to follow the fresh ski trail. A light covering of snow had fallen during the night and the runs were clearly marked, five parallel lines, with the stick holes deep beside them.

They can't have gone very far, she kept thinking as she ploughed her own way laboriously through the snow. Della would give up when she reached the clinic.

The clinic had not seemed quite so far away when she had made the journey by sleigh, nor on the way back with Stuart, but she reminded herself that the run back had been mostly downhill, and therefore, easier. Her arms began to ache and she seemed to be ploughing into the snow instead of skimming over it as she had been taught, and once or twice she stood still in her tracks, looking back to where she could see the dark, snaking road leading up from the fast dwindling village, wondering if she should have followed it for greater safety. There was no sense in turning back now, however, and there seemed no doubt about the marks on the trail. They were undoubtedly fresh, made since the overnight fall of snow.

The sun began to dazzle her eyes, even through her dark glasses, and then it did not seem so bright. The colors about her were sharp and very clear—the dark green of the pines and the vivid blue of the sky, with the pale turquoise of a distant glacier shimmering against the mountain wall. She remembered Stuart pointing it out to her, sharply defined against the high buttress of the northern peaks, a broad, arrested river of solid ice falling to the valley below with something vaguely disconcerting about its chilly aloofness.

The aching tiredness of her limbs increased, but her mind was closed to fatigue. She must find Della and dissuade her from this mad adventure at all costs, and her one hope remained that the ski party might have stopped at the clinic to rest or even take a meal there. She remembered Doktor Frey issuing the invitation to Martin Kirchhofer the evening before, but she could not bring the young mountaineer's reply to mind—or did not want to, because it might have been that Martin had refused, explaining that they wanted to press on as quickly as possible while the light remained good.

Their destination was the rest-hut at Neuhaus, far up on the plateau above the valley, and Jane prayed that Della had already abandoned the overnight project, realizing just how much it would entail. One of the young Swiss doctors at the clinic might have been able to reason with her.

Steadily the ski trail drew away from the road, winding closer in to the mountains, and then, abruptly, disconcertingly, it divided.

Jane stood in the churned-up snow where the small party must have stopped to consult their maps, staring in utter dismay at two distinct trails branching away to right and left. For some reason which she could not imagine, the party had broken up here, and she knew so little of trail running that no explanation presented itself. There was nothing for it but to use her own sense of direction and hope that the skiers had eventually joined forces again at the clinic.

Four people had taken the right hand trail and two had gone off on their own. Jane followed the four parallel lines and prayed that she might be right. Her idea was that Della and Mabel Kinross had left the male members of the climbing party and made directly for the clinic.

The mountains seemed nearer than she remembered them as she pushed on, and the sky beyond the peaks had turned milky, its vivid blueness overlaid with a thin film of cloud. The weather did not concern her at that juncture, however. Even if it snowed, she told herself that she would have reached the clinic long before then and made up with Della and the others.

Anger sharpened her thoughts as she labored on. Della was like a spoiled child in some respects, ungovernable, thoughtless of her own safety and the promise she had made to Stuart. There was also the promise Jane had made, the promise he had extracted, expecting loyalty from her in her work, at least. And Della had made all that so difficult!

The going became strenuous, her labored breathing audible in the stillness. There was very little wind, and the trees under which she passed seemed to pause, waiting. Once she heard an ominous rumble ahead of her and stood fascinated to watch a miniature avalanche of fine snow cascading down over the jutting rock face like powdered crystal, and perhaps it was then that she realized that she had come far too near to the mountain wall. The clinic and the clustering chalets on the plateau above it were farther to the west.

Yet, the trail remained. She stood for a moment, irresolute, wondering if she should turn back, but ahead the ski-runners had swerved to the left again and she bit her teeth into her trembling lower lip and pressed on.

The sun hid itself behind a cloud and a penetrating coldness struck her. She was nearer the glacier than she had imagined. She took off her glasses, but there was still glare on the snow and she was forced to wear them again. The aching of her limbs became like a numb, persistent pain at the back of her mind, but she would not give in. Stuart had demanded this of her. "Keep an eye on Della for me," he had said.

When the first flakes of snow settled on her windcheater she gazed at them, hardly believing what she saw, but the thought of the clinic had become such an obsession with her that she refused to examine the full significance of a fresh snowfall. It was still bright, and there were patches of blue in the sky over to the west, above the hidden valley. She would not think of Oberzach and Hilde coming home to find that she had gone. The maid would give Hilde her message and she would understand. She would telephone the clinic and, later, Doktor Frey would bring the sleigh and take Della home!

All easy enough to plan, but would it work out that way?

She banished the defeatist thought, forcing her unwilling limbs to carry her forward. She was climbing gradually along the side of a steep col and before her she imagined that she could see the squat turf roof of a little hut. Sheer fatigue and a desperate, gnawing hunger made her regard it with relief. Wherever she was, she had reached shelter, and the trail she had been following led upwards to the distant roof.

The hut proved to be further away than she had at first imagined and appeared to be reached by a narrow ice bridge spanning a terrifyingly deep ravine, but the trail went over it and she knew that she must do the same. Suddenly her confidence deserted her. Courage was sapped by fatigue and the very stillness of everything around her and she visualized herself hurtling down the sides of the ravine to dark oblivion.

Why had she listened to so many tales of adventure which had ended in disaster? She closed her eyes for a sickly moment, willing herself to go on, and then she was crossing the bridge and digging her sticks into the soft snow on the far side.

Laughing shakily, she reached the hut. It had windows on two sides and a stout pine door which was closed firmly against the rising wind. Madly she prayed that she might not find it empty.

Her knock did not bring any response and she almost collapsed into the one room of the deserted hut. All the evidence of recent inhabitation which lay about on the rough wooden benches and tables was of little comfort to her. The ski-runners had eaten their meal and gone!

She sat down at a table near the door, resting her head along her arm. Time seemed to be running out to some unescapable destiny, but for the present she could not care. Her aching body relaxed, the throbbing insistency of her thoughts was chilled.

When she raised her head after many minutes she saw the wood ash in the stone fireplace. It still glowed faintly, like fire under snow, and she crossed to it, nursing it into a flame with some shavings from the woodpile in another corner. There was nothing to eat in the hut and she had no provisions with her. She had travelled light indeed.

Wryly she smiled at the thought until the problem of her whereabouts pushed all other considerations into the background. She got up to look out of the window, but it was deeply set into the pine wall and she could not see to advantage. The snow had decreased visibility, too, although it was not yet very heavy.

She walked about the hut, finding a tin of drinking chocolate and some salt in a cupboard behind the door and also a tin mug without a handle. In another corner there was a wooden keg containing spring water, and she wondered if she should try to make herself something hot to drink, heating the water in the mug over the snow sparking logs.

For the first time sudden, paralyzing fear took possession of her. Supposing the snow trapped her up here in the mountains for days? A *strassenkarte* had been pinned up on the wall for the use of the summer climbers and it told her how far she had come from the road itself. The ski trail had led her directly to the mountains and now she was stranded at the first rest hut. There was nothing she could do but stay there until she felt capable of making the return journey or until another climbing party reached her. The second hope seemed to be the more forlorn of the two. Oberzach was not a popular resort and Martin Kirchhofer would probably be leading the only party of the day from the hotel.

The quiet of the little hut was suddenly rent by the now familiar sound of falling ice and snow as another minor avalanche cascaded down into a ravine, and black despondency descended upon her as she saw herself isolated in the deserted hut for days. It was minutes before she realized that the hut would probably be the first place a search-party would aim for.

With the comforting thought in mind, she built up the fire but she was scarcely prepared for an immediate response to her smoke signal. A heavy tread approached the hut and her heart began to hammer painfully as she crossed to the door.

Through the narrow, inadequate window she saw the blurred figure of a man propping his skis against the side of the hut. His face was turned from her and there was no thought of recognition in her mind. That one blind second when Stuart's name had rushed to her lips had passed in senseless and unreasoning disappointment and she opened the door to the stranger.

"Jane! Thank heaven I haven't been on a wild-goose chase!"

Tom Sark stumbled across the threshold, brushing snow from his clothes and stamping it from his heavy boots, and Jane could almost have laughed at the caprice of fate. Tom in place of Stuart!

"How did you get here? However did you come?" she gasped, relieved beyond measure to see someone she knew.

"I followed what I hoped would be your ski tracks." He took off his leather mittens and was rubbing his hands

131

together for warmth. "There was an awkward moment when I had to choose between right and left, but apparently I was lucky."

"I went wrong there, I think," Jane said. "I should have branched off the other way. At least, I feel that now."

"You came out after Della?" he suggested, watching her closely. "Why?"

"You shouldn't need to ask," she told him quickly. "She's still in no fit state to go out with a party on a whole day's run."

"But she *is* with a party," he pointed out. "Jane! what a fool you've been, risking this sort of thing under such conditions and alone!"

"I had to find her," Jane said desperately, realizing her own predicament perhaps for the first time. "I had to try to dissuade her from going on, and now I've made the most hopeless mess of everything!"

He did not try to contradict her. His eyes were on the scudding clouds which they could see through the tiny window and his own optimism was not particularly high.

"The idea being, I suppose, that you might reach Della before she had gone very far and persuade her to return with you? It was a hare-brained scheme, Jane, whichever way you like to look at it."

"I know—I know that now!" Jane realized that her first consideration had been the promise she had made to Stuart, but it was no use telling Tom about that. He just wouldn't understand. "All I can hope for is that Della and some other member of the ski party made the ski trail to the clinic."

"If that's where it went it might be the answer," he mused. "It would solve Della's problem, of course, but it is hardly likely to solve ours." He crossed to the *karte* on the wall. "As far as I can see, we're practically marooned up here."

"But the snow isn't really heavy," Jane protested. "We can go down by the way we came, over the bridge and back along the trail to the road, if necessary."

"Janey," he said, as if he were explaining something to a child, "we can't go back by the way we came. The ice bridge isn't there any more. I just got over it in time. It split and went down into the ravine with a sound like thunder."

Jane remembered the rumbling which she had taken for a distant avalanche, but she still continued to stare at him incredulously.

132

"There must be some other way," she said. "We must get back to Oberzach tonight."

He frowned, and then he laughed almost lightly.

"I can't think of one short of flying! Can you?"

She was forced to confess her own inadequacy, for she knew so little of this white countryside and its peculiar hazards.

"It's no use saying I wish I had never come," she observed miserably. "I do wish it, but that won't get us very far. What *can* we do, Tom? Can't you think? Can't you suggest anything?"

The fine edge of hysteria in her voice was apparent to him in the instant, and he said quietly:

"I'm as green as you are about mountaineering, but the fact remains that we are not miles from civilization. We're not very high up, either, and we're provided with adequate shelter. The people at Oberzach know where we were going, and even if the snowfall does obliterate our trail, they're sure to try the hut, sooner or later."

"You came from Oberzach, of course." Jane looked at him curiously. "How did you know about—this?"

"By the simple expedient of calling at Doktor Frey's after I had signed in at the hotel." His calm acceptance of their predicament was helping to steady her and he went on quickly. "The doctor's sister was not at home, but I gathered from a rather frenzied servant that you should never have set out in pursuit of Miss Cortonwell alone. Knowing what I do now, I am entirely in agreement with the fair Swiss miss!"

"You make it all sound—more than foolish," Jane told him ruefully. "Before you came I was quite convinced I could get back to the valley and perhaps reach the clinic by the road, but now that's impossible." She turned to face him, her eyes dark-shadowed with distress. "What *are* we to do?"

"Wait patiently till we're picked up." He came towards her, putting a comforting arm about her slim shoulders. "This sort of thing has happened before, you know," he pointed out lightly. "We are not the first couple to be stranded by an unexpected fall of snow, so take heart. It would be absolute madness to attempt to go down when we know so little about conditions round here."

"We might be here overnight—even for days!"

Jane saw the hours passing, lengthening into days, with Stuart returning to Oberzach at the end of them to be witness to the climax of her absurd adventure.

"Highly improper of us!" Tom grinned. "But excusable. Even Sir Walter Raleigh's famous cloak wouldn't be much use for crossing the ravine!"

"It's easier for you," Jane said, biting her lip. "You have no responsibilities. You're out here on holiday."

He swung round to confront her almost angrily.

"Look here, Jane," he said, "stop blaming yourself for everything! Della Cortonwell is old enough to know when she's being a fool, and even Hemmingway couldn't hold you entirely responsible for her mad schemes. You've got to believe that Della would have found some other way of exerting her ego if it hadn't been this."

"You don't understand," Jane protested. "I should have known it was coming. Stuart saw it and warned me——"

"And put you on your honor not to let his precious fiancée out of your sight? They are engaged, I suppose?"

"Not officially." The remaining color fled from Jane's cheeks. "Della's in love with him, of course," she added flatly.

"And he with her?" There was something watchful in Tom's brief glance at her distressed face.

"I suppose so. This cure he is hoping for will mean a great deal to him."

"But he wouldn't marry her as things stand? Well, it could scarcely be expected, could it, even to please Sir Gervaise and further his own career?" The thin edge of sarcasm in Tom's voice deepened. He did not like Sir Gervaise and he was envious of Stuart. "Cortonwell's the sort of man who would go out of his way to marry his daughter off to someone important, and if he thinks he has any hold on Hemmingway he'll use it without much compunction. He's as ruthless as hell. I've come up against him, and I know."

"The registrar's job?" Jane asked sympathetically.

"He kicked my application out," Tom admitted disgustedly. "It would have been a job after my own heart, but he had someone else earmarked for it, I expect, someone who could do him a bit of good! He's the sort who would cheerfully disinherit his own flesh and blood if it would benefit himself in any way."

The amazingly bitter remark struck Jane as being very unlike Tom, but perhaps he was disappointed about the registrar's job. There was no accounting for a man's secret ambitions and she felt glad that he appeared to have ambitions after all.

"Matron would be disappointed," she said, feeling that Conyers and Matron and operating days were very far behind her.

"She was," Tom admitted. "She's been very decent to me lately."

It was the first time Jane had heard him make such an admission, for Tom had been inclined to take things in the past as no more than his due. There had, apparently, been some sort of change in him, and she wondered if the blood transfusion incident and the inquest which had followed it had sobered him a little.

He strode to the fire, throwing more logs on to the flames and taking off his windcheater, which he hung to dry away from the heat.

"I was going to make some cocoa," Jane said. "There's half a tin full in the cupboard and a mug and some water."

"And I've got two slabs of chocolate and an orange!" He turned from the fire to grin at her. "We couldn't have done better if we had landed on a desert island!"

"At least, it would have been warm!" Jane shivered. He put his arm about her again, still protectively.

"Come on, then!" he encouraged. "We'll make the cocoa. I've always loathed the stuff, but it's amazing what you can drink if you try!"

They crouched before the fire, taking it in turn to hold the mug over the flames with a pair of wrought-iron tongs which might have been left there for the purpose, while outside the snow fell in a thickening blanket of white, obscuring the mountain wall across the narrow ravine and the broken ice bridge and the valley far beneath.

The complete isolation of their shelter was something Jane could not bear to think about when she remembered that she might still have been up here alone, and Tom seemed determined not to discuss it with her. He was still convinced that they would be rescued quite soon, although he did not attempt to explain how they were to be reached across the ravine.

When Jane heard footsteps for the second time, and men's voices, she could scarcely believe it.

"Tom!" she cried. "Tom!" and stumbled to the door.

It swung open before she could reach it and Stuart stood there in the grey half-light, tall and dominating, with the curtain of falling snow behind him and the light of relief in his grey eyes.

"Jane!" he said. "Thank God I've found you!"

Her heart bounded and every pulse in her body began to leap madly. Whenever he came it was the same. Her eyes clung to his for a long, breathless moment, searching, rewarded, and then his gaze went beyond her into the hut and he saw the man standing in the shadows beside the fire. He drew back as if something had leapt out and scorched him, and his face seemed cast in granite when he said:

"I had no idea you had a companion. I understood that you went out after Della, but apparently I've been misinformed."

Jane found herself struggling for words.

"I did go after Della. Tom and I followed the wrong trail."

He did not appear to be listening. His hard, expressionless gaze was taking in the scene in the hut and Tom's efforts at making her comfortable. The cheerfully-burning fire, the cocoa still steaming in the tin mug and Tom's resentful glare all might have suggested that they were not too greatly concerned about Della or her whereabouts.

Two men had come to the door behind him, villagers whom Jane had seen once or twice and remembered. They looked relieved that their search had ended so quickly.

"We'll push off right away," Stuart decided, taking command. After that first brief glance he did not seem to notice Tom. "We came up by a rather difficult route when we discovered that the ice bridge had given way," he explained. "We saw the smoke from your fire, of course, and realized that you must be up here."

Jane felt that there was nothing more to say. He had reached his own conclusions, and she felt too weak and mentally bruised to argue. When she struggled with the hood of her windcheater it was Tom who came to fasten it for her.

"Cheer up, Jane!" he urged. "Our fate is no longer in the lap of the gods—at least, not quite the same gods!"

She was in no mood to meet Tom's flippancy, and Stuart was waiting for them to start. He had damped down the fire and given a last cursory glance round the hut to see that everything was in order.

"We'll have to report the bridge," he said to one of the Swiss guides. "This was completely unforeseen."

Their way back skirted the edge of the glacier and he organized the convoy, roping Jane and himself together for further safety. Tom he sent on ahead between the two guides. They could not see the ice for the newly-fallen snow, but the chill of it smote deeply, finding Jane's heart. It seemed as if the end of the world had come.

Led by the two guides, they reached the valley in what seemed an incredibly short space of time, and Stuart said abruptly:

"The guides are going on to the hotel. Will you make sure that they get something to drink and a hot meal?"

It was the first time he had addressed a direct remark to Tom, and Jane saw Tom smile as he answered:

"I can look after that part of it. Thanks for all you've done for us, Hemmingway. It was an unfortunate accident, but I'm afraid these things just can't be helped, however efficient we may be otherwise."

Stuart turned to where Doktor Frey and Hilde were waiting for them in the shelter of the stone porch.

"In future I wouldn't take risks, if I were you," he said stiffly. "Oberzach isn't exactly as safe as Arosa."

"We knew that Stuart would find you and bring you safely back!" Hilde cried, embracing Jane with frank relief in her blue eyes. "It has all been so difficult, explaining to him, when he shot off like someone who has gone out of his senses after we tell him that you are lost!"

Jane turned into the ski-room and Stuart came in behind her, hanging his sticks up on the rack. He had stiffened at Hilde's remark, but he made no reference to it as Jane tried to unbuckle her skis.

"What happened to Della?" she asked.

"She's up at the clinic." He bent down to undo the frozen binding for her, his dark head bowed to the task, his face hidden. "The effort proved her wrong even more forcibly than I could have done," he added grimly. "If she escapes pneumonia she will be lucky."

"Please don't blame her too much," Jane begged. "Being Della, she just couldn't stand aside and see them go when she felt so fit."

"Being Della, she took the law completely into her own hands and hoodwinked you into the bargain," he said calmly. "This outside treatment has proved nothing but a farce, and I dare say I should have expected it."

"Perhaps if you had someone you could have trusted," she began bitterly.

He stood her skis side by side with his own against the wall, and they looked small and childish by comparison.

"Recrimination never did anyone any good," he said. "What you need now is a hot meal and a good night's rest."

"Will you leave Della at the clinic?"

"For the present."

His decision was inflexible, stamped inexorably in the set of his jaw and the hard line of his handsome mouth, and Jane could find no pity in him, for Della or anyone else. Why he had returned from Geneva two days earlier than he had intended did not matter. He had come and found her wanting, and he was making no secret of his anger.

Throughout the meal he listened to her description of the events of the day in stony silence, leaving it to the doctor and Hilde to comment on her adventure, and when their coffee was served he rose after gulping down a solitary cup.

"I'll get back up to the clinic," he said to his host. "Shall I see you up there later, or would you like me to do your rounds for you and save you the journey?"

Albert Frey shook his head.

"I'll come with you. I'd like to hear about your visit to Geneva, Stuart, and I obtained some information in Zurich today which I think will interest you. It may even have an indirect bearing on Miss Cortonwell's case."

Instantly Stuart's whole manner changed. He was alert, thoughtful, and most of the angry resentment seemed to have evaporated.

"Do you mean the new Loti theory?" he asked as he stood waiting for the doctor to find his coat. "I wondered when they would issue their results. You mean to try them out at the clinic, then?"

Albert Frey nodded.

"They are certainly worth a trial," he said.

Stuart turned to Hilde.

"I may stay up at the chalets for a few days," he said. "It might be necessary, if there are complications. Don't worry about me. I'll manage all right."

He had not looked at Jane, and she felt dismissed. He was going to be near Della, to give her the extra confidence of his love, hopeless though it might prove to be.

CHAPTER EIGHT

THERE WAS NO doubt that Tom Sark could make himself very agreeable, especially to people who he thought might be able to help him. He had come to Switzerland for three weeks, on holiday, but there was just the possibility that he might be able to prolong his visit. Specialized knowledge of an insidious disease could scarcely be acquired in a day or two, but he could still pick up quite a lot of useful knowledge by impressing Doktor Frey with his keenness. His disappointment over the registrar's job in Norchester had gone deep, and there was no very pressing reason why he should return immediately. It would be something of a feather in his cap, besides, to go back as an ex-pupil of the renowned Doktor Albert Frey.

To the simple, unaffected Swiss doctor his interest was both a compliment and a password to the Frey hospitality. He came to the house whenever he liked and the doctor eventually took him to the clinic.

Jane, with so little to do now that Della had gone, helped Hilde with her shopping and drank endless cups of coffee between attempts to perfect herself on skis, but gradually she began to feel that she was remaining at Oberzach under false pretenses. With Della being cared for at the clinic, her own usefulness had passed into other hands.

Immersed in his work, Stuart appeared to be avoiding Oberzach. She did not see him again until Doktor Frey told her she could visit Della.

Four days had passed since the abortive climb and their patient did not appear to be suffering from any ill effects, apart from the first desperate fatigue.

Tom drove her up to the plateau. Thoroughly self-possessed, he borrowed the Freys' sleigh whenever he wished to get about without propelling himself on his own two feet, and they drove through the crystalline afternoon air to the accompaniment of jangling harness and tinkling sleigh bells.

In the silence as they ran in the shadow of the pines, he said unexpectedly:

"What will you do when all this peters out, Jane?"

"I don't know." She held her breath. "It's—so different here—so free, and there's not so very much to go back to."

"Back to Norchester, you mean?" There was a pause, awkward with unsaid things, although Jane had honestly tried to put the memory of the past behind her. "I'm sorry about that unpleasant piece of misunderstanding in the operating theatre, Jane," he said at last. "If it would have helped, I would have spoken up sooner, but Hemmingway's evidence at the inquested settled the issue. The blood transfusion wouldn't have made any difference, anyway."

Jane did not want to discuss the matter. It was no use pointing out to Tom that his carelessness had cost her the job she had coveted and a great deal more besides.

"All the same," he mused, as if to dismiss any need for argument, "you've not done too badly out of it, have you?" He glanced about him appreciatively. "It must be costing old man Cortonwell a packet to keep you and Della out here."

Jane flushed.

"I've been thinking about that," she confessed. "If Della is to remain at the clinic, I must go home."

"And no one will decide that but Hemmingway, I suppose? He appears to be the master-mind hereabouts!"

"He's certainly the doctor in charge," Jane said frigidly.

They drove on in silence, covering the narrow road at a lively pace, the sure-footed horses responding to the whip with a toss of their long manes that sent the harness bells jangling madly and called wide-eyed children out to the chalet doors.

At the clinic Doktor Frey was waiting for them, his face wreathed in smiles. He led Tom away to the laboratories while Jane was escorted to Della's room by a trim maid in a grey dress.

"Hullo!" said Della, rising from the *chaise-longue* on her private balcony. "I wondered when Stuart was going to let me see you!"

So it had been Stuart's edict and not Doktor Frey's! Jane wondered if he really thought her companionship necessary to Della now that he was so contemptuous of her inefficiency.

Della did not look much different, except perhaps, that she was a little paler and a trifle more constrained.

"This place isn't so bad," she confessed when they were seated close to the balcony rail overlooking the long vista of snow-clad valley and towering, sun-kissed peaks. "It isn't run on hospital lines at all. One is allowed to remain a human being. Apart from Stuart, everyone is being most kind and terribly considerate."

Apart from Stuart! Della smiled at the question in Jane's eyes.

140

"He's furious, of course! You don't really expect him to be lenient after an episode like last week's, do you?" she asked. "His anger was the most perfectly leashed thing I've ever seen, but it was none the less effective for that! I duly crumbled before it, but it didn't seem to give him as much satisfaction as I thought it might."

"Possibly because his anger wasn't mainly with you," Jane said. "I was far more responsible for allowing you to go off like that."

"My dear Jane!" Della laughed. "You don't honestly believe that, do you? You couldn't have stopped me, you know, once I had made up my mind. We both know that, and so does Stuart."

Jane was not so easily convinced, however.

"I had a job to do," she said, "and I slipped up on it." She drew a long deep breath. "That is the way Stuart will look at it."

"You know him almost as well as I do!" Della declared. "He knew I wouldn't be able to get much farther than here, even on my stubborn determination, by the way, and now he looks on it as a good move, I suppose. It's proving his contention that sanitoria aren't the fearsome things one is inclined to imagine!" She studied Jane carefully for a moment. "He's terribly conscientious about his work. It means such a lot to him, and I know my case in particular is important, but nothing—no personal reason—will ever make Stuart deviate from a preconceived plan."

Jane got up and leaned against the balcony rail. Beneath her the black ribbon of the road wound down into the hidden valley and close at hand the white mountain-wall rose sheer above them into the blue sky. In the deep col above the ravine the ice of the glacier glistened coldly and she was suddenly shaken by the memory of her journey across it. Stuart had guided her unerringly, but his manner had been as frigid as the blue ice itself.

"Has Stuart arranged for you to stay up here, Della?" she asked.

"For the present." Della glanced round as her bedroom door opened. "He issues orders, but he never really tells me what he thinks," she added affectionately as Stuart strode across the room and came out to stand beside her.

She raised her hand to him and he clasped it for a moment before his fingers fastened over her pulse.

I've got to go, Jane thought desperately. Neither of them has any real need of me now.

141

When their tea was brought in Stuart shared it with them. Della was very gay. She appeared to have entirely forgotten the ski run and Stuart's righteous anger and was ready and willing to co-operate with him again in every way. Only once, when she asked about the Kirchhofer brothers did the old Della show through, the old irritation with her poor, frail body which refused to answer the dictates of her restless heart.

"I suppose they've gone on to St. Moritz," she said. "Martin is confident about the jump this year. He's on top of his form." Her voice shook a little. "Hans, of course, will win the slalom. There's no one to beat him!"

Stuart's lips were tightly compressed as he listened and he did not answer Della's statement. It was as if he had no immediate assurance to offer her.

Della drained her cup, saying quite naturally:

"This is my rest period. Why not take Jane up to the caves, Stuart? She hasn't seen them yet."

"Why not?" Stuart agreed, getting to his feet. "Doctor Sark is still busy in the laboratory."

"Oh!" Della said, glancing at Jane. "Is Tom Sark here? I thought Stuart went down for you. He said he would."

Tom had usurped that privilege, but it did not seem to matter very much, Jane thought. Neither did the proposed visit to the caves, although it would give her an opportunity of telling Stuart that she must go home.

He led the way downstairs, through the long, glass-protected verandah where Doktor Frey's patients greeted him as an old friend, eyeing Jane speculatively. They were ever eager for romance, even if it could hold no place in their own lives.

"How far is it to the caves?" she asked. "Do you think we ought to go?"

He paused to light his pipe in the shelter of the glass screen.

"That's entirely up to you," he told her enigmatically "Della believes that you should see all the local beauty spots while you remain here."

The last few words pierced her like a barbed shaft. In spite of the fact that she had already made up her own mind to go, she had not expected him to accept her decision as a foregone conclusion.

"Della can be the most thoughtful person I know at times," she said defensively, "but she is apt to forget that you are a busy doctor. Leisure was never your strong point, Stuart."

142

"Yet all work and no play has been known to make Jack a dull boy!" he returned easily. "Even doctors have to stretch their legs on occasion, and this one can take an order now and then."

An order from Della! There was something different about him this afternoon, Jane thought, a strange, almost boyish elation which took years from his age and made him the ideal companion for an afternoon's outing. She would let him take her on this walk to the caves, accepting his companionship as it came, the last intimate moment, perhaps, before they parted for good.

She knew now that she would not—could not—return to Norchester. It was too full of memories for her, too much a part of the past she was resolved to forget. She would find a job elsewhere, probably in Nottingham, where she would be near Hazel and Linda Jane.

The thought held consolation until she was confronted by the cold fact that Eric had decided to remove his wife and step-daughter to Nottingham so that he might not be pestered by unnecessary in-laws.

"Well, she thought, why be sensitive? With people like Eric possessiveness was natural. He was the primitive type who scented danger at every approach. She need not go to Nottingham. There were other cities. London, perhaps——

"Why the sudden preoccupation?"

"I was wondering what happens to a career that gets hacked about like mine," she answered frankly. "Does it always end up with the odd private nursing job, backed by the helpful specialist?"

"Either that or you get married," he said briefly. "I thought the alternative was fairly obvious."

"Not always," she flashed, hurt by his apparent indifference. "Marriage isn't the answer to every disappointment in life."

They had left the clinic behind and were on the pathway to the glacier, and in the shadow of the giant pines he looked down at her with a baffled expression in his eyes.

"I thought it was the culminating point of all happiness, though," he said. "Do you remember you once told me something like that? You said that your career could so easily be submerged in the little things of loving, of the everyday job of simply being a wife."

A sob caught in her throat, but she was determined to crush back emotion. He had reminded her of the past with a cruel deliberation, and she had no adequate weapon with which to fight back, but at least she had her determination to leave Oberzach as quickly as possible, which would not hurt Stuart at all!

"That applied in those days," she said huskily. "I'm older now."

"And wiser?"

"It's difficult to say. Perhaps one's values do change with the passing years."

"And sacrifices become easier, do you mean?"

She knew that he had considered her unwilling to sacrifice her life in England and her career for a student doctor's life abroad four years ago, but his continuing bitterness was difficult to bear.

"Sacrifices aren't a question of time or readiness," she said unevenly. "They are demanded of you at any time and you meet them according to your own conscience."

"But surely there must be some yard-stick of values?" he suggested doggedly. "Or does it all come back to love again? Either your love is great enough to sustain a particular sacrifice or it is not?"

They had left the shadow of the trees and were out on the broad snowfield with a hidden river rushing in its deep bed far beneath them and the glacier marking the sharp defile between the peaks. The sun had almost reached the mountain rim on the far side of the valley and the high plateau behind them was flushed with crimson fire. Jane felt that she could scarcely bear the beauty of it all, the silent trees and the snow, the distant blue of the glacier, and their complete isolation in a magic world so utterly devoid of sound.

"What does it matter?" she said. "Some people are born to sacrifice—others aren't. Talking about it won't do any good."

"I thought it might," he said. "I was foolish enough to think that it might elucidate many things, but don't let me distress you, Jane. The impulses of the past are entirely your own affair."

They reached the caves, low, blue-white caverns hewn out of the solid ice by the passing years, and he stood aside for her to go on before him.

The breathless quality of such an adventure should have entranced Jane, but their conversation on the way through the wood had obliterated all happier thought. Stalactites and stalagmites danced before her eyes in crazy, tortuous patterns, suggestive of pain and the vicissitudes of birth. The birth of reason? She imagined Stuart trying to present the past to her in reasonable perspective,

144

showing her how useless it was to harbor regret, but regret knew no laws. It scoffed at reason, twisting within her like some live thing, demanding utterance.

Blindly she turned to make her way out into the daylight and as blindly stumbled, twisting her foot on the rough slate of the cave floor.

An involuntary cry escaped her, and instantly she was caught up in Stuart's arms, feeling the wild beating of his heart against her own, the pressure of his mouth as it came down almost savagely against hers. The domed roof above them was obliterated by his dark head and nothing mattered but his nearness as she responded passionately to his kisses, knowing that there would never be another love like this in all her life.

It was Stuart who finally held her away from him.

"So the past isn't entirely a forgotten phase!" he said harshly. "For all your wild reasoning, Jane, it still matters to you!"

His eyes glittered in the weird blue light and she felt the cold from the glacier for the first time, possessing her, sinking into her heart. Could he have kissed her like that deliberately, punishing her, arousing love to throw it back in her face?

Shame submerged her as she remembered her own passionate reponse, her utter abandonment to his kisses, and she ran from him in blind fury, stumbling down the steep incline from the caves among boulders and rough shale along a rutted, half-defined path which led back to the snowfield.

She ran on, reaching the path which led among the trees, and here the ankle she had wrenched gave way completely and she sank ignominiously deep in the soft snow, waiting helplessly for Stuart to reach her.

He came striding along the path, tall, masterful, completely in control of the situation and his own emotions, and for that alone she felt that she hated him.

He helped her to her feet, supporting her with a strong arm about her waist and she felt the trembling of her body like a betrayal. His very touch had the power to unnerve her. She had shown him how much she cared and he was merely amused.

"Don't speak to me!" she sobbed unreasonably. "Don't touch me! I know that I hate you now."

He continued to hold her, patiently almost.

"Tell me that in a saner moment, Jane," he said as he bent to unclasp her snow boot.

145

Calmly, professionally, he set about the task of strapping up her ankle, using his handkerchief torn into strips. She hated him for his cold control of the situation, for the subdued sort of kindness which had replaced his former ruthlessness, and then all her emotions collapsed into the helplessness of despair. How could he have grown like this? By what bitter reasoning did he justify his treatment of her now for the errors of the past?

He led her, limping a little, back to the clinic and produced a more professional bandage for the injured foot.

"I could have done without this," she said unevenly when Della met them in the lounge. "It looks as if I'm going to be indoors for a day or two."

It was then that she remembered her decision to tell Stuart that she must leave Switzerland. She was doubly certain now. There was nothing between them but the bitterest enmity.

How true that was she did not stop to think. Her one desire was to put what distance she could between her and the scene at the caves.

Going back in the sleigh with Doktor Frey driving and Tom sitting under the bearskin rug by her side, she tried to perfect her plans.

"I'm going home, Tom," she said.

He smiled at her one-sidedly.

"Why, may I ask?"

"For one reason—Della is staying on at the clinic and will have no need for special nursing. At one time I imagined that she needed my companionship, too, but perhaps I was wrong."

"Why do you worry about anyone like Della?" he asked dispassionately. "She has everything she wants, and soon she will have her health back. I saw her latest X-ray plates this afternoon and they were highly satisfactory. Hemmingway showed them to me when I first went in. He was like a man who has just received a reprieve from a death sentence," he added carefully. "Della will marry him in a year's time and all will be right with their world. They'll go back to Norchester and be the celebrated Mr. and Mrs. Hemmingway. 'He's the great lung man, you know—right at the top of his profession'!" he mocked.

Jane could excuse his envy. Stuart did appear to have everything—even the love he had thought he might lose! Something that had survived anger and was small and hopeful and vulnerable died in her at the conviction. Poor dreaming fool, she thought. Were you seeking to recapture the past even now? No one had ever done that, made it just the same. She had been beset by a dream, a chimera reserved for moments such as this, the final groping of the tortured heart.

Stuart came to Oberzach that evening, following them down from the plateau on foot, and it seemed that his coming forced the issue of Jane's departure. He was like an elated schoolboy over the prospect of Della's recovery.

"This Loti treatment has proved a hundred per cent beneficial in cases like Della's," he explained when the doctor excused himself after dinner to write some letters. "It's quick, too. No tedious time-lag waiting for final results."

"Which means that Della has agreed to stay at the clinic until she can go home with absolute safety?" Jane asked.

"It will be essential," he said. "All the necessary apparatus is there, and Loti himself has promised to come up here as soon as he is free."

"I'm so glad!" Jane cried. "So glad for Della. She could never have accepted half measures."

He glanced at her keenly.

"You're pretty sure about that," he said, "yet you don't exactly apply it in your own case."

"I—don't come into this," she said harshly. "It's Della that counts. You're so certain of this cure and she has accepted the clinic. It isn't at all what she expected." She clasped her hands tightly, striving for the confidence and courage she knew she would need. "She'll be a model patient from now on. I feel sure of it!"

"And so," he added for her, "you wish to go home?"

Her eyes met his in a quick look of surprise.

"Don't ask me how I know," he mocked. "The indications are unmistakable."

"I can't stay on, Stuart," she said stonily. "My work here is finished."

"Don't you think I might be the competent judge of that?" he queried, rising to light a spill for his pipe from the crackling pine logs.

Jane met his calm gaze for the second time across the leaping flame which seemed to kindle an answering spark in his dark, grey eyes.

"I was Della's choice," she reminded him. "You could never have wanted me to come out here, Stuart."

"All the same," he said, "you came partly on my recommendation. And now you want me to send you home. Can you tell me why?"

His eyes remained steady on hers, probing, demanding an unequivocal answer.

"Because Della does not need me any more," Jane said. "She is entirely relaxed and happy at the clinic under Doktor Frey."

"Is that your only reason?" he persisted, standing squarely in front of her and taking the pipe from between his strong teeth. "Della's welfare? Della's happiness? What about your own happiness, Jane?"

She gripped the arm of her chair, praying that her voice would not quiver and betray her as she answered:

"I feel that I shall be happier back in England."

He bent to knock out the contents of his pipe against the stone hearth, as if it had no longer the power to soothe him.

"I see." He straightened, squaring his shoulders. "I take it that we can still depend upon you to a certain extent while Doctor Sark remains at Oberzach?"

"Yes," Jane said dispiritedly. "I shall probably travel back with Tom."

He did not refer to her decision again. He remained kind, but distant, encouraging her to visit Della but absenting himself from the informal little tea parties they shared on the sun-warmed terrace.

It was Jane who finally told Della of her decision to leave. She preferred it that way and Stuart had not interfered.

"Going home?" Della echoed in blank dismay. "But why, Jane? Why?"

"For the simple reason that I can't expect your father to go on paying a salary to someone who is no longer necessary in your scheme of things."

"What rot!" Della objected emphatically. "Anyway, that's not a very complimentary way to put it, is it? I need you now, as much as ever, Jane, if it's only to bolster up my morale."

"You'll have Stuart," Jane pointed out, "And Doktor Frey."

"Stuart can't stay here holding my hand for ever," Della said. "He's got work to do. He goes off next week, I believe, for a session in Vienna—a fortnight's conference, or something. You'll be letting me down, Jane, if you desert me now."

Jane smiled.

"It's nice of you to put it like this, Della," she said. "But I really have made up my mind to go."

"Because you're in love with Tom Sark?" Della demanded incredulously.

"No; that's not the reason."

"You're not even thinking of marrying the man?"

Jane hesitated. Had she been thinking of marrying Tom, accepting what Stuart had once called 'second best'?

"I don't know. He has asked me to marry him——"

"You'd be a fool even to think about it," Della interrupted impatiently. "Oh! whatever is the matter with everybody these days?" she cried. "Nobody seeing straight, everybody going about biting each other's heads off—nobody really happy at all! Am I going to be happy when I'm well again? 'There's the rub,' as our friend, Will Shakespeare, has it, I believe! We don't know. We don't know about anything! We rush around hoping for perfection and never gaining it and love takes the rap every time! Because we're in love we think we have a perfectly legitimate excuse for being as pig-headed as the devil. It makes us sensitive! It makes us fools, but somehow it can't make honest men and women out of us! Why can't we go and tell the person we love, fair and square, that life won't be worth a tinker's curse without them instead of bottling it all up inside and calling our stupidity by the name of pride!"

Jane had never heard her friend so eloquent before, and it seemed that Della had been haranguing herself as much as her audience. Yet, surely Della could not be unsure of Stuart's affection? Not now, when her cure was a certainty and the light of achievement was already burning in his eyes.

"It's so easy to see it like that, in theory " she said, turning away so that Della might not see her eyes. "We're all fools in practice though."

"And I could have sworn that Stuart was no fool!" Della mused, as the bedroom door closed on Jane's rigid unbending little back.

CHAPTER NINE

Two DAYS later Stuart left Oberzach for Vienna. An early *Föhn* was blowing and tempers were on edge in consequence. The snow had become sticky and moist and it was difficult to get about even on the sleigh. Then, overnight the wind changed and a freezing breath came down the valley from the north. Conditions on the roads became dangerous and inexperienced skiing was out of the question.

Housebound, Jane became restive. She knew that she must leave Oberzach before Stuart returned but the difficult part would be saying goodbye to Della and the Freys.

Della made it very difficult indeed.

"You're deserting your post!" she accused. "And that while the commanding officer is away too! I would not have credited you with such baseness. Does Stuart know about this?"

"Yes, he knows." Jane answered quite truthfully. Stuart had not put any obstacle in the way of her going except to ask if they could depend upon her while Tom remained there. As if Tom's being at Oberzach really mattered!

"I know Doktor Frey was going to offer you a job here at the clinic." Della went on and Jane was left wondering if Stuart had put his foot down on the suggestion as soon as it had been made.

She could not have accepted the job, anyway. She kept repeating the old formula. Her work here was finished. Della was getting well and would remain at the clinic until the new cure was completed.

"If you really mean to go," Della said at last, convinced that argument was no longer of any avail, "at least go and see Dad when you get back to Norchester. He'll expect you to report, and I'm determined to keep in touch, Jane."

It was easy enough to make the promise when she knew that she would have left Norchester long before Della returned there with Stuart. 'The celebrated Mr. and Mrs. Hemmingway.'

Tom's mocking words became reality, but she could not grudge Della her happiness now. They had come so far along the way together, even in such a short space of time, and Della had become her friend. Simple irony! Fate could think up the most improbable situations and drop them at your feet without a qualm!

"You've definitely made up your mind about going home?" Tom asked when he heard the news. "Could it mean that you've changed it, too, about marrying me?"

"It couldn't, Tom. I'm not thinking about marrying anyone."

The disappointment on his face would have been comical if it had not suddenly been sincere.

"I can't think why," he said. "At one time I imagined you were hankering after Hemmingway, but now you're not even waiting till he gets back from Vienna. Women never cease to amaze me!" He lit a cigarette. "How many times do you think I shall have to ask you before you say 'yes'?"

"I think—I'd stop trying now, if I were you," Jane said gently. "I'm sorry, Tom, but—it just doesn't seem any use."

"To use a well-worn platitude, you think you would only be offering me second best?"

She was amazed at his swift perception, but she could not deny the truth of his statement.

"What if I agreed to accept that? What if I told you it would be good enough?" he demanded.

"You'd regret it, Tom. Anyone would."

"I'm not an idealist."

"You're human, though. It would rankle in time."

He looked down at the glowing tip of his cigarette.

"I don't think so. I've never expected top-grade treatment from life, Jane. I've always had to be content with what came my way. Perhaps I've not been very grateful at times, but that's my way. Resentment is apt to get under your skin when you see the other fellow getting all the breaks, and then, if you're wise, you learn to snatch for yourself. I'll never make a very successful doctor, Jane, but I could try to be a conscientious one, if I had you."

Her eyes misted with quick tears.

"I wish I could promise you that sort of satisfaction," she said earnestly, "but it wouldn't really do any good, Tom. I haven't got a lot to go back to Norchester for, but I owe it to Della to report to her father."

"Sir Gervaise!" Tom jeered. "He won't consider he owes you anything once you've fulfilled your obligation to him. Don't make any mistake about that, Jane! You and I are the kind who will always have to stand on our own two feet. I wouldn't depend too much on Sir Gervaise's generosity, if I were you."

"I don't intend to depend upon anyone's generosity,"

she said proudly. "I'm not even hoping that Sir Gervaise will recommend me to another job. I think," she added breathlessly, "that I would prefer to find work away from Norchester."

That had been her decision in the first place, and she did not think she would have any reason to change her mind. The chilly fate which thinks up situations to disconcert its victims was still at work in her particular orbit, however.

Two days before they were due to leave the valley Tom made a final ski trip to the head of the plateau with the two guides who had come to their rescue that day when Stuart had found them in the hut above the glacier.

Jane spent the afternoon with Della, strolling as far as the wood on the way to the caves, but they turned back before they reached the ice and she was thankful beyond measure for something which felt like a reprieve.

The parting with Della was to be brief. They both wanted it that way.

"No regrets!" Della said. "Because we're sure to meet again."

Jane made her way back to Oberzach with a heavy heart. Doktor Frey was genuinely grieved at their parting and had made every effort to keep her. He could not understand why she insisted on going when she had made so many friends in Switzerland, he said wistfully, but he did understand that the ties of home were binding, too. Jane had no home ties, none in the way the kindly little professor meant, but she did not tell him so.

They were sitting together on the glassed-in terrace at the front of the house when the ambulance drew up at the foot of the steps and a white-faced maid came to call the doctor.

"It's the English gentleman!" she cried. "He has been hurt."

They carried Tom in on a stretcher, still in his torn windcheater and blood-spattered *vorlages*, his face white and distorted with pain, though he tried to smile in Jane's direction as he passed.

Calmly, Doktor Frey took charge. He was with Tom for more than an hour and then Jane could wait no longer. She crept up to the bedroom where the two ambulance men still remained and knocked on the door.

Albert Frey came out, closing the door firmly behind him.

"Can I help?" Jane asked. "Can I do anything?"
He shook his head.

"We've given him something to let him sleep for an hour or two," he said heavily. "It is the best we can do."

She stared at him, uncomprehending, not daring to think. The professor passed a hand across his eyes in a gesture of weariness.

"This is terrible," he said. "He is so young."

Jane moistened lips suddenly gone dry, but words refused to come.

"I must send for other advice" the doctor said moving towards the stairs. "We must have a second opinion before I can ask his people to accept my verdict."

"You mean that——"

She could not face up to the fear in her heart. There were no words in which to express it. Albert Frey gazed at her steadily.

"If he lives," he said quietly, knowing that she expected the truth "the chances are that he will not walk again."

"No! Oh, no!" The cry fell from Jane's lips and she dug her nails into the soft flesh of her palms in a frantic effort at control. "This other opinion you speak about Doktor Frey? It is the best that can be had?"

"Undoubtedly, the very best."

She had no need to ask. The Swiss were like that, generous and sure in their giving. All that was necessary now was to wait.

During the long watches of the night she sat by Tom's bedside, a fine perspiration beading her upper lip each time his breathing seemed to die in the silence of the quiet room, but by the morning he was still alive. His long spare body lay rigidly under the bedclothes, one arm flung outwards as if in mute protest at this sudden blow which fate had dealt, and Jane could not look at its latent strength without her lips trembling. To remain crippled for the rest of one's life! All the small weaknesses of his character were suddenly submerged in pity, and even when Hilde came to relieve her in the early hours of the morning she could not sleep while his future hung so precariously in the balance.

The specialist reached Oberzach by mid-day. Doktor Frey took him up to Tom's room and they remained there for over an hour, and when they came down again they found Jane still standing where they had left her in the lounge.

There's no hope, she thought, searching their shadowed faces.

"It is necessary to be very brave, Jane," Albert Frey told her kindly. "I know that Doctor Sark was your friend and it is true to say that he was very fond of you."

"Will he die?" Jane broke in. "Oh! Doktor Frey, is that what you are trying to tell me?"

His grey head bowed, Albert Frey moved towards her. "There is nothing that we can do," he said.

"How long?" she asked, after a pause.

"Three or four weeks, at most."

"Does he—want to go home?" she asked in a stunned whisper, wondering even as she uttered the words why she should ask. "Would it—hasten things if we moved him?"

The elderly specialist shook his head.

"It will make little difference. Stretcher cases are often taken back to England from our mountains, but, happily, not as this one. The sprained ankle or displaced thigh, perhaps. Often not so serious as they are painful."

Jane nodded dumbly, wondering if they had told Tom. "Does he know?" she asked.

"It would not do to tell him just now," Albert Frey said. "I shall send with you a full report to his own doctor in England." He brushed away a tear, of which he was not at all ashamed. "It is indeed tragic not to be able to help one so young and full of the joy of living."

Jane turned abruptly to the window. Her heart seemed to be bursting and a tight band pressed heavily across her brows. The headache had been there all morning, pent-up grief treading on the heels of disaster, and in spite of Hilde's kindness and her brother's ready sympathy she felt very much alone, responsible, almost, for what was to become of the man lying in the bedroom upstairs.

"He is asking for you," Albert Frey said. "You will go to him soon?"

"Yes—right away."

Jane went slowly up the stairs. In all her experience of nursing she had known nothing like this, the uncertainty of it, the sudden, devastating tragedy, and before she opened the bedroom door she had to dash betraying tears from her eyes. It felt like the calmness of despair that took her across the room to Tom's side with the shadow of a smile on her lips.

"Hullo Jane!" he greeted her in the ghost of his old voice. "I asked them to send you in when they had made me presentable." He indicated the chair beside the bed and she sank down into it thankfully. "You see, I didn't want you to go off to England without me!"

"I wouldn't do that, Tom " she whispered. "We hadn't planned to go till tomorrow."

"How long is it going to be till I'm able to get up?" he asked.

"I haven't asked Doktor Frey yet." She had managed to keep her eyes unwaveringly on his. "You may have to travel back as you are. It will be a—longish job, Tom."

"I had an idea it would." He stared up at the ceiling, his mouth twisting a little. "You'll stand by, Jane?" he asked. "You won't let me down in this?"

"No," she said quietly. "I won't let you down."

There was a long silence. He lay studying her face, noting its pallor and the dark shadows beneath her eyes.

"I thought we might be going back engaged to be married," he said slowly, the wisp of a smile straying at the corners of his mouth. "Foolish of me, I suppose, but there you are! Love knows no laws or laughs at locksmiths or something! You wouldn't consider it, Jane—not now that this has happened?" he begged on a more serious note.

Deep down in his voice Jane recognized the half forlorn tone of the schoolboy, the uncertainty which she had glimpsed in Tom once or twice before in spite of the thick shell of arrogance with which he had learned to protect himself.

"If you wish it," she said. "If it will make you feel happier—more secure."

She could not say why she had added these last two words, but the swift look of gratitude which followed the initial surprise in his eyes was answer enough. Tom was no more sure of his way in life than any of them, with the possible exception of Stuart!

The thought of Stuart stabbed deep, but she thrust it from her. He did not come into this. They would have left Oberzach before he returned from Vienna.

Tom moved restlessly on the bed.

"Get me back to England, Jane " he said. "There's something I have to do."

CHAPTER TEN

"IT'S GHASTLY!" DELLA cried. "Ghastly! I've been so full of self-pity, too." Her large amber eyes searched Jane's face. "Jane, does he know?"

"Good gracious, no!" Jane turned round from the window where she had been staring out at the snow. "There would be no point in telling him—no point whatever."

"And this engagement of yours?" Della looked as perplexed as she had been feeling ever since she had heard of Tom Sark's accident and the fact that Jane had promised to marry him. "I thought——"

Jane came across the room to stand by her side.

"Never mind what you thought, Della," she said gently. "Be a dear and make it all sound thoroughly natural when you go up to see him. Tom has been asking me to marry him for months."

"But what about Stuart?" Della asked still in that bewildered tone. "What is he going to say?"

"I can't see that it matters, since we will probably be in England before Stuart gets back here." Jane ran her fingers wearily through the soft waves of her hair. "The specialist and Doktor Frey both think Tom can be moved, so I don't think Stuart would object."

Della was still looking at her in a puzzled way when Albert Frey came in to take her up to Tom's room. I just don't understand Jane, she thought. She's changed so much in so short a time.

Della in an active mood was far more dynamic than even Jane imagined, however. When she had seen Tom and heard that he had fallen in with the idea of a swift return to England she permitted Doktor Frey to drive her back to the clinic in spite of the falling snow.

"Can't you do anything to stop them?" she demanded as soon as they had left Oberzach behind. "Jane can't be allowed to leave before Stuart gets here."

Events were moving much too rapidly for the mild little professor who liked his life to run to a set pattern, and he rubbed his hand in a perplexed way up and down his chin.

"Sometimes I am greatly confused by the English temperament," he confessed. "It is said that you are a cold race, not given to passion or hasty decisions, but I am not at all convinced of that. First, you do not trust me—or Stuart—sufficiently to come to the clinic and then you change your mind—so!" He snapped his fingers. "Then we have Jane, who seemed so much in love with Stuart, becoming engaged to this poor boy who has been so dreadfully injured. Is it out of sympathy, I ask myself, that she will do such a thing? Because, if it is so, it is a great mistake. There may yet be a miracle of healing and he will hold her to her promise. I have seen such miracles happen quite often in my profession," he added mildly.

For a moment it seemed that Della was no longer listening. She was staring into the snowy darkness above the horses' flanks, her eyes full of the old determination which Jane had come to dread.

"Stuart will have to know," she said. "At least he'll have to be told that they are leaving here."

While the little professor inspected a group of cultures he had been anxious to check up on in the laboratory she put through a call to Vienna. Stuart was not in his hotel, but the *concierge* would take a message to be delivered to him immediately he returned. Della's voice was calm and crystal-clear as she dictated it over the line.

"Just say, 'Come back at once. Most urgent.' And you can sign it 'Della'."

When she put down the instrument she sat staring at it for several seconds without moving, but when Doktor Frey came back into the lounge she had made up a table for bridge with three of his oldest patients. As he passed she made an odd little face at him, which he answered with his kindest smile.

Stuart reached Oberzach the following morning. Jane saw him get out of the hired car and could not believe the evidence of her own eyes, yet her first emotion was one of overwhelming relief.

"What's gone wrong?" he asked. "I've had a message from Della, but all it said was 'Come back at once.'"

So, it was anxiety over Della that had brought him, Jane thought, even as she recognized the unreasonable nature of the jealous heart-cry.

"It's Tom," she explained. "There's been an accident —a serious accident, but Della shouldn't have sent for you."

Her throat felt parched and she knew that she must look like death. Stuart took her by the arm and led her gently to one of the cane chairs on the covered verandah.

"Tell me about it as calmly as you can," he commanded. "When did it happen? Couldn't you have sent for me immediately, Jane?"

"Doktor Frey was here, and we've had a specialist since—from Zürich, I think."

His expression sharpened.

"What exactly is the trouble?"

"It's—his spine." She buried her face in her hands, all the accumulated misery of the past two days crowding in to sap her courage. "It's so unfair! He was so young—so vital——"

Gently he drew her hands away from her face, looking deep into her tear-filled eyes.

"How serious is this, Jane?" he demanded. "What was the specialist's verdict? Do you know?"

"There—just isn't any hope. There's absolutely nothing they can do."

"But, Good God!" he protested, "there surely must be something! They can't just abandon the case!"

"I think," she said slowly, stiffly, "Doktor Frey knew from the beginning. When they first brought him down from the mountains he said that—if Tom lived he would never walk again."

Numbly she was repeating Albert Frey's words, as if by the very repetition of them she could make something of them, at last.

Stuart straightened, his mouth grim, his eyes the color of slate.

"I see," he said. "It appears to be beyond their skill out here."

And therefore beyond human skill, Jane thought. The Swiss were among the greatest surgeons in the world and Tom had been given the benefit of Zürich's greatest name. If anything could be done, it would have been done here, on the spot.

She felt that Stuart knew that, too. He stood at the edge of the verandah staring unseeingly out at the freshly fallen snow, and then he wheeled round to confront her with the question she was expecting.

"Has he made any decision about going home? It was your intention, I believe."

"Yes," Jane said. "We were going together." She steeled herself for what she had to say. "We're engaged to be married Stuart——"

He stared at her as if he thought he might not have heard correctly.

"Good God!" he said, but that was all.

Albert Frey came in, greeting his arrival with obvious relief, and they went off together to see Tom.

Jane remained where she was, cold now that the sun had deserted the verandah, but hardly feeling it. She seemed too deeply plunged in unhappiness to move, and when Stuart came back downstairs he rang the bell and ordered some coffee.

"Strong and black, Erna," he said when the maid answered his summons. "When did you last eat?" he added, turning to Jane.

"Hilde brought me up a tray, but I couldn't eat anything," Jane answered. The thought of food was revolting. "I can't now, Stuart. Please just let me drink the coffee."

"If you don't eat something we'll have you collapsing on our hands next," he told her almost brusquely. "Some sandwiches, Erna, and plenty of coffee, there's a good girl!"

He sat watching while Jane ate, forcing the food down between gulps of the steaming beverage, and when she had finished he said decisively:

"I'm coming back to England with you. It would be impossible for you to make such a journey on your own."

"But—Della?" she protested weakly.

"Della will be quite safe here," he said briefly. "She'll be full of her own importance, having done the only sane thing in the past forty-eight hours."

How like Stuart that was! Della should not have wired him, forcing him into this situation, yet there was relief in the very thought of him and the knowledge that she need not make that nightmare journey alone. He would be there to share it with her.

"Do you know anything about Sark's relatives?" he asked presently. "I believe he spoke about some aunt or other, but his parents are the people we should contact first."

"He hasn't any parents," Jane explained. "This aunt he speaks of brought him up from infancy, I believe. He's very fond of her."

"He realizes, of course, that he can't go back there? No inexperienced person could possibly nurse him. We must find a bed for him at Conyers."

Until they were half way across the Channel Jane did not appreciate the fact that she was going back to Conyers. Tom was her one concern, but she knew that she would never have been able to make this flight if it hadn't been for Stuart.

He had arranged everything. He had even managed to make the parting with the Freys easier. somehow, encouraging Hilde not to break down in front of Tom. Della had come down from the clinic in the sleigh to stay the night before their departure, and she had parted with Stuart with what seemed unnatural brevity to Jane.

"You'll be seeing Dad, of course, Stuart," she had said. "Give me a good school report, won't you?"

"I'll do my best!" he returned with a slow smile. "Meanwhile don't forget that reports can also be sent by post!"

Della had laughed and blown him a kiss, flippant in the face of unaccustomed emotion, but when it had come to parting with Jane and Tom she had nothing to say.

"We may meet." Her lips seemed to stiffen and her eyes were suddenly opaque. "Until then—*au revoir!*"

Tom had held her hand for a moment and let it go. He did not say goodbye.

When the 'plane landed an ambulance was waiting. There were absolutely no hitches because Stuart had thought of everything. The long journey by road began with him sitting next to Jane, facing Tom across the narrow, confined space.

"We should get in about six," he said. "I phoned Matron from the airport."

Jane felt slightly sick. Reaction was setting in, but she was determined not to let it get a hold. What did it matter that she had been ignominiously dismissed from Conyers only a few short months ago? She was not returning there in her professional capacity. She was going back as Tom's fiancée.

The relationship had never seemed quite real, shadowed as it was by the future, but it was taking her back to Conyers in spite of herself.

When they turned in under the wide, arched gateway that seemed unreal too, unreal to be driving through it into the courtyard flanked by drab flower beds and the dejected looking rockery where Matron planted tulips in the spring and geraniums and lobelia for summer color. All so formal and, somehow, pointless, but Conyers was the whole of life to Matron.

The ambulance drew up at the side door. It was the visiting hour and the corridors would be busy. An orderly came round and opened the door for them and Stuart helped her out.

Momentarily Jane laid a hand on Tom's arm as they lifted him down.

"O.K., Jane!" he said. "No need to mention the stiff upper lip!"

She walked across the grey paving-stones to the door, and it was only then that she noticed Matron standing there in the shadows. Jane thought the older woman was about to faint.

"Matron!"

Agnes Lawdon pulled herself together with an effort. "Will you bring the patient in," she said in a stilted monotone.

How different her voice sounded, Jane thought. Surely Tom could not have meant so much to her? A woman like Matron had been trained to shock over a period of many years.

And training counted, of course. She led the way along the wide, downstairs corridor to the vacant bedroom next to her own office, holding the door wide to allow the stretcher-bearers to pass through. It was a room which was occupied only occasionally, when Conyers was un-usually full, for Agnes Lawdon liked nothing better than her own privacy. Jane had often thought of the empty room as a barrier erected between Matron and the outside world, a solid buttress against intrusion.

She stood now, tight-lipped and very pale, watching while her patient was lowered carefully on to the bed, and Jane passed her to go to Tom's side.

"Where will you be?" he asked. "Have you anywhere to stay?"

"I'll find somewhere," she said. "You mustn't worry about that."

"Jane." His voice was very tired. "Will you go down to Crale for me and have a talk to Aunt Ada?"

"Yes," she promised. "I'll go tomorrow, but she may be here before then."

"Did you write to her?"

"Yes. I thought I should."

"Good girl! You think of everything."

Stuart drew her gently away.

"He'll sleep now," he said. "You can leave him to Matron."

The silent figure by the door moved forward as he slid the hypodermic needle into Tom's arm. It was almost as if Agnes Lawdon had forgotten them—or dismissed them —as she stood looking down at the bed, and Jane followed Stuart swiftly from the room.

"I've booked accommodation for you at the White Hart," he said. "They'll take care of you there, Jane."

Tears stung her eyes at his kindness and constant thought for her.

"You must want to see Sir Gervaise," she said. "He'll be expecting you."

"He wired me that I must stay there, but it's rather far out. I'd like to be on hand."

In case Tom needed him? In case she needed him? It was the same thing now, but he would never know how much she needed him, his advice, the assurance of his protection at this moment of her greatest uncertainty!

"You've already done so much, Stuart—more than you need have—and—there's Della. She needs you, too."

"My responsibility for Della is almost over," he said. "You know, Jane, how much I owed to her father, and I feel that I have almost discharged that debt now, thanks to Doktor Frey and the Loti treatment."

"But you will go back to Switzerland," she said as if she expected it.

"Not because of Della. I think she will be coming home very soon."

He beckoned a taxi at the end of the lane and took her to the hotel.

"I'll come for you in the morning and take you across to Conyers," he promised as she signed her name at the desk. "Try to get some sleep, Jane. You look all in."

She could not sleep, even although every muscle in her body ached with fatigue. The torturing events of the past few days spun through her mind like a widening vortex, pulling her thoughts into its black, swirling depths. Stuart and Della! Tom and herself! They seemed like puppets dangling on the end of a string and manipulated by a derisive fate. She could not even think clearly. All she could do was to live in the present, to hope and pray that Doktor Frey's miracle would come their way.

When, finally, she dozed off in the greyness of the winter's dawn, her sleep was troubled by fantastic dreams in which she and Stuart and Della featured in unreal situations and she seemed to be pursuing Tom into some black abyss from which there was no return.

Day broke and the hotel stirred into life. She lay listening to the sound of the lift and the clatter down below in the kitchens, and then, at eight o'clock, when she could remain inactive no longer, she got up and began to dress.

Almost immediately the telephone beside her bed began to shrill. She stood staring at it for a moment, stark fear paralysing movement, thinking that it might mean that Tom had not survived the night. Would Matron ring her in that event—or Stuart?

It was Stuart's voice at the other end of the line.

"I've managed to borrow a car," he said. "If you like, I'll run you down to Crale. I heard you making the promise to Tom."

"Oh!" she gasped with relief. "If you would! It's such a difficult journey by train and bus."

"I've been to Conyers this morning, by the way," he said.

"How is Tom?" she asked breathlessly.

"Not too good. He had an unsettled night, which was to be expected, of course. Matron stayed up with him, apparently. She's a strange sort of woman."

"I've never really known her," Jane said. "I don't think anyone has—not really. When do you want me to be ready?"

"I'll pick you up in an hour's time," he said. "It's no use going to see Tom till the afternoon. We've given him something to let him sleep."

Jane was ready when he came for her, driving the big yellow car in which he had first brought Della to Conyers. He made room for her in the front beside him, wrapping a warm travelling rug about her knees and glancing critically at her pale face as he drove away.

"I hope you've had some breakfast, not just tea and toast," he said.

"I had an egg, but I really didn't feel like eating, Stuart."

His mouth, grim and disapproving, was mirrored in the windscreen, but he did not answer her as they left the town behind and drove swiftly through the bleak countryside.

"I've asked Sir Gervaise to have a look at Tom," he said. "He'll be the final authority, I'm afraid."

His tone said that he didn't hold out much hope, and Jane saw it underlined again in the tightly-compressed mouth and the slight dilation of the fine nostrils, but he had put Sir Gervaise's skill at her disposal and for that she had to thank him.

"You've done so much, Stuart. I shall never be able to thank you sufficiently for—for these past two days."

At eleven o'clock he pulled the car up before a wayside hotel and ordered coffee and biscuits. Jane drank the strong coffee thankfully, conscious of the chill in the Channel haze that struck coldly on her limbs, the damp, chill cold of England which she had almost forgotten in the crystalline air of the Alps.

She thought of Della still at Oberzach, at the clinic on the plateau where Stuart's lonely chalet awaited his eventual return. He would go back. She felt certain of that. He had only returned to England out of kindness, because of Tom's accident.

They drove on, reaching Crale just before twelve. Rose Cottage looked deserted and curiously woebegone as they approached it, its windows tightly closed and the sea haze wrapping it round. The garden which had been such a gay riot of summer flowers when Jane had last seen it lay forlornly under the pall of dank mist.

The door was opened to them immediately, however, and Ada Sark smiled when she saw Jane, although the marks of strain were heavily etched on her face.

"I got your letter," she said. "Will you come in?"

"This is Mr. Hemmingway." Jane introduced Stuart. "He helped to bring Tom home."

"You wrote that you were taking him to the nursing home," Mrs. Sark said, showing them into the parlor, as befitted the occasion, and stooping to light a noisy gas fire. "How badly is he hurt?"

She was looking more at Stuart than at Jane, as if she sensed that he would not beat about the bush, and he answered her appeal for truth.

"He's been pretty badly hurt, Mrs. Sark. We brought him home for that reason."

There was a painful, dazed sort of silence and then Ada nodded her grey head.

"I see," she said. "Can you tell me how it all happened?"

"He was skiing under rather bad conditions. He had not nearly sufficient experience."

"Foolhardy," Ada muttered. "He was always like that, full of adventurous notions."

"He'd like to see you," Jane said in a choked whisper. "He asked me to bring you. Do you think you could come back with us right away?"

"As soon as I've made you a bite to eat," Ada agreed, but Stuart cut in:

"No, please don't bother about food, Mrs. Sark. We'll get something in Bristol on our way back. When you are ready we'll push off as quickly as possible before this sea fret gets any worse."

Ada did not protest, hurrying off to do as Stuart asked, and although Jane wanted to thank him she could not. He was being kind—and distant. He was doing this for her as he would have done it for anyone in similar circumstances, a girl stunned by the knowledge that the man she had promised to marry was about to die.

Mrs. Sark had little to say on the journey northwards. She sat in the back of the car with her hands tightly clasped together over her handbag, as if she would offer a continuous prayer for Tom's recovery even in the face of Stuart's verdict, and she was out of the car before he could help her when they finally reached the nursing home.

Jane took her arm as they followed Stuart's tall figure through the swing doors.

"Matron is expecting us," he said. "Will you wait here for a few minutes till I find her?"

Ada blew her nose nervously as she turned to Jane.

"In all the years I've known Agnes, I've never been here before," she confessed. "I hate these places," she added vehemently. "I don't know how she has stuck it all these years, though the money was good when she got on a bit."

Jane remembered that Ada Sark and Matron had known each other for the greater part of their lives. They had, in effect, been friends, although friendship was a thing she had never connected with Agnes Lawdon. They did not seem the types to have struck up a lasting friendship, but she knew that these things happened. There was her own friendship with Della, for instance, blossoming in spite of their divergent temperaments and the fact that they were both in love with Stuart.

The sound of brisk footsteps in the corridor made her turn towards the waiting room as Agnes Lawdon came in, but the older woman did not seem to see her. Her eyes were fixed on her other visitor and she said quietly:

"Well, Ada! I'm glad you've come."

Jane stood back, but Mrs. Sark clung to her arm.

"You'll come, too, dearie?" she begged. "He was very fond of you, in his way."

Matron looked at Jane, but there was no antagonism in her eyes now, only a complete and utter weariness no wholly explained by the fact that she had sat up with a critically ill patient throughout the night.

They walked to the door of Tom's room, passing Stuart on the threshold.

"Don't wait too long," he cautioned, looking at Jane.

Ada Sark approached the bed, drawing Jane with her. Tom lay prostrate on his back, but he turned his head slightly when he saw them.

"Aunt Ada—kind of you to have come," he said. "What's it like at Crale? All the boats hauled up and the shore deserted?"

"And a sea fret in over the land!" Ada Sark's voice had all but broken. "It's not the time of the year for Crale, lad, or for boats, either."

There was a pause before Tom said awkwardly:

"I've never thanked you—never properly."

"That's all right, lad," Ada said steadily. "Crale was your home. There's no need to be thanking me."

A movement at the door made Jane turn in time to see Agnes Lawdon hesitate before she approached them. Her face looked grey and pinched in the rapidly waning light and she halted before she reached the bed.

"We'll have to leave him to sleep now," Jane said, touching Ada's arm. "We can come back later."

They went to the White Hart for tea. Matron had offered it to them in her room, but Jane had thought Mrs. Sark might want to rest afterwards and Stuart had arranged for her to stay at the hotel overnight.

Infallibly kind, completely thoughtful, but still distant, he had attended to the details of that long day for which Jane had found no heart, and at the end of it he would not let her sit up with Tom.

"It would be pointless, Jane," he told her with all the old firmness in his voice. "If there is any need, I will send for you. I promise you that."

She was forced to obey him. It seemed that Stuart was directing her entire world just now for a reason which she could not understand but which had ceased to puzzle her. Complete physical exhaustion had taken its inevitable toll and she felt that she could not even think.

CHAPTER ELEVEN

"It's a LAST resort, but I feel that the effort should be made."

Stuart sat back in the car besides Sir Gervaise Corton-well, watching the chauffeur turning it expertly into the early-morning traffic of Norchester's High Street while the older man digested what he had just been told.

"You appear to have more than the usual interest in this case, Stuart," Sir Gervaise observed. "Of course, you knew the fellow in Switzerland, didn't you?"

"I knew him slightly before he went there, too," Stuart said. "He was house physician at Conyers."

"Indeed?" Sir Gervaise was beginning to simulate a little more interest. "Is he a local man?"

"I'm not sure. He appears to have been brought up by some people down at Crale who adopted him as a child, and I believe he qualified somewhere in the midlands— Manchester or Leeds, perhaps."

"H'm! And I take it that you consider the case fairly hopeless from all you've just told me?"

"I'd like your final opinion," Stuart answered.

The car drove on.

"I've never had much contact with Conyers," Sir Gervaise mused. "Preferred to do my job at the City General, where my reputation was made, or send my patients in to Bristol. Still, I dare say they're efficient enough down there."

"Most efficient," Stuart assured him. "Matron is everything one could reasonably expect."

"We've never met," Sir Gervaise said somewhat pompously. "I believe she's only been here a year or two. I don't even remember having heard her name."

"She's a Miss Lawdon, I think." Stuart was giving his attention to the traffic, conscious of a dislike of being driven by someone else which he could never quite overcome. "I've heard it mentioned once or twice."

"Lawdon?" Sir Gervaise pondered. "I knew someone by that name once, but—it couldn't possibly be the same. It was years ago." He appeared to dismiss the thought. "No, it couldn't possibly be the same!"

"It's an unusual name," Stuart said, and left it there.

When they reached the nursing home and drew up at the front door he could see Agnes Lawdon standing behind the discreet net curtain of her office, looking out at them with the satisfaction of knowing that she could not be so keenly observed from their point of view. She was probably wondering about Sir Gervaise, of whom she must have heard many times. He thought of the slight starchiness of her manner which would be more in evidence than ever as she was presented to the great man, and then he led the way up the steps and through the swing doors into the hall.

Before the bust of Lord Conyers, who had presented the home to Norchester, banked chrysanthemums made the hall gay with color. Otherwise, the heavy oak doorways and solid panelling in which the old gentleman had delighted might have proved oppressive.

A maid came forward to take their coats. She was young and impressionable and fled with them immediately, like a child who has conducted some grave public ceremony and been swiftly overcome by shyness in the last few minutes.

Matron came slowly from the room facing them and Stuart heard a sound that was neither a gasp nor a denial but something between the two. It came from the man by his side, and when he turned to look at him Sir Gervaise's face was grey.

"Good-morning," Agnes Lawdon said steadily.

There was nothing in her manner to betray the fact, but Stuart knew that Sir Gervaise had been recognized in turn.

"This is Sir Gervaise Cortonwell," he introduced them with a feeling of futility, conscious of irony and something that was almost ludicrous in the situation. They had both tried not to give themselves away, and if Agnes Lawdon had succeeded where his patron had failed it was possibly because she had known all along whom she was about to meet. "How has my patient been these past few hours, Matron?"

"It's difficult to say, Mr. Hemmingway." Her voice was quite steady, her eyes dark and calm on his. "There appeared to be a slight relapse round about midnight again shortly after two o'clock, but—he has survived the night."

That fractional pause was the one concession she had made to emotion, if indeed she was capable of feeling acutely at all. Women in her profession often steeled themselves to reject pity, Stuart thought, sacrificing their womanhood in the process.

They turned and went quickly along the corridor, following the erect figure in the dark dress and stiff white headsquare until she paused before a door at its far end.

Her fingers fastened over the handle and lay there irresolutely for a moment before she pushed the door open and led the way in.

A nurse got up from the bedside and went noiselessly away and Matron picked up the chart from the chest of drawers and submitted it to Stuart.

While Sir Gervaise made his examination she stood back in the shadows, a lone, erect figure, watching and waiting for the final verdict.

"I believe you met my daughter in Switzerland," Sir Gervaise said as he bent over his patient. "Mr. Hemmingway has just been telling me that you stayed at the Oberzach hotel. I sent her away for a cure and I think it has worked. Wonderful fellows these Swiss, when it comes to lungs!"

Tom nodded.

"I'd like to have stayed there for a while," he said. "Doktor Frey was most helpful, but then I caught this packet and I wasn't a great deal of use." He gave the older man a long, searching look. "Hemmingway thinks you may be able to patch me up," he added slowly. "What are the odds?"

Sir Gervaise stroked his chin thoughtfully.

"It would be difficult to say," he evaded. "We'll have to be quite sure about your heart, for one thing, but you can safely leave that to us."

Stuart was conscious of Agnes Lawdon taking a step forward, as if she might intervene, but she did not speak. She stood aside as Sir Gervaise went out of the room, following them with a brief word to the hovering nurse.

As they paused outside her study door a telephone shrilled somewhere along the corridor and the brisk little secretary who had spoken to Stuart on several occasions came into the study on their heels.

"There's a telephone call for Mr. Hemmingway," she announced. "I've left it through in the office," she added to Stuart as he turned to follow her.

When he had gone the silence in the room deepened until it became tension and it was the man who finally broke it.

"Agnes!" he said. "It must be all of thirty years——"

Agnes Lawdon looked at him across the breadth of the room, unsmiling and remote.

"Every minute of them," she said. "Thirty years is a long time, Gervaise. We've both come a long way since then."

He appeared to clutch at some wisp of dignity, subconsciously straightening his stooped shoulders.

"Yes, indeed, I've done quite well for myself," he admitted. "And you?"

"Well enough." Her eyes were hard, forcing him to meet their steady, prolonged gaze. "Are you going to operate on this case?" she demanded harshly.

He looked away.

"The indications are all against success——"

"Is that all you care about?" she asked savagely. "Success! Never to operate on a poor chance in case your precious reputation might suffer in the process of failure? I tell you," she added more slowly, mistress of herself again, "you *must* operate! You're the man for the job and—it's the least you can do." The dark eyes still held his, compelling him. "It's the very least you can do," she repeated firmly.

In the tense, waiting silence which followed her ultimatum he moved towards her, a man groping in the mists of the past.

"What are you trying to tell me?" he demanded. "This boy? What does he mean to you?"

"He is my son." The calm voice stated the fact without emotion. "I never told him the facts of his birth because I knew how they would cripple him. Ada and Joe Sark adopted him and I paid them for his keep. Afterwards, I was able to put him through college—make him a doctor."

She flung the details at him one by one, as if they scarcely mattered. They were the shabby fabric of the past and all she was concerned with now was the present and perhaps the future. The man facing her moistened his lips twice before he spoke.

"Are you trying to tell me that—that——"

"I am telling you that the boy you have just examined is your son," she said quietly. "But for this accident, you would never have known."

He looked for a moment as if he would strike her and then his hands fell to his sides.

"Why didn't you tell me—long ago?" he demanded. "I had a right to know."

"What right?" She put the question calmly, watching his heated face grow pale again as he was forced to meet her eyes. "You would have given anything for a son of your marriage, but that was denied to you, yet you would not have recognized my child. You married well, Gervaise, and your marriage took you even further than you had hoped, for I still do not think you were a very brilliant doctor in the beginning, although I made my own particular contribution to your career." She paused, adding when he did not answer her. "I thought I could guide my son's life, hoping that he, too, would marry to his advantage, but recently I've wondered if that was where I went wrong. Love and faithfulness may count in a man's life, after all. This girl he's fond of," she continued almost introspectively. "Maybe she's the type who will make him happy. I tried to split their friendship up by getting rid of her, but Tom got the better of me there. He went out after what he wanted. He was determined sometimes—as determined as you were."

Her voice ebbed into the silence of the room while Sir Gervaise stared out of the window at the spires of the cathedral church across the way. His face was quite colorless when he turned to look at her again.

"I couldn't operate, even if I wanted to," he said. "It's hopeless, I tell you—hopeless!"

"You are the authority," she told him inexorably. "You have operated in a case like this before. I have followed your career, Gervaise—very closely."

"You're asking the impossible!" he cried. "Knowing—realizing all you have just told me, how could I?"

"Would it have been easier for you if you had not known?" she asked coldly. "You were never an emotional man, Gervaise. You took what you wanted even in your youth. Your daughter came here and I found her very like you—selfish and headstrong, considering herself before everything else. She had, however, the saving grace of charity."

He strode back to the window.

"What does all this add up to?" he asked more cautiously. "You want my help. Very well, but I must ask for you silence as payment."

For the first time she allowed emotion to distrub her expression. Her lips curled perceptibly.

"You shall have it," she promised. "After thirty years, it should come easily enough."

When Stuart came back into the room they were still standing with its width between them, the silence fraught with a thousand unsaid things.

"Are we ready to leave?" Sir Gervaise asked, glancing at his watch. "I have another appointment at the City General."

When they were safely in the car Stuart looked at his companion keenly.

"I propose to operate on that case," Sir Gervaise said stiffly.

"But sir——"

The older man held up a cautioning hand.

"Allow me to be the best judge of this, Hemmingway," he said. "I have my own reasons for going on with the job."

Suddenly, as if something in him had crumbled, he leaned forward and put his face in his hands.

"You're ill, sir!" Stuart said. "Let me stop the car."

"No! No, I'm all right! Just a dizzy spell." He mopped his brow. "Working too hard, I expect. After this—business is over I may go out to Zürich and join Della for a few weeks." He looked at Stuart anxiously. "You're quite sure this cure is working in her case, my boy?" he asked. "You did say it was practically a hundred per cent., didn't you?"

"I might go so far as to say that it *has* worked with Della," Stuart assured him, "but I think you would be wise to keep her out there for the remainder of this winter. Doktor Frey will co-operate, and I'm quite sure Della herself will be willing if she is told that she may do a little judicious skiing later on. She could even go up to Zermatt for the end of the season."

"She'll need that nurse of yours if she leaves the clinic," Sir Gervaise said, frowning. "I was surprised when you said you had brought the girl back with you, by the way. Her salary was a mere flea bite."

"Miss Calvert came back with Doctor Sark," Stuart said stiffly. "They are engaged to be married."

He watched the remaining color recede from his companion's face, leaving him grey and haggard looking.

"Too much rests with me," he said thickly. "I would have done what I could for the boy under other circumstances——"

"You still mean to do that," Stuart reminded him rather grimly, for he had little faith in the success of the operation. "It is—very generous of you."

There was no reply, and after a few minutes Stuart asked if he might be dropped at Jane's hotel.

"The City's only a couple of blocks farther on," he said, "but if you like I'll come the rest of the way with you, sir."

"There's no need," Sir Gervaise assured him, hastily swallowing one of the tiny capsules he kept in a phial in his waistcoat pocket. "I shall be all right. Have dinner with me tonight, my boy, and we'll talk about Della. I think you should still be keeping an eye on that girl of mine, you know!" he added with heavy playfulness.

He drove away, and Stuart was left on the pavement, frowning and wondering what had upset him so much during those few minutes at Conyers when he had been left alone with Matron.

The telephone call had been from Jane. She had spent the morning curbing her anxiety in order to allay Aunt Ada's suspicions and it had not been an easy task, but even when Stuart had answered her call he had not been able to tell her very much.

So often in her own nursing days she had used the old, noncommittal formula, 'as well as can be expected,' and now Stuart had used it to her. How different it was to be on the receiving end of such a message! How keen the sense of frustration which trod so swiftly on the heels of disappointment and sudden, unreasoning irritation! Really, she knew that there might be literally nothing more to be said.

When she saw Stuart getting down from Sir Gervaise's Rolls she almost ran across the foyer to meet him, restraining herself with the utmost difficulty and ordering coffee to be brought to their table instead. She was on her feet as he came towards her.

"Is there any news, Stuart?" she asked. "Anything definite?"

He just avoided meeting her eyes.

"Sir Gervaise is going to operate," he said.

"Then—there *is* hope?" Her eyes were suddenly misted with tears and relief flooded over her like a great tide. "There's bound to be if he's going to take the risk!"

"Don't force me to a platitude, Jane," he said almost wearily as he sat down.

"But quite often it is true that where there's life there's hope," she reminded him. "You're tired, Stuart. You've done so much!"

"No more than anyone else would have done for you in the circumstances, Jane. 'Old acquaintances,' remember!"

Cynicism sat uneasily upon him for the first time. Jane wondered what he would do about Della, how soon he would go back to Switzerland to be with her, but she could not ask. Probably this affair of Tom's was keeping him in England longer than he wished to stay.

Yet it could not be helped. She would have felt it like desertion if he had gone.

When the coffee came Ada Sark began to pour it out with an unsteady hand. She had listened to their conversation without a word, plunged in her own unhappy thoughts of Tom.

"Maybe I should go home for an hour or two," she said, pursuing the domestic pattern of these thoughts. "I never really shut up the house—not properly, and I'd have to ask a neighbor to see my cat. I'll want to be here, of course, when Tom goes through this operation," she added firmly. "You'll tell me when it's to be?" she asked Stuart plaintively.

"Jane will know," he said, getting to his feet. "I'll keep in touch with her, Mrs. Sark, and she'll bring you to the nursing home when you get back." He bent to take the plump hand in his, holding it firmly for a moment. "Try not to worry too much about Tom," he advised. "These things are in higher hands than ours."

"He's such a nice young gentleman," Ada Sark mused as she watched him stride away towards the swing doors. "It's funny that he's never found himself a wife, isn't it?"

CHAPTER TWELVE

STUART WENT straight back to Conyers. To say that he was worried about Tom Sark was an understatement, and he had to force himself to accept Sir Gervaise's decision to operate as encouraging. It could not be that the old man was slipping. He had been an authority on this sort of thing for years, more years than Stuart could count as his lifetime.

Tom was asleep when he got to the nursing home and he would not have him disturbed for a routine check-up. He stood looking down at the still figure on the bed, conscious of a growing unhappiness about the whole business for which he could not account. The issue involved him because of Jane, and she seemed to be demanding the future from him, Tom's future and her own.

His eyes ran over the fair, ruffled hair on the pillow, the high, narrow brow and the suggestion of weakness about the relaxed jaw, not critically but with a new compassion. The man had so much to live for that it seemed almost sacrilege to voice his own grave doubts.

He turned away, going slowly along the wide corridor to the main door where a draught of freezing air met him, and when he turned the corner he was confronted by a small girl in a scarlet coat holding open the swing door for the slim young woman who followed her.

Mother and daughter, he thought idly, meeting two pairs of identical blue eyes. Surely they must have misunderstood about the visiting hours?

"I wonder if you could help me?" He saw without its making a great deal of impression on his mind that the mother walked with a slight limp. "I'm looking for my sister. I had a letter from her from Switzerland saying that she was coming home and the only address she could give me was this one. Do you think I could see her? Do you think she might be here?"

"I've no idea." His mind was still very much with Tom Sark and Jane, "But if you will tell me your name, I'll ask Matron to see you."

"We've met before," Hazel Bridgewater told him. "You came to Heppleton once to see Jane."

Stuart stared back at her, as if Jane's name could only have been an echo of his own bitter reflections, and then he opened the office door, ushering mother and daughter into the warmth of a glowing electric fire.

"We can talk here in comfort," he said. "Of course, I remember you now! Please forgive me for not recognizing you straight away. I travelled back from Zürich with Jane and Doctor Sark," he explained, wondering if she had been told about her sister's sudden engagement. "We're quite old friends, you know."

Hazel bit her lip.

"I wondered—when you came to the house," she said. "You—you were engaged to Jane at one time, weren't you?"

He nodded briefly, as if he did not want to remember that time.

"Yes. I believe you lived in Devon then. Jane was to take me to see you, but she never did."

"It—all ended so suddenly." Hazel paused, as if what she had been about to add had suddenly become difficult, and then she raised stormy blue eyes to his. "Why did you throw her over like that?"

Stuart took a swift turn to the window and back again. "Did Jane tell you that I threw her over?" he demanded.

"She couldn't very well." Hazel was still frankly resentful. "It happened round about the time of the accident, I guess. My husband was killed in a car crash and I was so severely injured that it was thought I might have to be pushed in a wheel chair for the rest of my life."

Stuart wheeled round, staring down at her incredulously.

"You say all this happened four years ago?" he asked slowly and deliberately, like a man weighing up evidence. "And afterwards Jane gave you the impression that I had 'thrown her over'? That was the way you put it, wasn't it?"

"Well, it was true!" Hazel retorted belligerently. "I've never see anyone so unhappy as Jane was at that time and for years afterwards, yet she was always kind and considerate to me. She had to work to help support us all, too. I had very little left when my husband's affairs were straightened out, and my mother was a widow. There was Linda Jane, too." She looked across at the child sitting in the sunlight on the broad windowsill. "She was little more than a baby at the time and I could do nothing for her. Mother looked after her through the day and Jane took over when she had time off from Conyers."

"Go on," Stuart commanded stonily.

"There isn't a lot more to be said, is there?" Hazel asked. "You let Jane down in the cruellest way possible when she must have needed the comfort of your love most. You went abroad or something, didn't you?"

Stuart knew that Hazel was prepared to dislike him, but he could do nothing about that at the moment. In five brief minutes she had given the lie to four of the bitterest years of his life, vindicating Jane, turning the past upside down. At first it was difficult to believe, but there was no gain-saying the proof before his eyes—Hazel with her slight limp which would always remain as evidence of the accident which had changed so much in all their lives, and the fair-haired little girl who was not quite five years old.

Why had Jane done it? Why hadn't she come to him and explained everything? He knew the answer before the question had formed properly in his mind. He had been desperately poor, a penniless graduate determined to rise to the heights, and she had seen herself and her family as a drag on his career. He might have been able to support a wife in comparative comfort if he had been willing to stay in England and accept a regulation hospital job, but his heart had been set on that post-graduate course in Zürich which his ability as a student had made possible and Jane had known that she could not leave England. Nor would she saddle him with the responsibility of her family or even the choice of making a decision!

He saw it all now quite clearly. She had not permitted him any choice because she had known of his ambition, how much his career meant to him.

He felt sick with the knowledge, revolted by his own unforgiving bitterness which he had been at little pains to conceal from her even after four years. He had been harsh and intolerant at their parting and again at their meeting at Conyers, and now he saw the years when she had stayed behind in England and fought her battle alone. Much that had puzzled him about Jane during these past few months came into clear perspective at last. He saw the reflection of hurt in her eyes at his own unkindness and recoiled at the thought of all he had said and done to her. What paltry satisfaction had he hoped to get out of it? In what way did he believe himself justified?

Linda Jane came across the room to lean heavily against her mother's knees, surveying him with candid blue eyes.

"Why don't you take me to my Aunt Jane?" she demanded. "We've come from Nottin'ham to see her—on a bus."

He pulled himself together with a supreme effort.

"I'm going to take you straight away," he said. "She's living at a nice hotel quite near here where we can have something to eat. Would you like to come with me in my car?"

"Oh! yes, please!" Linda Jane's eyes fairly shone. "I like riding in a car. There's a big yellow one outside."

"We'll go in that one," he said. "Shall we?"

The question was directed to Hazel as well as to the excited Linda, and Hazel rose as her small daughter offered Stuart a confidenthand.

"Whatever you believe about what happened four years ago, Hazel," Stuart said quietly, "let me take you to Jane now. She needs someone at this moment as much as she did then—perhaps even more so."

He could not tell Hazel about the sacrifice her sister had made all these years ago, could not explain that it was Jane who had refused to go abroad with him in that moment of her family's greatest need. He did, however, ask a rather blunt question, which was typical of him.

"You've married again, of course?"

A faint color dyed Hazel's cheeks.

"Yes. At first when the doctors thought I wouldn't walk any more I suppose I was difficult to deal with," she confessed as they went out to the car. "I didn't think life was worth living and I must have caused Jane and my mother endless heartache, but then, gradually, I began to respond to a new treatment they tried at the hospital and after about a year I could sit up and there was just the chance that I might eventually be able to walk again." She drew a deep breath as Stuart opened the car door for her to get in. "I don't know why I'm telling you all this," she added. "Perhaps it's because you're a doctor and will understand, though you didn't understand Jane very well."

No, he hadn't understood Jane! He had shot off at a tangent, blaming her bitterly at the first defection, and the desperate fact remained that he couldn't turn back the years. You couldn't undo the past! Jane was now in love with someone else. Suddenly he was thinking that she had made a similar sort of sacrifice for Tom Sark. Taking the rap for the blood transfusion business had cost her a good job at Conyers and it hadn't really been necessary, after all. He had often wondered why Matron had wanted to get rid of Jane and seized on that small mistake in the operating theatre as the ideal opportunity.

"It was another year before I could even stand," Hazel went on, as if she felt compelled to recite the whole story once she had begun. "And all that time Jane worked at Conyers and took care of Lindy in between. Then, quite

178

suddenly, my mother died. I was able to walk by that time, but I still couldn't cope with an outside job. Jane and I decided to keep on the house. I could manage that, and Lindy, too, after a while, and I really liked housekeeping best. Then, about six months ago, I met Eric." She paused, momentarily confused by the grim expression which had crossed her companion's face. "Jane thought I should take my chance of happiness." she told him a little breathlessly. "She wouldn't stand in my way."

"Of course, she wouldn't," he answered dryly. "Jane's like that."

There was a long silence. Hazel wished she didn't feel so uncomfortable, and really he had no right to make her feel that way! Hadn't he let Jane down, too, four years ago?

Stuart brought the car to a standstill under the stone portico of the White Hart. He was not quite sure how he was going to meet Jane, but certainly she must see her sister.

The White Hart was busy at that hour, but he found the receptionist, who made the necessary inquiries for him. She came back after five minutes to say that Jane had gone out for the day.

"But that's impossible," he said. "I saw her here less than a couple of hours ago! Just after eleven, as a matter of fact."

The receptionist nodded.

"She went out at a quarter to twelve, sir, saying that she might not be back much before seven in the evening. She did mention, though, that she would ring the hotel in case there was any message for her from the nursing home."

"I see." There was nothing for him to do but accept checkmate. "Thank you very much. I don't suppose Miss Calvert would say when she intended to 'phone you?" he inquired as an afterthought.

"About four o'clock, sir."

"You've no idea where from?"

"No. I'm sorry!"

Well, that was that! He turned back to the waiting Hazel and Linda Jane, who was growing tired and restless.

"I'm afraid we've drawn a blank." He was not thinking so much of Hazel as of Jane's possible disappointment when she eventually heard that she had missed her sister. "Jane appears to have gone off for the day somewhere—or, at least, till seven o'clock this evening. Could you possibly stay here overnight?" he asked without much hope.

"I couldn't possibly," Hazel told him. "There's Eric, you see. He'll be in at six, expecting his tea. We didn't come to stay, only to see Jane for an hour or two."

"If you are here at four o'clock you will perhaps be able to speak to her on the telephone," he suggested, wondering what he was to do with them till four. "That would be better than nothing. In the meantime, let me give you some lunch."

"Oh, I really couldn't!" Hazel protested, remembering that she hadn't exactly minced her words when they had first met and she had accused him of deserting Jane. "I—we'll get something at a café somewhere. I know Norchester quite well."

"You should do," he said with a warm smile which somehow cleared the air a little. "All the same, Hazel, I insist that you have your lunch here with me."

The man was used to giving orders, Hazel thought. It was typical of him, but behind the hardness was a sincerity and kindness which she could not doubt.

"Please, Mummy," Linda Jane put in, "I'm hungry now!"

"That appears to settle everything!" Hazel laughed, meeting Stuart's eyes. "Though I don't know why you should insist on being so kind."

"Put it down to my friendship with Jane," he said enigmatically, and Hazel was left to wonder what could possibly have come between him and her sister when his personal charm seemed all that could be desired. Could it, she mused, have been Jane's fault, after all?

During the meal she was aware of Stuart having to make an effort to sustain interest in her conversation. His thoughts were apparently elsewhere, and Hazel rose from the table a trifle piqued and said that they would go.

Linda Jane had clambered on to Stuart's knee, her initial shyness completely dissipated by the promise of another ride in the yellow car, and he looked up at Hazel in some surprise.

"I thought you would want to speak to Jane," he said, glancing at his watch. "It's almost three o'clock and she may telephone earlier than she said. It seems a pity to miss her for the sake of half an hour or so when we have waited so long. Isn't there a later bus you could get?"

"There's one about five." Hazel hesitated. "I'd like to speak to Jane," she confessed. "It seems almost as if I am running away now that she needs help."

During the meal Stuart had told her about Jane's engagement, feeling that it would be expected of him. He had also explained about Tom's accident, since that was the reason why Jane was keeping in such close contact with the hotel. For the past hour he had been wondering where she could possibly have gone, but the simple explanation, when it came, did not surprise him.

Jane had gone down to Crale with Tom's aunt. Confronted with the hurried journey following upon the news of Tom's accident, Ada Sark had begun to feel the weight of her years. She confessed to Jane that she was dreading the journey to Crale and back and heaved a sight of the utmost relief when Jane eventually offered to go with her.

"It will mean there and back with very little time to spare," she had warned, but Ada had accepted the condition without demur.

They reached Crale shortly after one o'clock, had a quick meal in a deserted café on the sea front, and went to the cottage to see to the cat and pack Mrs. Sark's small week-end case.

At quarter to four Jane went down the lane to the Post Office to 'phone through to the White Hart. The line was very clear, but the swift, anxious beating of her heart seemed magnified a thousandfold as she waited in the tiny booth.

"Oh, Miss Calvert!" the receptionist said at the far end. "There's someone here to speak to you."

Jane could not answer. Two strangling hands seemed to have reached up and encircled her throat and a loud buzzing sounded in her ears so that she was afraid she would not be able to hear at all. Through it she recognized Stuart's voice.

"Jane, are you there?"

She thought that she knew what he was going to tell her. His voice sounded concerned, with a new urgency about it which stunned her senses.

"Is it—Tom?" she asked. "Have you heard from Conyers?"

"No. As far as I know, everything is much the same there," he said to her utter relief. "I 'phoned about half an hour ago. Matron was with him and he was still asleep. She doesn't think he should have any visitors until later in the evening."

"I thought—when you asked to speak to me that it must be—bad news," Jane gasped.

"Not always!" he said with a hint of the old cynicism in his deep voice. "Your sister is here, Jane," he added.

"Hazel! But how——?"

"She came through from Nottingham for the day to see you when she got your letter—the one you posted in Zürich. We've had a meal together—and a long talk."

He seemed to have added that last sentence deliberately, and there was something in his voice which she could not quite understand, a restraint and an excitement combined, which seemed very unlike Stuart, the Stuart she had come to know during the past four months.

"She's waiting to speak to you now," he said. "I can't take up all the call, but, Jane, I must see you as soon as ever you get back! Where are you now?" the quiet voice went on. "Is it near enough for me to come and fetch you?"

"I'm at Crale," Jane answered dazedly. "I came down with Aunt Ada."

The name struck Stuart like a blow in the face. It was the measure of her relationship with Tom Sark, for plump, cheerful little 'Aunt Ada' would be her aunt by marriage if Tom lived!

It made no difference to the fact that he must see Jane immediately, he told himself doggedly, though something had gone out of his voice when he said:

"I'll be waiting here at the hotel when you get in. Unfortunately, it looks as if you're just going to miss seeing Hazel. Here she is, though. I'm putting her on now."

Jane almost wept at the sound of her sister's voice, the blessed relief of contact with one of her own family, at last. There wasn't very much they could say. Just that Jane would come to Nottingham whenever she could reasonably get away—when Tom was safely out of the wood. Yes, her engagement had been sudden, but she had known Doctor Sark for quite a long time. Hazel remembered him coming to Heppleton, of course? Was Linda Jane there? Could she just manage to say 'Hello?'

Hazel held Linda up to the instrument and a second or two later the time signal went.

"Don't forget, Jane! If there's anything I can do."

"I won't forget, Hazel. Goodbye, dear!"

There was nothing Hazel could do, Jane thought. Nothing anyone could do. It all rested with Providence. Jane had ceased to call it Fate now. She stood in the hot little booth for several minutes, staring at the silent instrument on the wall. What was it Stuart wanted to say to her that was so urgent? What lay behind the deep insistency in his voice when he had told her that they must meet without delay?

CHAPTER THIRTEEN

IT SEEMED AN eternity till seven o'clock. She walked back along the lane to Rose Cottage, wondering if they could possibly catch an earlier bus from Crale, but Aunt Ada had prepared tea for them and she would have been hurt if Jane had refused it.

"Mrs. Cartwright next door will take Toddy," she explained the small details of her household. Toddy was the ginger kitten Tom had given her for Christmas, the seventh in a long succession of cats who seemed destined to meet untimely ends. "I can stay a day or two when I know he's being cared for properly."

Jane smiled at the thought of Tom naming the kitten with a glass in his hand, but immediately her eyes darkened as she remembered Conyers and the verdict that was yet to come.

The bus journey seemed interminable and once or twice she failed to answer Aunt Ada when she spoke. Quiet, generous Aunt Ada seemed almost garrulous by the time they had reached Norchester and pulled into the bus station.

"There now, isn't that kind!" she exclaimed even before Jane had noticed the waiting car. "Fancy him coming to meet us at the bus! I said from the beginning what a thoughtful young man he was!"

Stuart was coming towards them and Jane's heart raced to meet him. It was madness, she knew, but such necessary madness. If she tried to smother her emotions at every turn something would give way in the end. She had time to compose herself, waiting in the crowded bus till the passengers before her got down.

Stuart helped Aunt Ada, taking her shabby leather case and propelling her by the elbow across the busy street. He had looked at Jane directly as she stepped on to the pavement, a long, searching look which had quickened her pulses but told her nothing. Evidently he meant to see Mrs. Sark safely to the White Hart before he told her what he had to say.

They reached the hotel at quarter to seven. He had ordered dinner for them for half-past.

"Can you spare me that time?" he asked Jane as Aunt Ada was whirled up in the lift. "This is most important."

"Yes," she said. "There should be plenty of privacy in the lounge."

183

Had he wanted privacy? She could not guess and knew that it did not matter very much. She seemed to have reached the end of a very long journey, not the journey from Zürich which had ended at Conyers, but a steeper, more uphill road where she had been bruised and cut upon the way. If her feet faltered now it was from very tiredness, the desperate fatigue of the spirit which surpasses any physical weariness and is not so readily replaced.

Stuart led the way to the alcoved lounge and she was glad that it was empty, after all. For some unknown reason she felt ready to weep, the tears choking against her throat. Stuart rang for drinks, forcing her to accept one.

"I told you I had spent part of today with Hazel," he said quietly when they were alone again. "Jane, why couldn't you have told me the truth four years ago?"

There was no doubting his meaning. She did not need confirmation of the fact that he now knew why she had refused to go to Zürich with him and share his student struggles, but it did not seem to matter now, not as it had done once, when she had lain spent with wishing and praying that just such a miracle as this would happen. In the interval had come Della, and now there was Tom, dependent upon her, relying upon her strength in this emergency. Their lives, which had once been entangled in misunderstanding, were now bound up by honor and a sacred promise.

"Jane," he said thickly, "forgive me. There's nothing else I can say. All those unrepeatable things—the bitterness and the accusation—could never be shame enough for doubting you in the first place."

He rose and paced to the window, standing with his back to her, and Jane felt as if a deadly weight was pressing her to the earth, the weight of hopelessness, of a love forced to cry 'too late!'

"That's what we do with our youth and our love," he said, coming back to stand beside her. "We tear it to shreds without question—for pride, and hurt, and jealousy, and we learn to suffer for these things afterwards!"

"And afterwards," Jane said with her hand at her throat, "afterwards there may be compensation—for one or the other."

He looked down at her, his eyes dark mirrors of pain.

"You told me once that compensation was as good as saying 'second best.' You don't believe that now, do you?"

Jane's hands clenched hard by her side.

"I don't know what I believe," she said. "I only know that I'm glad you've learned the truth at last, though it can't make any difference now."

He stared at her, the old Stuart, with all his cold composure gone and a beaten look in his eyes which made her turn her own away.

"Well," he said, "I had to tell you. I couldn't let you go on believing that I didn't know. I can't blame you for not wanting to forgive the way I've treated you—the fury that drove me to want to hurt you in return. All I can hope for is that you'll come to it gradually, possibly when you've reached some other sort of happiness with Tom."

She could not look at him. He had spoken of her own happiness, yet there was happiness for him, too, with Della.

Why did Della seem so unreal, of a sudden, so much the chimera of her own fancy? Was it because so many miles lay between them, because Della was not there in the flesh to claim Stuart and did not seem strong enough to claim him in spirit?

"There's no question of forgiveness," she managed. "We made a mistake, that was all. I should have told you the truth."

There was no immediate answer, and when she looked up his eyes were blazing, dark and passionate in his thin face.

"My love was no mistake," he said roughly. "It meant everything to me and it did to you once! Whatever the truth would have done to us, Jane, it could never have reduced us to this!"

He had gone before she could utter one cry of protest or try to stop him, and she sank back into her chair, crushed and defeated and utterly spent by the swift progress of events which had filled her long day.

When the telephone shrilled in her bedroom twenty minutes later she lifted the receiver with the thought that nothing else could possibly happen in a day that was already overcrowded with events.

"Yes, this is Jane Calvert speaking. Who? Matron! Oh——"

Agnes Lawdon's voice came across the line with measured persistence.

"Doctor Sark is sinking. He has asked for you. Can you get in touch with—his aunt?"

"Yes." The word had been no more than a whisper. "Yes, Matron, I'll come at once."

It was a formula, a repetition from the old days at Conyers, and Jane followed it up automatically. Don't panic in an emergency. But what an emergency! She grew sick at the thought of having to tell Aunt Ada, of seeing the round, homely face stricken with grief, the gentle eyes full of tears, yet there was no one else to do it. In all the years of her training Jane had never become hardened to this sort of thing. Death was for ever a tragedy to those left behind.

Ada Sark took it very well. In some ways, Jane realized, Aunt Ada had expected it. She would see Tom again. That was the main thing.

When they reached Conyers Jane got out of the taxi first, looking instinctively at the long windows on the ground floor which she knew so well. The curtains had been drawn in the room next to Matron's. Tom was dead.

For once in her life shock could not be absorbed in activity. There was nothing for her to do. Matron had done it all. She came to the door of the room when they knocked and followed them to the bed, but she did not speak. If anything, she was paler than ever, with a thin, withdrawn look about her which made Jane feel sorry for her without knowing why.

"Will you come into my room and take a cup of tea?" she asked.

In the corridor they met Sir Gervaise Cortonwell and Stuart, and she seemed only to see the older man.

"You're too late," she said beneath her breath. "Doctor Sark died half an hour ago."

Her eyes were stony as they rested on Sir Gervaise's face, and Jane thought how grey the older man looked. He was more stooped than ever as he turned away, suddenly and inexplicably aged. Was Matron blaming him for Tom's death, she wondered, thinking that he should have operated more quickly?

They went into the study and sat on the chintz-covered chairs, Ada Sark and Jane together near the window and Matron facing them across the hearth. They did not speak for a very long time.

"I can't believe it," Ada said at last. "It seems no time since he was a lad at school, no time at all." She drew a deep breath. "It will leave a gap in our lives," she sighed. "He was such a live wire, was Tom."

Matron collected their cups on to the tray and Jane rose, as if at a signal.

"I think we ought to go now," she said. "Thank you, Matron, for the tea."

They walked together to the door and Agnes Lawdon said almost harshly:

"I'm sorry about the way you left Conyers. If you wish a public apology, I shall make it."

Jane shook her head.

"It doesn't matter now," she said. "I shall have to find work, of course, but it will be away from Norchester."

"I see." The older woman still seemed to hesitate. "You are a good nurse," she said awkwardly. "I think it would be wrong for you to give up your profession. If you should change your mind about working here, let me know."

Jane drew the collar of her coat up under her chin, smiling faintly.

"I couldn't come back to Conyers, Matron," she said quietly. "I think you will understand."

"Perhaps you are right." The momentary weakness had passed and Agnes Lawdon was herself again. "You are young enough to be able to make a fresh start elsewhere," she agreed. "You will let me know, of course, when you need a reference."

"Yes, Matron," Jane said. "I shall let you know."

In the dark, rain-washed courtyard outside she caught gleam of a yellow car and Stuart stepped towards them out of the night.

"I waited, Jane," he said. "Let me take you back to your hotel."

"My! how kind you've been!" Mrs. Sark sighed with relief as she settled back against the softly-cushioned upholstery. "You were a good friend of Tom's, I expect, at the hospital?"

Stuart tucked a heavy fur rug round her knees.

"I didn't know him very well," he confessed, "but that makes very little difference. Will you stay the night at the White Hart, Mrs. Sark, or would you like me to run you down to Crale?"

Ada hesitated. Hotels had never seemed very homely places at the best of times, and when one faced the shock of sudden death home held its comfort.

"It's very late," she pointed out. "It would take us all of two hours to get there."

Stuart looked at his watch.

"It's not quite nine o'clock. I'm perfectly willing to take you if you would like to go."

187

"I—think that would be best."

He looked at Jane as he closed the car door.

"You'll go with her? I'll see to everything here."

"Why should you do it all?"

His fingers fastened securely under her elbow as he led the way round to the far side of the car.

"Because you're about all in and haven't realized it yet. You've taken about as much as any human being can stand without cracking up, Jane. Go down to Crale with Aunt Ada and I'll bring you back whenever you want to come."

The insistence behind the words was not to be disobeyed. This was the new, authoritative Stuart speaking, the man in command of the situation who would not take no for an answer. Jane felt that he could see the way ahead far more clearly than she could, and with the admission she acknowledged a sudden weakness, the desire to give in to any suggestion which would shift some of the weight of these past few days from her drooping shoulders.

A desperate tiredness had taken possession of her and she did not want to think. At least Crale would be restful and far enough away from Norchester to let her plan for the future without the memory of the past rising up at every street corner to mock her.

She stayed at Crale for three weeks. Ada Sark made no pretense about her sudden loneliness. It was nice, she said, to have someone young about the house, someone who had known Tom. Jane felt the days passing slowly, irretrievably, bearing her away from the past, yet she had still to make a definite decision about the future. She had seen Stuart at Tom's funeral, but that was all. He had not come to Crale since. Perhaps he had even gone back to Switzerland, back to Della.

There was no pain in the thought now, just a dull resignation, an acceptance of the way life must be. She had nothing more to give to regret, nor to hope, nor sorrow.

When she told Mrs. Sark that she must go, Ada accepted that, too.

"I couldn't hope to keep you," she said.

Jane made her plans, conscious of a numbness of spirit such as she had never experienced before, aware that the pattern she was weaving for the days ahead had no real place in her heart. Then, two days before she was due to leave Rose Cottage, Stuart came to Crale.

She was so convinced that he must have returned to Zürich that for several seconds she stared at the yellow car unbelievingly. It was a gusty day in March with a brisk

188

wind beating up the Channel and the hills of Wales gloriously clear against the western sky, an English day with the first promise of spring about it, a day for renewed hope and new beginnings, and she had come for a walk along the sea front to clear her mind of its final indecision. The car had pulled up facing her at the far end of the promenade and Stuart got out and came striding towards her.

"Jane," he said, "have you a minute or two to hear what I have to say?"

She nodded wordlessly, the surprise of his coming too great to permit of speech, the spell of his nearness too disturbing to what she had tried to call her new-found peace of mind to allow her to look at him for very long.

He opened the car door, standing aside for her to get in, and then he drove northwards, out of the village a little way until they were high on the cliffs and alone. He pulled the car up and turned towards her.

"Jane," he said slowly, "I'm going back to Switzerland."

Her heart seemed to turn over, in spite of the fact that she had believed him already there.

"I—thought you had gone," she said. "It seemed—a long time to stay in England when—when all you wanted was out there."

He stretched across the wheel, taking her hands and holding them in a grip that hurt.

"All I wanted!" he repeated. "You still think my career matters most! How blind you can be, Jane—how unsure of yourself! I'm asking you—begging you to come with me."

She raised her head, compelled by the insistence in his voice, the hardening grip of his strong fingers.

"Because of Della?" she asked miserably.

"Della?" He sounded as if he had momentarily forgotten all about Della. "What has she to do with it? I'm asking you to come because I love you, because I've never ceased to love you in all these years. I'm asking you to come, Jane, for the second time."

Because I love you! The words sounded in Jane's heart like the breath of spring itself. They were all she wanted to hear.

"Oh! Stuart," she said. "Oh, Stuart——!"

He gathered her into his arms, then, kissing her gently, and it was as if the years between now and their first loving had never been. A great restfulness stole over Jane, an undisputed peace. She lay in his arms as if she had always belonged there, the memory of their parting receding with every breath she drew.

It was minutes before reality came crashing back, before she stirred in his arms, thrusting him from her.

"And Della?" she cried. "How can you say all this when Della's happiness is involved, too?"

For the second time he looked frankly puzzled by the mention of Della's name.

"Della will be as pleased about all this as a dog with two tails," he said with complete assurance. "I've just heard from her, as a matter of fact. The Kirchhofer brothers are back in Zürich and Della and Martin Kirchhofer are engaged to be married. The marriage won't be for some time yet, until there's absolutely no doubt about her health, of course, but I don't think they need worry unduly. Della will be cured. That was what I owed to the Cortonwells, Jane," he said, taking her in his arms again with a determination that would brook no opposition this time. "Sir Gervaise did a great deal for me when my people were killed during the war and he made it possible for me to go on with my studies afterwards. At times I've thought him strange—hard and even bombastic about his personal success—but he gave me my chance and when he put Della in my care it was something like a sacred trust to me. Now that she will get well I feel that I have more or less discharged my obligation to them. Della will be happy with Martin. There has never been anyone else for her since she first met him at St. Moritz years ago, but she knew that they couldn't contemplate marriage while her health remained in danger."

"Martin Kirchhofer!" Jane said. "Oh! I should have known! I should have realized how much it mattered to Della when she couldn't make the pace, when she believed that an ability to meet him on equal terms—to climb to the heights with him—was essential to their love!" Suddenly she was shaking, clinging to Stuart passionately. "Oh, Stuart! what a fool I've been, loving you all this time and not knowing—not being *sure* that nobody else could matter quite so much once we had loved!"

"I made it difficult for you, didn't I?" he said gently drawing her towards him and crushing her head against his shoulder. He spoke with his lips close to her hair, caressingly: "It wasn't easy, Jane, and we didn't exactly help each other. I went out to Switzerland in the utmost bitterness determined to build a life without love against a background of success and accumulating wealth, but it didn't work out. Not the way I imagined it would." He let his lips linger on her hair for a moment. "That day in the chalet above the clinic I realized just how wrong I had been, but I had lived out my disappointment there, day after day, along with my regrets, seeing you there with me as you should have been—imagining so many things." His arm tightened about her. "I took you there that day— the day after Tom phoned you from Arosa—to prove to myself that my love was dead, to see you in the chalet which would have been our first home and not care, but it was no use! I did care. I still loved you more than life itself, and there was an end to pretense. It was then that I realized what it would mean to me if you married Sark."

"I had nothing to give Tom," she said unsteadily, "except assurance while he needed it."

"Yet, when you seemed bent on marrying him, I thought you were trying to be content with half measures for some reason best known to yourself, and even when you told me you were leaving Oberzach together I still couldn't accept the fact that you were in love with the fellow. I tried to convince myself with the knowledge of the sacrifice you had made for his career—the kind of sacrifice I thought you had once refused to make for mine—but it was useless. You belonged to me by every right of love. You were mine! I could see no other way than that, although you held me off at every turn." She stirred in his arms, but he held her closer. "That's why I came back to England with you, I suppose. I couldn't be convinced that your love was dead, and there were so many things to prove that mine remained a living torture in my breast. That awful moment when I followed your tracks through the snow to the broken ice bridge will be with me for ever, I suppose. I imagined you hurtling down into the ravine an hour or only seconds before, and then I came round by another way and found you in Tom Sark's arms!"

Jane twisted round to look at him.

"You don't believe that? You don't believe any of that now?" she implored.

For a full second he gazed back into her eyes, and then, purposefully, he bent his dark head to kiss her full on the lips.

"No, my darling, I don't believe any of it," he said. "All we must ever believe is that we are in love, that nothing can alter that now!"

What readers say about Harlequin Romances

"I feel as if I am in a different world every
time I read a Harlequin."
A.T.,* Detroit, Michigan

"Harlequins have been my passport to the
world. I have been many places without
ever leaving my doorstep."
P.Z., Belvedere, Illinois

"I like Harlequin books because they tell
so much about other countries."
N.G., Rouyn, Quebec

"Your books offer a world of knowledge
about places and people."
L.J., New Orleans, Louisiana

*Names available on request